DOUBLE
CROSS

Tracy Gilpin was born in Cape Town, South Africa, and has an anti-apartheid struggle background. The moral dilemmas of pacifism versus armed conflict continue to intrigue her and have become the theme of much of her writing.

She has been a member for some years of Greenpeace and People for the Ethical Treatment of Animals. The plight of women around the world continues to inspire her to use her writing to spread the message of their continuing struggle.

Although Tracy's formal training was in journalism, she has worked mainly as a communications practitioner. She is the author of a non-fiction book, and has had more than thirty works of short fiction published internationally.

DOUBLE CROSS

TRACY GILPIN

BLACK STAR
CRIME™

First published in Great Britain 2008
Black Star Crime
Eton House, 18-24 Paradise Road, Richmond, Surrey TW9 1SR

© Tracy Gilpin 2008

ISBN: 978 1 848 45005 9

Set in Times Roman 10 on 11 pt.
081-1108-74747

Printed and bound in Spain
by Litografia Rosés S.A., Barcelona

Red
who was there at every word

1

IN A country rated number three in the murder stakes, keeping an eye out for violence was first, not second nature; and never more so than on a dark winter morning heavy with fog and that stillness before rush hour. Still, Dunai failed to see the legs sticking out the doorway of a restaurant. She tripped, staggered forward, righted herself, then turned back to stare cautiously at the wrapped bundle. It was adult-sized and for a moment she felt sick with fear, then it twitched, squirmed and a head appeared.

'God*dammit*, Mr Bojangles, I'm going to get you fixed with traffic cones and hazard lights.'

He was wrapped in plastic, which he'd tied in place with string, then wriggled under a blanket that looked sodden and smelled of ice and old sweat.

'Ai, Dunai,' he said, baring his gums in what was not a smile.

She called him Mr Bojangles because he'd never tell anyone his name. She thought he was schizophrenic, one of the mentally ill who'd slipped through the cracks and landed on a pavement where nothing seemed real and no one could be trusted.

She opened her tin and took out a handful of biscuits, raising them to her nose and breathing in ginger spice to replace the scent of homelessness. She made sure their fingers didn't touch as he reached for them.

'Been a bad night,' he said, reclining on an elbow and shaking his head.

'Cold enough to freeze a squirrel's arse.'

He fixed his black eyes on her. 'Cold, yes, but there's been other things.' He hesitated. 'Goings-on.'

'You should've gone to a shelter.'

With a plastic crackle the old man leaned forward. 'The devil come out there.' He pointed to Dunai's building. 'I seen him. Big black devil, red eyes.'

'You're off your meds again.'

'I seen him,' he said, raising his voice. 'I seen the devil. The preacher in the square say the devil's all around.'

'He's off his meds too.'

'You don't believe me!' he shouted. 'I seen him!'

'Okay,' Dunai said, impatient to get out of the cold. 'I believe you. Thing is, as long as he didn't see *you*, you're okay.'

Mr Bojangles squinted up at her and she sighed. 'You got money for coffee?' she asked. The old man shook his head. 'Get them to put it on my tab at Food on the Square, then find a place in the sun when this fog clears.'

She hoisted her heavy tote higher on her shoulder and started across the cobblestones of Greenmarket Square to the old four-storey yellow and white building where she worked. Beyond the wood and glass doors the foyer was in darkness and she wondered if there'd been a power cut. She glanced across the square to the baroque façade of the Old Town House. Nope, no power cut.

She inserted her key in the security door but it wouldn't budge. 'Oh, *crap*,' she said, giving the gate a tug. It flew open and slammed against the jamb. She jumped back and nearly dropped her tin. Some idiot had forgotten to lock it. Worse was the same idiot had forgotten to lock the doors into the foyer. That was asking for trouble. Dunai secured everything carefully behind her.

The foyer looked different without the brass chandelier burning overhead. Her heart did a little skittish number in the second it took her to realise the shadow in the mirror was her own. She shook her head, decided she'd had enough exercise for the morning and took the lift to the third floor.

When the doors slid open she noticed the passage lights were out. But there was light coming from under Siobhan's door. She felt something cold brush the back of her neck. Get out. Leave the building now, she told herself.

But what if Siobhan had simply made an early start? There was a logical explanation for all this. She knew nothing about electrics, but she'd heard people talk about circuits. Perhaps only certain circuits were out. Before she could change her mind, she moved quickly along the passage, then stopped to listen at the door. Not a sound. 'Siobhan? You in there?' Nothing. She half-heartedly pushed the door; there was a click and it swung open. It was only her concern for Siobhan that prevented her breaking a land speed record on her way out.

She stepped inside the office and was hit by a smell of urine. At first glance the room looked empty, the toilet door wide open. Then her eyes flew to the orange tasselled skirt and brown loafers sticking out from behind the desk. She rushed forward, only to stop suddenly at what she saw. Siobhan lay on her back, staring at the ceiling with eyes that were blood-red and glassy as playground marbles. Dunai's heart pumped blood and hysteria along a thousand course ways; she tasted vomit at the back of her throat.

Sinking slowly to her knees beside the body, she let her bag slide to the floor. The tin landed with a clang and she almost jumped to her feet, her eyes flying to the darkened doorway. But she was drawn back to Siobhan's body, to her wild dark hair spread across the carpet, two broad streaks of silver lying limp alongside her head like broken wings. She raised her hand to stroke back Siobhan's hair but recoiled at the coldness of the forehead beneath her fingers. She stared at the broken capillaries beside the bridge of her nose, along her eyebrows and hairline. Her lips were blue-grey, shrivelled and drawn back tightly against her teeth. Dunai became aware of the rigidity of the body, arms stiff at her sides, fingernails bloodied, torn almost completely from the middle fingers of her right hand. Her throat was a mess of bruises and torn, blood-caked skin.

A wave of revulsion swept over Dunai and panic rode that wave like a frothy white cap. She jumped to her feet, stumbled away from the body, fell over her bag and landed hard on her backside. She scrambled back up and rushed around the desk, grabbed the telephone, but it dropped from her hand, clattering loudly against the desk. She reached for it with two hands and, trembling uncontrollably, carefully took one hand away to dial.

'Hello?'

'Bryan, it's Dunai.' Her voice sounded like she was shivering from cold.

'Hi'ya, hon.'

'Bryan, something terrible's happened.' She tightened her jaw to keep her teeth from chattering.

'Dunai? What's wrong?'

'Siobhan. She's dead, Bryan. She's dead—'

'Dunai! What's— Where are you?'

'Office. The office. She's dead, Bryan. She's… Somebody's murdered her. She's been murdered.'

'No… My God.' There was silence on the other end. Dunai's voice rose. 'Bryan?'

'Wait there. Wait for me. Don't touch anything. The police. Have you called the police?' She shook her head, then remembered to say no.

'I'll call them. I'm on my way. Is the door locked?' Dunai's brain refused the leap in logic. 'The door, Dunai,' Bryan almost shouted. 'Are you locked in?'

'No.'

'I'm going to ring off. Then I want you to lock the door. Take the key out so I can get in with mine, and don't open for anyone. You hear me, Dunai? I'm going to call the police. Now lock the door. I'm on my way.'

She dropped the receiver back into place, then stared at the open door. Beyond, the dark passage was filled with every monster that had ever haunted her childhood. She had to force herself to move and, keeping her eyes averted from the darkness, slammed the door shut, turned the key, then slipped it into her pocket.

Alone with Siobhan, she pressed her back to the cold wall; its iciness crept through her coat, her short denim dungaree dress and jumper till it touched her skin. It was then her mind began to ask why and when and who would do such a thing. My God, who would do this? And suddenly she was filled with anger; a familiar rage that made her feel possessed by another animal entirely. One that wanted to bite and claw, hit out and scream at a fucking awful world till her throat was raw and her energy spent.

Why today? Dunai wondered. Some dislocated part of her brain registered the strangeness of this thought. Could there have been a better time to find Siobhan dead? But today she'd planned to surprise her with biscuits and a gift. It was her second anniversary at STOP and two years was a record for Dunai, who'd been fired from almost every job she'd had.

She'd met Siobhan right after she'd been fired from a department store for calling the wife of a CEO whose company experimented on animals 'the Eva Braun of the cosmetics world'. Ejected from the building by a security guard, she'd heard someone call, 'Excuse me. I want to talk to you.' She'd turned to see a woman rushing towards her. She was about Dunai's height, which was one metre seventy, very thin and had angular features. Her very long, slightly frizzy brown hair had a thick streak of silver-white at either temple.

'I'd like to offer you a job.'

'I just got fired.'

'I know, I saw.'

'Then you know I'm a troublemaker.'

'Yes. That's why I'm offering you the job.'

'Doing what?'

'As my assistant. Someone who'll be as much at home on a protest march as she'd be in an office. I'm a social activist. Founder of STOP—Strategies for Targeting Over-Population.

It's an NGO pressure group. I'm offering you the job if you want it, Dunai. That is your name?'

'It means the physical embodiment—'

'Of Earth Mother. I know.' Dunai was impressed. 'Well, think about it. I'll give you my card, then call when you've decided.'

'I'll give it a try,' Dunai said, 'but my typing's crap.'

'That can be fixed. But there's nothing wrong with your social conscience. My name's Siobhan Craig.' She stepped forward and stuck her hand out. Dunai shook it.

In the twenty-six years before Dunai had met Siobhan, life had disappointed her beyond her wildest dreams and she knew she too had disappointed, but Siobhan had changed all that. She had become friend, family and mentor. Two years, Dunai thought, and not once had she felt the deep disappointment that had begun to make her feel tired and worn out though still in her twenties. Siobhan had been like a mother to her. There, she'd said it. She'd lost another mother. No, she hadn't lost either woman; one had given her away, the other had been taken.

Dunai had never known her mother. She'd grown up at St Mark's Home for Children after being left there as a baby; she'd been no more than a month old. Pinned to her jumper had been a scrap of paper with the word 'Dunai' scrawled on it. This had caused some debate amongst the Dominican sisters since a dunai—pronounced doonie—was the 'physical embodiment'—Sister Finbar's words—'of the pagan Earth Mother'. Probably on Sister Raymunda's insistence, they'd let her keep the only thing that was truly hers and she'd been baptised Dunai Marks.

Now, twenty-eight years later, she found herself cut adrift again. She stayed still, felt her rage become something definite—cold, hard and very real. She slid down the wall, curled her arms around her wellington boots and pulled her thighs to her chest. From here she could see Siobhan's skirt and shoes, but didn't have to look at her face. She would watch over her till Bryan arrived and she'd make a promise.

'Siobhan.' It came out as a croak; she tried again. 'I'm going to make them pay for this, Siobhan. I swear to you, I'm going to make whoever did this pay.'

IT FELT AS IF ten minutes had passed but it had to be more than that because there was a policeman in the room, helping her to her feet and she was obliging, thanking him even, when she wanted to stay alone with Siobhan so part of her could believe the situation could still be fixed somehow.

'Where's Bryan?' she asked, eyes fixed on Siobhan's skirt, trying hard not to look at her face.

'Mr Larsen's in the passage. That's how we got in, with his key. I'll take you to him.'

Bryan Larsen was STOP's American statistician, but he was so much more than that. Dunai rushed to meet him, her eyes fixed on all he represented—strength, reliability. The perfectionist who brought order to Siobhan's brilliance.

But her eyes found an altered Bryan this morning. He looked as if he'd dressed from the laundry basket; one lapel of his corduroy jacket sat higher than the other and a shirt button had come loose on the summit of his small paunch. His light brown hair that started just beyond the crown stood out at the back of his head as if some furry animal, ever slipping, was holding on for dear life. His pale blue eyes were rimmed with red, and the bulbous tip of his nose was a muted shade of raspberry. Any other day they'd have ragged him about the transformation.

'What the hell is going on?' he asked, almost accusingly. Dunai stretched a hand out to him but he ignored it.

'She's dead, Bryan.' The words felt like a lie; something horrible she'd said in the heat of the moment to hurt someone. Words she'd later take back and claim she'd never really meant. Bryan looked at the policeman still standing beside her. He nodded.

Bryan held his arms out to her and she tipped towards him, allowing herself to be drawn to his chest, her hair brushed gently the way she'd seen him comfort his daughters. Having never had a father, even in this ghastly moment it was a contact she treasured.

'I can't believe this is happening,' Bryan said in disbelief as SA Police Service tape was pulled across the office doorway. 'Siobhan…' He shook his head.

The lift doors opened and light spilled into the passage. Dunai drew away from Bryan as figures in white jumpsuits and blue gloves stepped silently into it and looked about them. They placed metal toolboxes on the carpet, pulled blue coverings over their shoes, then walked towards the police tape and moved beyond the light.

A man in a blue windbreaker, another with a doctor's bag and a woman carrying a camera glanced their way as they passed, but said nothing, just pulled on the foot coverings and ducked under the tape. The remaining white suit spoke briefly with a policeman, then unfolded a ladder, rummaged inside his toolbox, climbed up and began inspecting a light bulb as the policeman aimed his torch from below. Dunai jumped at the metallic sound of the closing lift doors and they were once again left in near darkness.

Finding herself on the periphery of activity, she put her arm around Bryan's waist and steered him towards the office next to Siobhan's. She snapped on the light, left him standing silently in the middle of the room, then went to draw back the vertical blinds. The square was still covered by fog, nothing visible except strange smudges of light.

She turned away and started for her desk, her eyes falling on familiar objects that seemed somehow altered this morning—the old desks painted yellow for herself and navy-blue for Bryan, two steel file-cabinets, the fax, television and DVD on a pine table, the old twill sofa and coffee table, and the floor to ceiling book-case with its eclectic collection of books.

'Here, let me take that,' Bryan said as she reached her desk and realised she was still clutching the biscuit tin. She handed it to him. He pushed a diary out of the way, placed the tin on the desk in front of her and guided her into her chair.

The policeman who'd led her from Siobhan's office appeared in the doorway. 'They want you next door, Mr Larsen.'

Bryan kept his eyes fixed on her face. 'You'll be okay till I get back?' She nodded.

She still hadn't moved when he returned, pale and shaken, with the man in the blue windbreaker. He was younger than she'd first thought, perhaps in his late twenties, blond and blue-eyed, the boy next door except his eyes were bloodshot and he looked somehow depleted.

'Dunai Marks? I'm Detective Inspector van Reenen, the in-vestigating officer.' He held his hand out to her and she shook it. 'I'm sorry for your loss, Ms Marks,' he said in a heavy Afrikaans accent. 'D'you think you'll be okay to answer some questions? It'll help us try to find who did this.'

No, Dunai wanted to say. They'd be just questions and an-swers to him, something he'd done a thousand times before, an-other part of the daily routine. But she said none of this, only nodded and indicated a chair.

'You said Ms Craig told you she was working late. She do that often?'

'She usually took work home. But she was working on a pre-sentation to government so she needed her reference material. There was too much to take home.'

Bryan appeared with a tea tray and she opened the biscuit tin, offered it to the policeman. He hesitated, then took one of the ginger biscuits. She offered them to Bryan but he shook his head.

'I've been working here two years today; that's why I made these.' Dunai stared at the biscuit tin. 'I know why this happened.' She fixed her eyes on the detective's face. 'Enemies in Siobhan's life were as common as junk mail. She was desperate for people to realise what's going on, and for that they said she was evil.'

'What's going on?' DI van Reenen asked without the least curiosity. His eyes followed Dunai's to a large poster on the wall. 'Oh, that,' he said.

They both stared at the image of a pressure cooker jammed full of people trying to claw their way out, pushing against a lid that threatened to blow. Beneath the picture was printed: *Only idiots fill a pot with more than it's able to hold. STOP. Think.*

'Dunai's right,' Bryan said, pulling a chair up to the side of her desk. 'Siobhan was guided by conscience, no matter what it cost her. Unfortunately, hate mail and death threats were part of the job.'

'She keep any of it?'

'Not that I know of.'

'What was this presentation she was working on?'

'Seven years ago we started an impact study in Khayelitsha township. Built a centre with eight satellite clinics that offered contraception, abortion services and female empowerment programmes. The effect on population growth has been impressive.' Bryan waited for the detective to finish scribbling in his notebook. 'It sounds simple but you have to understand what Siobhan was up against.'

He went to a small television on the pine table, selected a DVD, popped it into the machine, skipped to a point, then hit play.

The screen showed a building site. A female voice said, 'The woman was returning home after an abortion at a STOP clinic when she was grabbed by a mob and brought to this building site. A kangaroo court was held, then she was beaten and her genitalia and uterus mutilated with several objects found at the scene.'

There was a long shot of an officer in a green forensics vest placing a metal pipe into a plastic bag.

'By the time the police and ambulance arrived the woman had

bled to death. As yet, no arrests have been made.' The young Indian reporter stood beside a large pool of blood that had saturated the soil. 'This is Prim Govender for E-News, Khayelitsha.'

Bryan stopped the DVD, then turned in his seat to look at DI van Reenen. 'That was two years into the project,' he said. He looked down at his tightly laced fingers, then up again and there was the ghost of a smile on his face. 'Siobhan's always been at her most magnificent when provoked. She hired a private investigator who gathered enough evidence to convict the woman's boyfriend and eight others. She got the support of a local struggle hero and the co-operation of community leaders, even managed to shame them into accompanying her to meetings and on house visits.

'That clinic is our biggest success and we make a presentation to government in a month. If they like the results, a committee will draft legislation for the Population Control Bill based on our model and, if passed, facilities will be set up all over the country. We'd hoped to go sub-Saharan, then the rest of the continent, but without Siobhan…'

He reached across the desk and covered Dunai's hand with his. 'I see all these women's faces. All the ones we haven't reached… There are too many to give up now. We'll just work harder, be even more determined.'

Dunai nodded. There was silence for a heartbeat, then Dunai asked a question she knew would deliver another sucker-punch. 'What's going to happen to her now? Her body, I mean.'

'The medical officer you saw earlier has confirmed the death and they're taking photos and footage of the scene. We're waiting for the pathologist, who'll give me some preliminary information to start with, then her body will be taken away for post-mortem.' There it was—post-mortem, the sucker-punch.

'I want to go over again the last time you saw Ms Craig alive.'

Bryan nodded. 'Dunai and I decided to call it a day just before seven. We locked up here, then stopped by Siobhan's office to let her know we were off.'

'She have any appointments for the evening?'

'No,' Bryan said. 'Nothing that she mentioned.'

'Wait!' Dunai said, her back ramrod straight. 'In the foyer on my way out I stopped for a chat with someone who works in the building. A man came in and said something to our guard like, "Just stopping by Siobhan's office." When I turned to see who it was, he was waiting at the lift.'

'Who was he?' the detective asked.

'I don't know.'

'What did he look like?'

'Dammit,' Dunai said. 'I didn't take special note of him. We work with social workers and volunteers and it isn't unusual for them to come by when they have time. They don't always make appointments.'

'And you, Mr Larsen?'

Bryan shook his head. 'I went straight back upstairs to fetch my diary I'd left behind. I was back down in a couple of minutes. I must have missed him.'

'You'd be surprised what you can take in at a glance,' the detective said to Dunai. 'Was he black, coloured, Asian or white?'

'White,' Dunai said.

'Can you remember what height he was?'

'Um. About my height—one metre seventy.'

'Clothes?'

'I think he was wearing part of a suit. Suit trousers—black, maybe. He was wearing a parka, navy or black, and I don't remember seeing a tie.' Dunai closed her eyes. 'He had brown hair. I'm almost sure he had a receding hairline…or a high forehead. And he had a broad face, strong bone structure.'

She opened her eyes. DI van Reenen pulled a mobile from his pocket. 'I'm going to get an officer in here with an Identikit.' But before he could punch in the number, a uniformed policeman appeared in the doorway, walked over and bent to whisper in his ear. The detective looked annoyed, then surprised. 'I'm needed outside for a minute,' he said, then left the office.

Dunai's bladder was full so she got up and headed for the toilets at the end of the passage. She was about to open the door when she saw the flash of a blue windbreaker just before the fire escape door closed with a soft pneumatic whoosh. She remembered the look of surprise on DI van Reenen's face.

There was no reason to follow. No reason at all to go to the fire escape door, but she did, her fingers curling around the handle and pushing it open. It was the low, urgent tones that made her move towards the railing. The voices were pitched too low to pick out individual words. Peering down the stairwell, she saw the top of DI van Reenen's head. He was saying very little. Most of the talking was being done by a man in a charcoal suit. Other than his clothing, all she could see was a head of thick, dark brown hair.

DI van Reenen began arguing and his voice rose. 'This is a *police* investigation. If burglary's where the evidence leads, then fine, but otherwise…' He shook his head. The man leaned towards the detective and spoke without raising his voice. She could make out none of his words. He was still speaking when, without warning, he tipped his head back and she got a glimpse of fair skin and regular features before ducking away from the railing.

With heart pounding, she headed for the fire escape door, yanked it open, rushed into the passage, then into the toilet block. She headed for the furthest cubicle, slammed and locked the door quickly. Surely he wouldn't follow her in here. Did they think she'd overheard something she shouldn't? Had she? 'If burglary's where the evidence leads, then fine, but otherwise…' And what had the detective meant by, 'This is a *police* investigation!' If not a police officer, then who was the man in the charcoal suit?

She stayed stock-still, waiting for the sound of footsteps but they never came. She used the toilet, then went to stand at a basin, staring at herself in the mirror, expecting her face to have changed too in the last hour.

Large, slate-coloured eyes stared back at her—familiar eyes

filled with emotions she didn't recognise. Her pale skin looked as if she'd had the life drained out of her, except there were two bright splotches of colour on her cheeks. She splashed water on her face, then blotted it with paper towels. She smoothed her dark shoulder-length bob and the fringe that ended an inch above strong, dark brows.

Out of the corner of her eye she saw it—like a shimmering, monochromatic caterpillar crawling across her eyeball. It was how her migraines started. Her sensitive eyes picked up the minute flickerings of the fluorescent lights and she began to feel sick and disorientated. She quickly headed back to her office.

'You okay?' Bryan asked. DI van Reenen was back in his seat, looking up at her, watching her closely, Dunai thought. She nodded for his benefit and took her seat. While the men resumed their question and answer session, she rummaged in her bag for the nose spray she used to treat her migraines, and gave a squirt in each nostril.

'The detective's been telling me they think it's a burglary,' Bryan said.

'What?'

'They think it's a burglary,' Bryan said. 'Her watch was gone, her laptop, mobile. The fax and coffee machine are missing.'

Dunai shook her head. 'Why kill her?'

'Some people don't need a reason,' the detective said.

She heard the words again: 'If burglary's where the evidence leads, then fine, but otherwise…'

Dunai tried to focus on the detective but it was like seeing only half his face through thick fog. 'I don't believe for a minute Siobhan died for a coffee machine.'

'The unlocked doors,' Bryan said. 'How would…?'

'You mind if I…?' The detective reached over and Bryan moved the biscuit tin closer.

'D'you think somebody who works in the building arranged it?' Bryan persisted.

The detective finished chewing, nodded. 'Somebody leaves the door open, or passes the keys to their friends, who come in and sweep the place. Or someone walks into the building during the day and steals a set of keys.'

'Then they'd have broken into other offices in the building,' Bryan said.

'No, they could've started next door. The top floor is closed off for renovations, so Ms Craig's is the first office on the highest occupied floor and there's no security gate.'

'Maybe somebody killed Siobhan for a reason and made it look like burglary,' Dunai said. 'Then, while the police are looking in that direction, they get away with it.'

There was silence.

'It can't only happen in films,' Dunai said.

DI van Reenen swiped a hand across his mouth. 'This is the seventh capital crime on my shift. I've got about eighty open dockets and I've been doing this for seven years. Most crimes that get solved are pretty much what they appear to be.'

Dunai resisted the urge to come out with what she'd heard on the stairwell; she'd have to admit to eavesdropping and he'd probably deny it anyway.

'But you are going to look at other possibilities. What about the man on his way up to Siobhan when Bryan and I were leaving?'

'An officer will work with you to compile an Identikit. We'll look into it, but right now primary evidence points to burglary and that's where we're going to direct our enquiries.'

He began to put his notebook into his pocket.

Dunai needed to put her head down till the medication kicked in, but for Siobhan's sake she fought it.

'I know there's something more going on here. At least question the people who were openly hostile to her. You can't imagine how volatile this sort of work is.'

'I think I can,' the detective said, getting to his feet. 'I deal with people all the time who're doing their bit to reduce the population.'

Dunai ignored this. 'Look, I know she was killed by someone who wanted to stop *her*, not steal the fax machine. You agree, Bryan.'

It was a statement, not a question. Bryan looked at her; curiously, she thought.

'When I called you, you told me to lock the door, not to open it to anyone except you or the police. You must have thought we were all in danger.'

Bryan ran a hand over his face.

'You agree?' The detective sounded even wearier.

'Before I knew it was a burglary, yes.'

'So you'll look at other possibilities?' Dunai was having difficulty forming the words.

'Not unless the evidence points in that direction. For now, we'll concentrate on the building's occupants. I'm waiting for the pathologist to arrive. When I've got his findings I'll finish my shift, but you can speak to one of my colleagues if you think of anything, otherwise you can get hold of me tomorrow.'

When he'd left, Dunai turned to Bryan. 'It wasn't a burglary. There's more to this than that policeman's letting on. I heard him talking to someone on the stairwell who seemed to be trying to get him to look at it as a burglary.'

'What exactly did they say?' Bryan asked, frowning.

'He said, "If burglary's where the evidence leads, then fine, but otherwise..." and then the other man interrupted but I couldn't hear what he said.'

Bryan shook his head. 'Listen, hon. This has been one hell of a shock, but we have to let the police take care of it. We need to carry on here; don't forget that in all this. There's Siobhan's vision and I know this is such a cliché, but it's what she would have wanted us to do. We're so close to attaining everything we've worked so hard for. We need to do this now more than ever.'

Dunai nodded because she wasn't capable of arguing any more. 'I've got a migraine.'

'Okay, let's get you onto the couch.'

She didn't get migraines often but when she did they knew the drill. She lay on the old brown twill sofa while Bryan went off to fetch a blanket. He covered her, then crouched down and patted her head. 'Try to rest. I've got to get on with things, but I'll be right here. You need anything, call.'

She woke with a start and looked around. The office was empty; it was the sounds coming from the passage that had woken her. The migraine was gone but she felt groggy and her stomach grumbled. She sat up and pushed the blanket aside.

Outside, in the passage, the scene-of-crime officers were packing up and the lights blazed overhead again, hurting her eyes. A moment later a stretcher carrying Siobhan's body, zipped into a body bag, was wheeled towards the lift.

She felt Bryan putting an arm around her shoulders but she didn't respond. It had just occurred to her how she'd begin the search for Siobhan's killer. It would mean depending on someone she disliked and dreaded approaching. It might not even work, but if it did she'd have a real chance of fulfilling her promise to Siobhan. And a little lost pride would be a small price to pay.

DUNAI lost the next seven hours in a blur of activity. Bryan took most of the calls, fending off the media and telling the story repeatedly to the people who'd known Siobhan. Dunai worked with a police officer on the Identikit that would hopefully reveal the identity of the last person to see Siobhan alive. Then she called Barbara, her next-door neighbour, who cared for her son during the day. She always went home for lunch and made sure she was there to put him down for a nap. Today, of course, she wouldn't make it.

'I don't know what to tell him,' she admitted to the ex-kindergarten teacher.

There was shocked silence on the other end, then Barbara's response sounded stiff and automatic. 'Better not say anything. He'll ask when he's ready and then, whatever you tell him, keep it simple. At two and a half he won't understand the concept of death, no matter what you say.'

Dunai spent the rest of the afternoon sending out e-mails, making cups of tea and coffee and going out to buy lunch, which neither of them ate. Siobhan's husband, anti-globalisation activist, Philippe Baobi, returned their call from France later in the day and she watched as Bryan stuttered over the horror of it, stopped, then started again as he tried to explain to the African expatriate what had happened to his wife. Dunai left her desk and went to perch awkwardly on the arm of Bryan's chair, her arms around his shoulders. He broke down for the first time that day when the call ended but Dunai refused to open the floodgates of her own grief just yet.

Bryan left soon after four, having told her how much he needed to be with his family. As much as Dunai longed to go home too, she stayed on for another half hour. What she was about to do, she knew Bryan would not approve of.

She went through her usual end of day routine—began the systems backup on the server, tidied her desk, got the coffee maker ready for the next day, put on her coat and slipped the back-up tape into her pocket. But, instead of leaving the building, she climbed one floor down and walked to the end of the passage.

The glass door was fronted by a thick wrought iron security gate that hadn't been closed properly. Next to it was a buzzer. Dunai pressed it. No answer. She pulled open the security gate and tried the handle. The door swung open.

The small reception area was cold and dim, with only one fluorescent tube buzzing overhead. Dunai filled her lungs with extra oxygen and strode across the room to the open doorway of the interlinking office. That was where she found him.

He wore jeans and a white T-shirt under a suede jacket. He was at his desk, turned sideways from the door, feet up, a drink in his hand. Dunai did a double take, but it was the room rather than the man that surprised her. A large bookcase covered one wall, a TV cabinet another, its shelves filled with ceramics and a collection of carved masks. Wooden shutters were fixed to the inside of the windows above a suede sofa—plush, chocolate brown and scattered with raffia- and ochre-coloured cushions. There were two cream upholstered chairs facing an oak desk that was cluttered with manila folders and loose pages. The chair behind the desk was high-backed and leather, and the man in the chair was Carl Lambrecht.

The ex-police detective was subject to more rumours than the Stock Exchange. She'd heard whispers about him in lifts and stairwells and it was usually women doing the whispering. The only thing that had sounded like fact was that he was in his mid-thirties, divorced, and had turned to private investigating after leaving the police force. Dunai wasn't sure she thought he was good-looking. He probably had been at some stage, but that had been before life had happened to him. His nose looked as if it had been broken and he hadn't bothered to fix it. His grey eyes had the same expression chimps got after being kept in small cages. His thick, light brown hair was mussed and his jaw line blurred by stubble.

She glanced again at the room of creams, browns and ochres—Afro-chic, masculine and tasteful, although it contained more dead animal skin than a curio shop. She looked back at Carl Lambrecht and shook her head. The man's lack of grooming had in no way diminished the feminine attention that had probably been his since birth. His deep voice with a slight trace of Afrikaans accent seemed to add to the attraction. Even Siobhan had been affected by him, taking extra care with her appearance whenever they'd met to discuss the investigative work he'd carried out for her from time to time. But not Dunai; she didn't like him. He was a cliché and she suspected his ego matched his size.

'Stand there any longer and I'm going to start charging.'

She jumped and blurted out, 'It's a case.'

'What's a case?'

'I want to talk to you about a case.'

'I'm closed.' He hadn't even turned to look at her. Rude bastard, Dunai thought.

'My friend was murdered today so if you're incapable of compassion you could at least be polite.'

All six feet plus of him swivelled to face her and Dunai's immediate reaction was to run, but she stood her ground, fighting the urge to drop her eyes to the carpet as his bored into her.

'Siobhan Craig,' he said after what was probably meant to be an intimidating pause. She nodded.

'You want a drink?' he asked.

'No, thanks.'

His eyes travelled over her. They reached her face. Dunai forced herself to hold his stare.

'Dunai. That spelt d-o-o-n-i-e?'

'No.' Dunai spelt her name for him.

'Never heard it before.'

'It means the physical embodiment of Earth Mother.'

'Your parents hippies?'

She shook her head impatiently and scowled. 'This isn't about me. I'm here for Siobhan.'

'Well, then, Ms Physical Embodiment of Earth Mother, what can I do for you?' He got to his feet, bowed from the waist and indicated a chair. She chose to ignore the mockery in his voice; she had a job to do so she sat.

'The police think Siobhan was accidentally murdered in a botched burglary. I think one of her enemies killed her.'

'Her enemies.'

'Don't say it like I'm a nutter. Yes, I know it's a cliché, but why is everyone having such a hard time believing it? Siobhan was advocating drastic measures to curb population growth that flew in the face of at least a dozen radical groups. It makes more sense that she was killed by one of these people than murdered because she stood between someone and a fax machine. And there's another aspect to this that everyone's ignoring. If Siobhan was killed because of the work she was doing, then Bryan and I could be in danger.'

Carl was slumped back in his chair, watching her while he tapped two fingers on the desk.

'Well?' she demanded with more force than confidence.

His eyes narrowed. 'I spoke to a couple of uniforms and techs and I don't think you have a case. It'd be pointless hiring—'

'I'm not hiring you,' she snapped, not even trying to fight her usual impatience. 'You don't have to do a thing. All I'm asking is that you give me some tips on how I can investigate this myself.'

'Tips.'

'Yes, tips. I'll do it with or without your help, but I know Siobhan hired you a few times and I also know she liked you.' Dunai realised that doubt must have shown all over her face because it provoked a smile that transformed Carl's features. 'I'm not asking for myself. I'm asking you to give me a few pointers for Siobhan's sake.'

Carl said nothing, just stared at her. She stared back. She wasn't leaving this office without his help. So he was being a hard-arse; it was nothing less than she'd expected. But she still had an ace up her sleeve.

'There's something else you should know.'

She told him about DI van Reenen's meeting on the fire escape with the man in the charcoal suit and, although Carl's body seemed relaxed still, his eyes had taken on an alertness that told her he was really listening now.

When she'd finished he sat forward and this time there wasn't a trace of mockery in his voice as he said, 'You need to think about this carefully, Dunai. Ask yourself how far you'd be prepared to go.'

'How far I'd...' She swallowed, dropped her voice and a little pride. 'Siobhan was like a mother to me; how far do you think I want to go?'

Carl looked at her intently, then sighed and nodded. 'Okay. The guy your detective was meeting on the fire escape was probably NIA. One of the uniforms I spoke to seemed to think intelligence was involved.'

'But why would the National Intelligence Agency come to the scene of Siobhan's murder?'

'Hmm. Something she was working on?'

'It's possible. The government was interested in her work. But still...National Intelligence.' Dunai couldn't quite believe it. 'And then there's the guy who was on his way up to see Siobhan when Bryan and I were leaving. He was more than likely the last person to see her alive. I don't understand why the police aren't making that the focus of their investigation.'

'Probably because the pathologist's preliminary finding is that the time of death was between ten and midnight. Your mystery visitor arrived at seven, which means he had a lot of time to kill before getting around to Siobhan.'

Dunai grimaced. Carl kept tapping his fingers on the desktop, looking thoughtfully at a spot just past her left shoulder.

When she couldn't take it any more, she said, 'So are you going to help me or not?'

'Tell you what, Dunai,' he said, leaning his forearms on the desk. 'You bring me proof of motive, or something pretty damn close, and you've got a deal.'

'I've started making a list of people she's had run-ins with.'

'Not good enough. Proof of motive or no deal.'

'Shit. Okay, deal.'

Dunai jumped to her feet and stuck her hand out. Carl looked at it, then shook. She could tell he was trying not to smile and that infuriated her.

'You an alcoholic, Mr Lambrecht?'

'Get out before I change my mind.'

She turned to go.

'Oh, and one other thing, Dunai. You ever call me Mr Lambrecht again, the deal's off.'

Dunai was so angry she almost told him to stuff his help, but she needed him so she bit her tongue and left the office quickly before that unruly appendage could work its way clear of her teeth.

As she hit the square she remembered Siobhan's cat. If she hadn't made it home last night he probably hadn't eaten. So, instead of going home, she headed for the flat in Queen Victoria Street. Grief would have to wait another hour.

4

DUNAI was almost certain she was being followed. It was an unusual car: olive green Valiant right out of the seventies. Any other day she'd have put it down to coincidence, but not today. And there was something familiar about the car but at dusk with headlights blazing it was impossible to see inside. About a quarter of her wanted to march up to the window and hammer on it, but she was three quarters coward so the overwhelming urge was to run like hell.

Without waiting for the lights to change, she leapt off the pavement, dodging bumpers and blaring horns. Instead of turning right into Queen Victoria Street, she jogged along Wale Street past St George's Cathedral. She made as if she were moving towards the Slave Lodge, then turned suddenly right into Government Avenue: a pedestrian walkway that ran the length of the Company Gardens. This way, if she were being followed, her stalker would have to follow her in on foot.

The Company Gardens had started life as a humble vegetable patch planted by the Dutch East India Company in the seventeenth century. It had become what some claimed was one of the world's most attractive city parks. It was also dangerous after dark. But it was still dusk and the risks seemed to outweigh the benefits, so she opted for quick passage through the gardens, hopefully keeping well ahead of her pursuer.

She had jogged halfway down the avenue when her calves began to cramp. She slowed to a brisk walk and looked behind her. A figure moved towards her. He wore a dark coat but was too far away for her to see any detail and she sure as hell wasn't going to wait around till he passed under a lamppost.

Gunning her long legs into action, she started to jog again, doing her best with the heavy tote over her shoulder and her muscles backchatting at every step.

If she had a mobile she could call Bryan from a hiding place and stay put till he arrived with the police. But of course she didn't carry a mobile because of the non-biodegradable nature of the product and the decimation of primates in West Africa where one of its components was mined. Now, thanks to her ecological stand, Dunai Marks might be next for extinction. She didn't have the option of finding a hiding place; she had to get out.

She knew she'd reached the centre of the gardens when she saw the sundial up ahead and the statue of the Virgin on a marble basin and plinth. The temperature was dropping and the air smelled of damp foliage. She jogged on past the old slave bell and the aviaries, and towards the statue of Cecil John Rhodes pointing north to the endless potential of the hinterland. These days everyone was rushing south, including Dunai.

It happened as she rounded the statue; a dark figure stepped into her path. She instinctively flung up her arm. Her wrist was caught in a strong grip.

'I'm not going to hurt you, Dunai,' the woman said, but Dunai yanked wildly against the restraining hand. 'I've been sent to talk to you. That's all I'm going to do.'

Her voice was low and calm. Dunai stopped struggling; it wouldn't do much good anyway. The woman's jeans and leather duster coat held within their seams a six-foot frame of muscle and strength that kept her rooted to the spot with no effort at all. Her eyes were dark in the fading light—no colour Dunai could discern. Thick, dark hair was pulled tightly off her face, accentuating a strong, almost masculine bone structure. A gold pendant of two crosses melded together glinted against the black of her polo-neck jumper.

'How d'you know my name?' Dunai asked.

The woman let go of her arm. 'That's not important now. What you need to know is that Siobhan was not killed in a burglary.'

Dunai felt stunned. She asked the next question tentatively. 'Who killed her, then?'

'We don't know yet.'

'Well, how do you know it wasn't burglary? How do you know Siobhan?'

'It isn't my task to answer these questions.'

Dunai faced the woman square on. 'I want to know.'

The woman's gaze was steady. 'Siobhan was a meticulous record-keeper but her documents have been removed for safe-keeping. There's nothing that'll incriminate her.'

'I don't know what you're talking about.'

'You will,' the woman stated with absolute certainty. 'We'll do everything we can to protect you but with so much focus on the situation there's only so much we can do to intervene.'

'Who is *we?*'

The woman's gaze did not flicker, nor did her voice alter a decibel. 'I have no directive to divulge that information. You must be patient, Dunai. Find who murdered Siobhan. The task is daunting but there is help available and it'll be extended when absolutely necessary. The purpose of this meeting has been to tell you this.' She nodded once. 'Good luck, Dunai.' Then she turned and strode towards the aviaries.

'Don't just… Hold on.' Dunai went after her. 'You can't say these things then disappear. Please just *wait*. You have to tell me what's going on. *Please*.'

The woman merely lengthened her stride, then disappeared around one of the cages. Dunai rounded the corner just seconds later but the avenue was empty. She stopped, stood there, arms dangling at her sides, and felt an overwhelming urge to burst into tears; this time out of frustration more than grief. But she fought it; right now she needed to get out of the gardens.

She walked quickly to the exit to Queen Victoria Street, pausing behind the pillars and giant conifers. No one rushed into the rose garden behind her and there was no sign of the Valiant in the street when she peered around the shrubbery.

She darted across, glancing over her shoulder as she unlocked the gate into the garden that fronted Siobhan's block of flats.

She fumbled a bit with the lock, got the door open and stepped inside. She locked it quickly behind her and turned on the passage light, then moved to the kitchen; the room was empty. She went to the study, then the lounge, crossed the room and drew the curtains. On her way back she touched the head of the dunai in the corner. The statue was just over a foot of polished wood, its breasts and belly enormous, face smooth and featureless, feet not important enough to carve.

Siobhan had bought it long before she'd met her. Sometimes when she'd visit, Dunai would get a soft cloth and linseed oil, sit cross-legged on the brown thick-pile carpet and polish it while they talked. Her son had taken his first steps on a Saturday afternoon using the statue for leverage.

'If anything happens to me, take it, it's yours,' Siobhan had said that afternoon.

Dunai decided she would, but first she had a cat to find. 'El Nino?' she called. No answer. She tried again—nothing. That was odd.

She went to the bedroom and flicked the switch, letting out a breath as the room filled with light.

Siobhan's slippers lay discarded close to Dunai's feet. A T-shirt had been thrown across the unmade bed. The chest was piled with folded laundry, books, a tube of hand cream and a foolscap notepad. Dunai felt tears on her cheeks and this time did nothing to stop them.

Life would never be the same without her. For two years Dunai had been desperate for her approval. Beside her childhood obsession with Pippi Longstocking, Siobhan had become her hero. She was everything in Dunai's character she'd grown up being mildly embarrassed about. Siobhan had taught her to prize these aspects of herself. All the things people had told her to quash, temper, Siobhan had encouraged her to cultivate, live out. Now what? The entire concept of death was too ridiculous to grasp; like a completely implausible ending to an otherwise good book. Here today, gone tomorrow applied to loser boyfriends and badly managed money. Not *life*. Surely not.

Wiping her eyes, Dunai looked round. She thought she'd heard something—a muted meow. 'El Nino?' It came again, from the direction of the cupboard. She rushed across the room and yanked open the first door. Nothing.

She opened the second door and the cat's silvery-grey body flew past her and landed on the carpet. Dunai pressed a hand to her heart. 'What the hell were you doing in there?'

He stopped in the middle of the room and let out a wail. Dunai withdrew the hand she'd extended. He wailed a second time, then a third. He couldn't possibly sense Siobhan was never coming back, could he? Superstition, Dunai, she heard Siobhan say. He was just hungry, probably thought he'd been abandoned. She couldn't understand why he'd been in the cupboard, though. Last thing Siobhan did every morning before leaving the flat was fill his bowls and make sure he was settled for the day.

Dunai stuck her head inside the cupboard. No mess, no smell of urine so he couldn't have been in there long. But then how had he gotten in after Siobhan had left the flat? Perhaps she'd forgot to close the cupboard door and he'd climbed in and been trapped when the door blew shut behind him. Dunai looked at the bedroom windows; they were closed.

She turned again towards the cupboard. It was obvious he'd made himself comfortable on top of a parcel wrapped in tissue paper. Something glinting on the shelf caught her eye and she reached up and pulled it out. It was a long, heavy gold chain and crucifix pendant of yellow gold with a second crucifix in white gold melded just to the right of the crossbar. It was the second time in half an hour she'd seen this pendant. She remembered it around the neck of the woman she'd just encountered in the gardens.

Dunai went to the bed, sat on its edge and stared at the pendant lying on her open palm. The cat's cries eventually penetrated the fog and she stood up slowly. 'Time to feed you, catman,' she mumbled. He wailed all the way down the passage and kept it up as she opened a tin of food. He stopped only as his head dipped to eat.

In the bedroom she picked the pendant up off the bed where she'd discarded it and put it back in the cupboard. She left the lamp burning in the bedroom and the kitchen light on; tonight she really didn't care that coal was a non-renewable energy source. After spending a minute scratching the cat behind the ears and assuring him Siobhan's husband was on his way from France, she let herself out, the statue of the dunai tucked under her arm.

5

It took Dunai fifteen minutes to reach the outskirts of Bo-Kaap, the area she called home.

Bo-Kaap meant 'above the Cape' and was tucked into a fold of Signal Hill above the City of Cape Town. Three hundred years ago the area had been home to skilled and educated slaves, who had been deported from the Indonesian archipelago and eventually freed. Their descendants had stayed on and over the centuries the twelve or so blocks had become peculiarly theirs. It was a labyrinth of brightly painted cube houses on narrow cobblestone streets that swept steeply up the hill where even the trees grew at an angle. There were spice shops, corner grocers and home industries and almost a dozen mosques, attracting a new mix of affluence and alternative lifestyles to the area. And at twelve on the dot every day except Sundays, the old cannon boomed from the top of Signal Hill, even though the glorious ships of the past no longer shifted at anchor below.

Dunai had just crossed Buitengragt when she noticed the Valiant approaching the Wale Street intersection. 'Oh, shit, oh, shit, oh, shit,' she said, fumbling in her bag for her phone card and heading for the public call box ten metres away. If she never made it home, it was imperative she tell someone about the car. Bryan picked up the phone.

'Bryan, there isn't time to explain. I'm being followed by an olive-green Valiant. I'm at the call box just past the Wale and Buitengragt intersection. Its lights are on so I can't see the registration or who's inside but it's an olive-green Valiant.'

'What the hell's—?'

'I've got to go.'

'Okay, okay, I'm on my way. I'll call the police. I'll get my mobile. Call me back so we can stay in touch. But you don't have… Shit. Okay—' Dunai put the phone down. Bryan would just have to find her.

The light turned green and the Valiant started up Wale Street. She needed to get off the street. She was making it too easy for them to pull up, drag her inside and drive off. She decided to take a back way that would be almost impossible to follow by car.

Few houses in Bo-Kaap had gardens. Some backed onto alleyways, others shared a courtyard or small paved area where adults parked their cars at night and children played football or cricket during the day. Dunai passed one of these squares on her left. It was dark now. There were a few parked cars, no children. Not a soul was out in the cold; it was supper time. Lights showed in windows and glowed from street lamps in golden puddles on the paving.

Just beyond the square a steep stairway was bordered on the right by the blank wall of a mint-green double-storey house and, a couple of metres on, a candyfloss coloured house straddled the walkway, a section of its lower storey creating an arched walk-through to the street on the other side—Chiappini Street and home. A nearby street light lent some faint illumination to the interior of the tunnel.

Dunai hoisted her bag higher on her shoulder, tucked the statue against her chest and descended the stairs at a trot, picking up pace as she stepped past the arches into the walk-through.

Something hit her between her shoulder blades and she went down on all fours, pain shooting through her knees. The statue clattered against the bricks. Another weight landed in the middle of her back, forcing her flat against the ground. Her attacker grabbed a fistful of hair and ground her cheek against the paving.

'Don't you fuckin' *move*. You look at me, I'll kill you.'

She didn't move. Her lungs felt crushed; it was hard to breathe. She tried not to panic. The voice was male, young. A voice from these parts. A voice of the Bo-Kaap. Her assailant, still with a foot on her back, began to tug at her coat. She was going to be raped. Surely not. Not me, Dunai thought. There had to be something she could do. Not just lie here like this. If she could just *think*.

'Your turn now, *bitch*,' her attacker growled and bent forward to get a better grip on her coat.

Dunai let out a bellow and in one motion heaved to the side and grabbed the dunai as she went. She threw her arm out sideways in a wide arc and felt wood connect with bone. Her assailant howled, let go of her. She twisted on the ground, got a glimpse of a black glove clutching the side of a balaclavaed head.

He came for her again before she could scramble to her feet. There was a shout and the sound of a car door slamming.

'Bryan!' Dunai screamed, scrambling to her feet. His name choked off as she saw the green Valiant and a man running towards her. There were more of them. They had her cornered and she couldn't fight them all. They'd drag her into the car, do God-only-knew-what to her, then kill her like they'd killed Siobhan.

She jumped back as her original attacker grabbed her bag from the ground and ran for the stairway. She felt dizzy and began to tremble, but she steadied herself for the attack, holding the dunai in front of her like a weapon as the man from the Valiant came rushing towards her. He wasn't at all what she'd expected, being middle-aged and wearing a white crocheted skullcap and grey beard.

Dunai began to feel battle rage and crouched lower as the Valiant's passenger door opened. She kept her eyes on the man coming towards her. Let them come. She'd damage every fucking one of them.

'You okay?' the man said, stopping a couple of feet from her. The words refused to compute. 'We saw that *skollie* attack you. My wife's calling the police. You okay?' he asked.

All she could think was: wrong question.

'You hurt?' he tried again. 'You want us to call a doctor?'

Dunai shook her head.

'My goodness,' the man said, tugging his beard, 'what is this neighbourhood coming to?'

A woman's scarfed head appeared on the passenger side of the Valiant. She was lit up by the car's interior light. 'Police are on their way,' she called, one plump leg still in the car, her hand clutching the doorframe.

'That's it,' Dunai said into the darkness. 'No more.' She noticed a strange look pass between the couple.

'Let us help you,' the man said, holding a hand out to her.

She avoided him, stepped into Chiappini Street and started walking, the statue cradled in her arms. The couple got back into their car and cruised very slowly behind her. She passed the mint-green house, yellow, baby-blue, lavender and her own turquoise house. Her bag was gone, along with her keys.

She stopped when she got to the pink house next door to her own and knocked. There was no answer. She hammered her fist against the wood.

'All right, all right,' she heard from inside.

The door opened and Gavin stared at her in horror. 'Oh-my... What *happened*? Rory!' he shouted. 'Something's happened to Dunai.'

'I've been attacked,' she blurted out. 'Siobhan's dead and I've got no idea how her cat got in the cupboard. I can't fetch Jesse like this.'

Gavin tucked his chin in, half turned. Rory's wiry frame, clad in psychedelic golf trousers that involved a lot of pink, red and orange, came down the passage towards her. He was wiping his paint-covered fingers on a rag. 'What's going on?'

'She's had some sort of breakdown,' Gavin said.

'Oh-my...' Rory said as he took in her dishevelled clothes, her mussed hair, bloodshot eyes and bleeding cheek. He opened his arms to her and she flew into them.

'We saw what happened,' the man from the Valiant said. He and the woman now stood on the stoep.

They all turned at the sound of brakes, as Bryan's blue Citroën and a police car came screeching to a halt at the pavement.

'That's it,' Bryan shouted, rushing towards the group. 'That's the car. Olive-green Valiant.'

Two policemen got out of their white standard issue Opel Kadet and walked cautiously towards the car that stood with its doors open. The group on the stoep looked from the policemen to Bryan as he stopped in front of Dunai and stared at her in horror. 'Who the hell did this to you?'

'I was attacked.'

'I can see that, but who did this? Who owns that Valiant?'

'I do,' the bearded man said.

'You did this to her?'

'No! That was a mistake,' Dunai said. 'He tried to help me.'

The policemen joined them on the crowded stoep.

'But why was he following you?' Bryan asked.

Dunai was far too confused to even hazard a guess. The accused man's head whipped in Bryan's direction and he pointed to his chest. 'Me? No, I wasn't following her.'

'I've seen your car before,' she said softly, trying to make sense of it. 'Then tonight in Longmarket Street, Church, Burg and Wale, now Chiappini.'

'What're you talking about? Following you?' the woman said angrily. 'He was coming to fetch me.'

'My wife works in Greenmarket Square,' he explained. 'After I picked her up, we went to her sister's flat in Kloof Street to fetch curtains. She makes curtains.'

'We've got them in the car,' the woman said triumphantly.

Her husband pulled at his beard and turned to the policemen. 'We were on our way home. We live further up in Stadzicht Street. Then we saw her being attacked in the walkway.'

'I thought you were...' Dunai said slowly. 'Oh, my God, I'm so sorry.'

She needed to sit down, which she did, on the step. Gavin came out of the house and pressed a tumbler of brandy into her hand, tissues into the other.

'I need you to go next door,' she told Gavin, 'and tell Barbara what's happened. I'll fetch Jesse as soon as I can.'

Gavin nodded and headed for the lavender house two doors down.

It took another ten minutes of explanations and apologies before the misunderstood couple drove away in their Valiant.

Rory, who worked from home as an artist, had a spare key to Dunai's house in case of an emergency, which this obviously was. Once he'd fetched the key, they all moved next door to Dunai's turquoise house. Gavin, who'd just returned from his errand to Barbara, went to the spare room to babysit the animals, which was a labour of love since he had allergies.

One of the policemen stood in Dunai's living room, looking aghast at all the second-hand paraphernalia she collected to sell at her Greenmarket Square stall every second Saturday. The other policeman went over to her small half-moon table, looked undecided for a moment, then chose to sit at the straight end.

'All this stuff yours?' the standing policeman asked.

'I didn't steal it,' Dunai said and took another gulp of brandy. She coughed, felt embarrassed but didn't put the tumbler down.

'What happened?' the seated policeman asked, his pen poised above a form.

'Why don't you sit first?' Rory suggested from the old wrought iron garden chair she'd picked up on municipal refuse day some years ago. She went to her favourite seat, which was a garden bench she'd found discarded near a children's park. She'd painted it pale pink and put cushions on it—good as new. Bryan sat beside her.

'Officer?' she said, shifting closer to Bryan and patting the bench beside her.

'I'm fine,' the standing policeman said, his hands clasped behind his back as his mother had no doubt taught him to do when surrounded by breakable goodies.

The only relatively new piece of furniture was a cream sofa Siobhan had given her because she'd said she was sick of sitting on the wooden bench with its flaking paint whenever she came to visit. Dunai tried not to look at it as she recounted the events of the evening. The seated policeman never once looked her way as he scribbled non-stop and fired questions over his shoulder.

He did look up when she said, 'I think this might have something to do with my friend who was murdered last night.' Even the standing policeman managed to tear his eyes from her bric-à-brac.

She told them about Siobhan, but left out DI van Reenen's argument on the fire escape with the man in the charcoal suit and her visit to Carl Lambrecht. She also said nothing about the woman in the Company Gardens and the necklace she'd found in Siobhan's flat. She concluded with, 'So it's obvious what he meant by, "Your turn now, bitch.".'

'Maybe not,' the seated policeman said. 'Seems like more of the same thing we've been seeing in this area lately.'

Dunai bit back a retort and tried to sound as rational as she possibly could. 'Look, I know all this sounds crazy but today hasn't exactly been a sane day. The person who just attacked me could be the person who murdered Siobhan. Would you at least run this by DI van Reenen?'

'You bet I will,' the policeman said with a note of sarcasm in his voice. He collected his forms, managed a muttered 'night' and headed for the door.

The policeman who'd stood throughout the interview said, as if he'd just had a revelation, 'You buy all this stuff, then do it up and sell it, right?' Dunai nodded. 'You make good money?'

'Some.'

'Hmm,' he said thoughtfully as he left.

'Shit,' Dunai said as she locked the door behind them. 'Why do people like that become policemen?'

'Failed their undertaker's exam,' Rory said.

Dunai's legs felt suddenly as if they'd had their bones removed. Never in her life had she felt so completely drained. She watched as Rory opened the door of the second bedroom. There were the sounds of a brief scuffle before Gavin came bounding down the passage sneezing. The cats, Tommy and Annika, made for the living room with Mr Nelson, an African grey parrot, waddling down the passage behind them. Her dog, Horse, a Bouvier des Flandres who was as big as a pony, rushed past Mr Nelson, who shouted, 'Bosh!' as he tottered dangerously in the dog's slipstream. All four animals headed for Dunai, who sat a little straighter, ready to give out greetings, pats and scratches with nothing less than the usual enthusiasm they'd expect of her.

6

DUNAI had cancelled her stolen cards while Bryan got a locksmith to change the locks, then he'd gone to the chemist for painkillers and ointment while Dunai got Jesse ready for bed. Somewhere in her exhausted body she'd found the reserves to behave almost as if nothing unusual had happened that day.

She thought about the woman in the gardens who had said she'd removed documents that might incriminate Siobhan, and the NIA man in the charcoal suit who wanted the murder treated as a botched burglary. Again she heard Carl Lambrecht's words: 'You bring me proof of motive, or something pretty damn close, and you've got a deal.' She'd been hearing them all evening and they made her stomach twist into a knot, so she forced herself to think of something else every time they came to her. This time it was her son.

He stood beside her bed, bare-bottomed in nothing but a pyjama top and red Winnie-the-Pooh beanie. Tufts of dark hair sticking out the bottom of the beanie were plastered to his face. Dunai made a mental note to get his hair cut. After a brief battle of wills, she managed to get Jesse ready for bed and tucked him in. Feeling exhausted, she sang him to sleep, then went to find Bryan, who'd returned from the chemist.

He was in the kitchen, bowl of eggs in one hand, whisk in the other. He paused to give her the painkillers and rub ointment between her shoulder blades then, despite her protests, insisted on

staying to finish dinner for her. Dunai gave up, left him to it and
went to the lounge where she curled up on an oversized bean-
bag that smelled of buttermilk rusks and Jesse.

Horse plodded across the room and began to fuss over her,
sniffing her face and hands and snorting. She stroked his rough
grey and brindle coat. The large dog stood utterly still for a full
minute, then once satisfied his guardian was in no immediate
danger, went back to the kitchen only to return moments later,
his loyalties divided between Dunai and the smells in the kitchen.

Dunai forced herself to eat the omelette and tried to ignore
Bryan's look of deepening concern every time the wind rattled
the old sash windows and made her flinch.

'We need to find who's doing this, Bryan, irrespective of what
the police think.'

'You could get into trouble, interfering with a police investigation.'

'Getting into trouble doing something I believe in has never
been a deterrent for me and this isn't the sort of thing to leave in
a stranger's hands. Not only is Siobhan dead, but there's a very
real chance you and I could be in danger. What about our children?'

Bryan shook his head sadly.

'You're not taking me seriously,' Dunai said.

'Dunai, all I'm asking is that you try to see this from the police's point of view,' he said. 'All evidence points to the fact that
Siobhan was killed in a burglary gone wrong and the logical explanation is that the attack on you tonight is part of a bigoted
campaign to get rid of outsiders in the area. Think about it, Hon.
It's pretty damn obvious in the cold light of day.'

'There're too many coincidences, Bryan, and what if you're
wrong? We could wind up dead.'

Bryan seemed to think about this for a moment, then shook
his head. Dunai felt anger bubble in her chest. 'Guy in the bala-
clava wasn't the first person to jump me tonight.'

The comment had the desired effect. 'What are you talking
about?'

She told him about the woman who'd accosted her in the Company Gardens. She also told him where she'd found Siobhan's cat and described the pendant, identical to the one worn by the amazon.

Bryan was silent for a moment, then ran a hand over his face. 'Siobhan's murder's been all over the news, Dunai. That woman could have been any crackpot. As for the pendant…' He shrugged. 'When things have settled I'll clear it with her lawyer and get someone to take a look at it.' Again he ran a hand over his face, the gesture more agitated this time. 'But right now I just don't know.'

Dunai had never heard him sound so weary before and she felt a little guilty. He'd been holding the fort, dealing with lawyers, the media and STOP associates all day. He too had been close to Siobhan; had known her a lot longer than Dunai and was having to deal with his own grief.

'We can talk about this some other time,' she said, leaning over and squeezing his hand. 'Why don't you go home and get some sleep?'

'I still think you need to speak to someone. Belle has a friend who's a grief counsellor—'

'Bryan.'

'No, I want you to listen to me. Just hear me out. Siobhan was so much larger than life. She had this enormous life force.' The last two words caught in his throat. 'And when someone like that dies we desperately want to find some meaning in it—a reason. But sometimes there just isn't any.'

Dunai gritted her teeth.

'What I'm saying is there're better ways to deal with grief. I'm worried about you in this state. Matter of fact, I want to you to pack a bag for yourself and Jesse and come spend some time with Belle and me.'

'I've got my animals to think about.'

'Rory can keep an eye on them.'

'I won't leave them, Bryan.' Dunai shook her head and Bryan knew better than to argue.

'Yeah, okay. You want me to stay?'

'Thanks, but I'll be okay.'

'You need anything, you call. And I mean that, Dunai. I can be pretty mean when one of my loved ones is threatened, so you call, you hear?'

'I hear.'

'Good. And stick to well-lit streets from now on. No more gardens or tunnels. And get home before dark or get someone to drive you. And let this thing go, Dunai. Give the police time to get on with the investigation. You and I already have our work cut out for us.'

Dunai nodded. Yes, she'd give the police all the space they needed. They could disappear into a black hole for all she cared. She had her own investigation to get on with because she had every intention of finding a motive for Carl Lambrecht, even though she had absolutely no idea how to go about it. Thing was, from now on she'd keep further developments to herself.

7

SIOBHAN is dead. Siobhan is dead. Dunai woke with these words looping through her mind. Feeling hollow inside, and trying to ignore the pain in her cheek and back, she got the morning routine underway with breakfast for Jesse and the animals, only managing a couple of mouthfuls of cereal herself.

She'd made sure she was running late for work this morning, dropping Jesse off with Barbara at a quarter to eight. Never a day went by that she wasn't grateful for Barbara's wise presence in her life. The ex-kindergarten teacher, who had lived almost all her forty years in Bo-Kaap, had decided to make do with her husband's social worker salary so she could stay at home with their son who was almost three. The mothers had become friends soon after Dunai moved in and it wasn't long before Barbara had offered to look after Jesse during the day for a reasonable fee. And, since they shared a tiny courtyard, the back doors of both houses were left unlocked so the animals had companionship and increased space during the day.

The third floor of the office block was silent and Dunai braced herself for the walk past Siobhan's office. Concentrate on the details, she told herself. Like how she was going to find a motive for Carl Lambrecht. She wasn't even sure if he'd meant motive as in having pretty good grounds for suspecting someone, or whether 'proof of motive' meant something that would prove someone's guilt in a court of law. As far as Dunai could tell, this was paramount to tracking down a murderer, which really irritated her. If she'd known how to find these sort of things she wouldn't have gone to him for help in the first place.

There were fifty-two messages on the answerphone. She worked her way through them, deleting calls from the media and all the people who said they wished they'd done it, the ones who were convinced Siobhan's murder was God's retribution, and the person who clapped and laughed on the other end.

By the time Bryan arrived at nine from a meeting with Siobhan's lawyer, Dunai was busy with a grocery list for Philippe, who was on his way from France and would be staying at Siobhan's flat, which was not well stocked even at the best of times. Although the pair had loved each other for some fifteen years, their devotion to their work had led them along divergent paths. Spending eight months apart every year would signal the death knell for most marriages but for Siobhan and Philippe it had suited their independent natures, their rejection of societal convention and their belief that their lives had a higher calling. If anything, it had seemed to only deepen their relationship over the years.

Bryan was on the phone taking down Philippe's flight details and Dunai had just crossed out 'croissants' and written 'bagels' when the word Bojangles popped into her head. Mr Bojangles! She gasped in surprise and Bryan shot her a worried look. 'Just remembered something,' she said, pretending to go back to the list, but Mr Bojangles's voice was like an accusation in her ears: '…there's been other things. Goings-on.' Mr Bojangles pointing at their building. 'The devil come out there.' She tried to remember his exact words but couldn't.

More delusions, more voices, she'd thought, and she'd been impatient with him, turning her back and walking away. Now she realised Mr Bojangles just might have seen the person who'd murdered Siobhan. It took an enormous effort to stay in her seat, keep her pen hovering above the grocery list.

As soon as Bryan left the office, she rushed to the window.

It was miserable down there, with stall owners huddled beneath colourful squares of tarpaulin. She strained to see Mr Bojangles's navy cap, but the distance was too great and there were too many trees.

She returned to her list, but kept trying to think of all the places Mr Bojangles could be. At midday, DI van Reenen stopped by the office.

'We've identified the man who came to see Ms Craig the evening she was murdered,' he said. 'His name's Dan Cowley.' He waited for a reaction; both Bryan and Dunai shook their heads. 'He's a property developer. Built the chain of Millennium Malls across the country, owns The Cowley Building on the foreshore.'

'What did he have to do with Siobhan?' Bryan asked.

'He heads up the South African chapter of Men of The Covenant.' Again Bryan and Dunai shook their heads. 'It's a Christian men's group,' DI van Reenen said. 'They packed out Newlands Rugby Stadium last month.'

'I don't see what business he'd have with Siobhan,' Bryan said. 'She was an atheist. As far as I know, she had nothing to do with religious groups of any kind.'

'And a *men's* religious group…' Dunai shook her head.

'He came to see Siobhan,' the detective said, 'because he'd heard about her work with abused women. He offered the counselling services of Men of The Covenant to men who abuse their partners.'

'To which Siobhan said no,' Dunai stated with certainty.

'Seems that way,' DI van Reenen said, consulting his notebook. 'She thanked him for his concern but said she avoided affiliation with religious groups because her programmes were about female empowerment and she didn't want the women who came to her for help to feel they had to adopt a certain ideology to get that help. Mr Cowley told Ms Craig that the offer stood if she changed her mind. She assured him she wouldn't and he left around seven-thirty.'

'So it's a dead end,' Dunai said.

'Seems that way,' DI van Reenen said. 'The post mortem will be done today, but it's unlikely time of death will change much. When Mr Cowley exited the building the security guard had left for the day but a tenant remembers him well. She was on her way out when she found him standing in the foyer. He'd come all the way downstairs, only to find the doors locked and had been about to go back up when she arrived. She confirms she let Mr Cowley out at around seven-thirty and locked up after him. Ms Craig's time of death was around ten, which means she was alive long after he'd left.'

'So we're back to the burglary scenario,' Bryan said.

'We never abandoned it,' van Reenen confirmed.

It was then Dunai almost told him about Mr Bojangles but all she really had was a gut feeling that he'd seen the person who'd killed Siobhan. She'd find the vagrant herself, try to get a description, then take it to the police. Or it might be better to go to Carl first.

When the detective left, Dunai grabbed her coat and bag and told Bryan she was popping home for lunch.

'Just a minute,' he said, going to his desk drawer. He took out a mobile phone and handed it to her. 'Here's the booklet that goes with that. I've written your number on the cover. Get familiar with it, Dunai. I want you to carry it on you at all times. I know you've got environmental concerns, but after what happened last night I think those are moot points.'

Dunai nodded, holding the mobile in one hand and the information booklet in the other. 'It's necessary in the circumstances,' she agreed. 'Thanks, Bryan, I appreciate this.'

'And make sure you take time off whenever you need to,' he said, closing his desk drawer. 'We've got the presentation to prepare but Philippe will be here soon to help and it's not like we can go on as if nothing's happened.'

'How are you doing?' Dunai asked.

'I've got Belle and the girls.' He shook his head. 'They're amazing. Sometimes I can't believe I had anything to do with producing them.' Dunai watched his Adam's apple bob. 'I didn't think I was going to get to have a family. Thought I'd die a lonely old man so not a day goes by when I'm not grateful for them. But you don't want to hear all this. Off you go, Dunai. Go home and feed your family.'

Dunai headed across the office, then turned back at the door. 'Bryan, what's going to happen with the house in Chiappini Street? I've always paid rent to Siobhan. I don't know anything about this friend of hers overseas who's the owner. I don't even know who'll be administering the property now that she's… You don't think we'll have to move, do you?'

'I honestly don't know,' Bryan said. 'But don't worry, I'll look into it.'

But Dunai did worry. She'd never be able to afford another property in the city. She'd have to move into the suburbs. She didn't have a car and she'd lose Barbara, and Rory and Gavin. She'd have to find day care for Jesse with some stranger… One step at a time, she told herself. And the next was to find Mr Bojangles.

Dunai searched the square in vain, even asking the security guards in the foyers of surrounding office blocks. At ten to one, rain was falling and the cold had seeped through her clothing. Despondent, she headed towards Bo-Kaap with two questions on her mind: how would one know if a vagrant were missing and, if he were, how would one go about finding him? The best answer she could come up with was: ask another vagrant.

If Mr Bojangles had seen the killer he might be in danger. She thought about going to the police but dismissed the idea. She knew what they'd say if she pitched up at the station with a story about a vagrant called Mr Bojangles who had told her he'd seen the devil in black with red eyes. No, she'd just have to find him on her own. He'd lived on the streets for who knew how long. His survival skills just might be enough to outwit the devil.

After lunch with Barbara, her son and Jesse, Dunai went back to the turquoise house, took two of the painkillers Bryan had bought the night before, went to her bedroom, drew the curtains and climbed under the duvet with Jesse. She closed her eyes tightly against the throbbing in her head. She felt the animals hop onto the bed but was too exhausted to chase them off.

She dreamt she was in the Company Gardens, crouched behind the statue of the Virgin. Siobhan and the amazon were fighting; blood poured from the larger woman's head. Siobhan was bleeding from the nose. She wanted to scream at them to stop, but she stayed behind the statue, hating herself for her cowardice. It was the dunai they were fighting over. Siobhan clutched it tightly to her chest and screamed, 'Back up!' as the amazon came towards her. Neither woman had noticed that the carving had changed from warm wood to cold, black stone. She heard herself scream as the statue's eyes began to glow red.

She woke to a loud thud, a shriek of surprise from one of the cats, a shout of 'Bosh!' and a deep warning rumble from Horse. She sat up quickly, her heart hurling itself all over her chest.

The thud had been the sound of the dunai hitting the floor—it now lay at Jesse's feet—and the cats, who'd probably climbed onto her bedside table and drawn his attention to the statue, turned their backs on the scene and sauntered from the room.

Sometimes Dunai wondered why she put up with them. Animals and children seemed essentially ungrateful to her. Tommy she'd taken in two years ago when he'd arrived at her door. From his battle scars and the mean look in his eye, she'd been sure the ginger was hungry, homeless and the cause of many unintended pregnancies around the Cape. For his sins she'd had him neutered. Annika she'd stolen. The small black and white cat had been living in filthy conditions in the backyard of a house next to a home used by some of the older orphans from St Mark's. Dunai and the man who had become Jesse's father had broken into the yard and taken the bundle of skin and bones to the vet. He thought she'd probably had several litters of kittens already. Annika never left the house now, except when they went for walks.

'Vaughn,' Jesse said, scooping the statue into his arms with some difficulty. It was the best he could do with Siobhan's name. 'Where Vaughn?' he said, tottering towards the bed.

Dunai swallowed. 'She's gone away, Jes.'

He hoisted the dunai onto the bed, then scrambled up after it. He reached for the statue and turned it upside down.

'I don't want you playing with this, Jesse. It isn't a toy and you might break it.' She reached for the dunai but Jesse pulled back with a sharp, 'No!'

Something clicked in Dunai's brain.

'Back up,' she mumbled to herself. 'Oh, my…'

She leapt off the bed and ran to what should have been the dining room but was a study, animal and storage room. There were two boxes on the table beside the computer. One held backup tapes labelled according to the days of the week—copies of STOP's computer files kept off site—but it was the larger box Dunai unlocked.

About a month ago Siobhan had asked her to store a CD with the backup tapes. It was the only time she'd ever done this and Dunai had failed at the time to wonder why Siobhan needed a CD of reports stored off site when they'd already been copied to the backup tapes.

She flipped through the disks until she came to one marked 'Progress Reports—Siobhan'. She slipped it into the computer and brought up the disk's contents. It contained only one Word folder called 'reports' but when Dunai tried to open it she was prompted for a password. She tried all the obvious names and dates but nothing worked. She glanced at her watch; it was twenty to two.

She went back to her bedroom, where Jesse was putting the dunai to bed, scooped him up, then rushed next door to the pink house. Rory answered her knock wearing a white poet's shirt splattered with paint and trousers sporting thin yellow and green vertical stripes.

'You look like a gherkin,' Dunai said as he stepped back into the passage to allow them to pass.

'I do?' Rory said, bending forward to look at his trousers. 'Oh, my gosh, I do, don't I?'

'Don't worry,' Dunai said. 'Impersonating a pickle isn't a crime. Gavin isn't here, by any chance?' She held her breath.

'You're in luck,' Rory said. 'How're you, big boy?' he said to Jesse.

'I *am* big boy,' Jesse said proudly.

'You're the man,' Rory said, holding up his hand. Jesse high-fived him. To Dunai he said, 'Hold on a sec; I'll get Gavin.'

Gavin was not only Rory's lover, but also a techno-wiz who owned an IT consultancy. He worked in the city and often came home for lunch.

'You feeling better today?' he asked, stepping into the living room.

Not knowing what to say, Dunai simply cocked her head to the side.

'Suppose not,' Gavin said. 'I'm terrible in situations like these. Never know what to say.'

'Don't worry about it,' she said. 'I need your help.'

A wary look crossed his face.

'With an IT problem,' she said.

Gavin relaxed. 'What can I do for you?'

'How difficult is it to get into a password protected Word document?'

'Easy,' Gavin said.

'I need to access one of Siobhan's folders. D'you think you could get me in?'

'Don't see why not.'

It took him less than ten minutes to tell her, 'Password's *Ubuntu*,' before he returned to the pink house to finish lunch.

There were thirteen files inside the folder. A surname had been used to name each file. Dunai recognised 'Cowley', the man who'd come to see Siobhan the night she had been murdered. She opened the file and began to read. Her hand trembled on the mouse as she opened another file, then another and read the list of transgressions, followed by what looked like passwords to computer files and a log of dates, digits and telephone numbers.

It took her a while to realise she was reading carefully documented blackmail records. It still didn't mean Siobhan had collected the information. She might have stumbled onto someone blackmailing these people and been killed for it. But the dates didn't lie. Too many of them coincided with co-operation Siobhan had managed to pull out of the hat at the last minute or the inexplicable backing down of powerful opposition to some aspect of the pilot project. She recognised the large cash injection STOP had received from a wealthy supporter and plans that had been passed unexpectedly by local government.

But why give Dunai such an incriminating disk? Perhaps she'd thought her life was in danger and she'd wanted her to know who had a motive. Or she might simply have wanted somewhere safe to keep the backup, never expecting Dunai to disregard the password.

The file name—*Ubuntu*—showed a level of cynicism Dunai had never encountered in Siobhan. The word meant 'humanity' in Xhosa and represented an ancient African principle of individuals working together harmoniously for the good of the whole—'I am because we are'.

'Mummy, I firsty.'

Dunai became aware that she was rocking back and forth, stunned beyond belief. Siobhan had done this. There was no getting away from it.

'Mumm-yyyy.'

'Okay, okay, I'm coming.'

Dunai printed out the password pages, then placed the disk back in the box. She put the box in the desk drawer, locked it and slipped the key into her pocket.

She got a drink for Jesse, then took him next door to Barbara, rushed back, threw on her coat, tucked the password sheets into a pocket of her jeans and went again to the pink house next door.

Gavin was reluctant to go to Siobhan's flat, insisting that since Dunai had the passwords she didn't need him.

'Trust me,' she said. 'Nothing since yesterday morning's turned out right. I might still need you.'

The small second bedroom in Siobhan's flat had been turned into a study. There was barely enough room to move between the bookcases and cluttered desk where her computer was kept. A file fell to the floor as Gavin sat at the desk. He shot up again.

'Shit!' he said. 'You sure we're meant to be here?'

He looked towards the door as if expecting a couple of Keystone Cops to burst in at any moment.

'What do you mean?' Dunai asked, pulling up a chair and putting the cat on her lap.

'Aren't the police meant to go through her stuff or something?'

'It's not a murder scene, Gavin. And anyway the police are convinced she surprised a burglar in her office. They're overworked and underpaid and not interested in looking any further. Sit,' she instructed. Gavin sat.

For the next ten minutes his fingers flew over the keyboard, not letting up even as he muttered to himself and tipped forward from time to time to peer more closely at the screen.

'*What?*' she said, when she couldn't stand it any longer.

Gavin slumped back in the chair. 'Computer's been wiped.'

'What do you mean, wiped?'

'It's all gone, Dunai. Every last shred of data. Usually when files are deleted they're no longer visible to the user but remain on the hard drive and that data takes a long time to be overwritten. You can't even wipe a hard drive by submerging it in water; you'd have to physically destroy it. I bet if we opened her up we'd find she's been toasted. Whoever did this knows their stuff.'

Gavin sounded impressed; Dunai wasn't.

'What about backup disks?' she asked, pulling open the top desk drawer. It was empty except for a few items of stationery. 'This is where Siobhan keeps her disks. It's usually full of them.'

She put the purring cat on the ground and searched the rest of the study but came up empty-handed. 'I can't believe this is *happening*,' she said, pressing the heel of a hand to each temple.

'There was nothing wrong with this computer a couple of days ago and all her backup disks were in that top drawer. Who the hell is *doing* this?'

'She have a laptop?'

'Yes, but it was stolen in the so-called burglary.'

'Then I'm fresh out of suggestions and late for a meeting.'

Gavin got to his feet. The cat brushed against his leg. 'Yes, you're gorgeous,' he said, peering down, 'but I'm allergic.'

'Thanks for helping,' Dunai said, feeling frustration turn to despondency.

'You want a lift back?'

'No, you're late. Go on. I'll see you later.'

When Gavin had left, she went back to the study and stared at the computer.

'Siobhan was a meticulous record-keeper but her documents have been removed for safe-keeping.' That was what the amazon had told her in the Gardens. 'There's nothing that'll incriminate her,' she'd said.

'I don't know what you're talking about.'

'You will,' the woman had said with certainty. They'd erased all trace of files on Siobhan's computer and taken her disks, which was probably when the cat had been closed in the cupboard. Only they didn't know Siobhan had given Dunai a backup disk.

Dunai stayed to feed the cat and give him some attention. Sitting in the middle of the living-room carpet with him dozing in her lap, and a deep pain in her heart, she wondered who Siobhan had really been and, more pressingly, what life-threatening activity she'd been mixed up in.

8

DUNAI'S arm was twisted into staying for dinner by Bryan's wife, Belle, and she watched with fascination, as she always did, a world she'd never been part of. Nothing was lost on her. Bryan's varying expressions as his daughters, named Amy and May in honour of their mother's triumph over dyslexia, recounted their day. The degree of synchronicity in the family's speech and humour. The way Belle took off her specs halfway through dinner and gazed short-sightedly at her family around the dining room table. The small smile on her lips.

Dunai looked over at Jesse, who was propped up on cushions spooning mashed potato into his mouth. At his age she had no idea what it was like to sit around a family dinner table like this and she felt a sense of achievement that, even though she'd failed to create a nuclear family of her own, Jesse was at least experiencing it on a regular basis.

It was unfortunate that tonight she had more on her mind than the pleasures of family.

It was eight o'clock when Belle finally took the girls off to bed. Dunai told Bryan she needed to speak to him on his own. She tucked a blanket around Jesse, who'd fallen asleep on the sofa, then went to Bryan's study. The room showed nothing of his American heritage. Zulu pot lamps, a dark wood and wicker desk, the Mbali cushions and woven throws covering chairs and sofa, and the chiwara, a stylised antelope head symbolising agricultural prosperity, atop an Ashanti stool in the corner, were proof of roots planted deeply in African soil now. The only décor of a global nature were the numerous family photographs and children's artwork on walls, desk, bookcase and cabinet.

'Don't you miss your home country?' Dunai asked.

'This is my home country.'

'But still…'

'The poverty's greater here, Dunai, but so's the honesty.'

'Honesty.' Dunai repeated the word with a twinge of nostalgia.

'Hmm,' Bryan said. 'In America people are indoctrinated with the American dream while forty per cent of its children live below the poverty line, there's racial segregation in schools and half the country's wealth is owned by less than two per cent of the population. And very few people feel the need to do anything drastic about it. It disgusts me.'

'I see what you mean,' Dunai said. 'But if your parents were still alive you'd want to go back to visit them.'

Bryan shook his head. 'You grew up without parents. I wish I'd at least grown up without a father.'

Dunai frowned.

'My mother did her best,' Bryan explained. 'But my father was a bastard; always quick with the strap. I swore I'd never hit my kids and I haven't. I've always tried to raise them with encouragement and compassion.'

Bryan looked over at a photograph of his daughters and his face softened, lost some of its tension as he recounted an anecdote. It was a while before Dunai was able to tell him her reason for coming here tonight and, even to own ears, her words about murder, blackmail documents and missing computer files sounded melodramatic and surreal amidst all this homeliness. Bryan said nothing when she'd finished.

'Say something,' she finally said. 'Just don't tell me you knew about this all along.'

Bryan, who'd been sitting with his legs crossed, leaned forward suddenly. 'Of course I didn't.'

Dunai didn't believe him. 'Then why aren't you shocked? You don't even seem surprised.'

He fixed her with a sad stare. 'That's because I'm not.' He sighed. 'I've always suspected Siobhan didn't play by the rules. There were too many things that didn't add up. Times we should've been completely derailed but she managed to keep us on track, strengthen our position even.'

'But you said nothing.' Dunai didn't want to sound angry but she did.

Bryan held up a placating hand. 'No, I didn't keep quiet. I tried to bring it up on several occasions but you know Siobhan. She didn't like being questioned. I tried to speak to her again…it must have been six months ago, but she questioned my loyalty to STOP. There was an argument. I didn't bring it up again. I suppose, after that, every time something went inexplicably right for us, I convinced myself it was Siobhan magic.'

'Who the hell was she, Bryan? Can you tell me that?' Tears slid down Dunai's cheeks and she swiped at them angrily with the back of her hand.

Bryan got to his feet, went to sit on the arm of her chair and put an arm around her shoulders. 'This changes nothing,' he said vehemently. 'Siobhan was everything you knew her to be. Now you find out there's more, so what? How many people do you know personally who'd sacrifice everything to fight for people too self-centred or short-sighted to realise our survival as a species is at stake? Siobhan fought the good fight, Dunai. Don't ever forget that.'

Dunai felt deeply disappointed. Bryan had a strict code of ethics and she'd never known him to compromise.

'So now blackmail's part of the good fight?'

'Look at it from Siobhan's point of view. How long d'you watch people self-destruct before you take drastic action? I warned her about breaking the law, but I understand why she did it. Siobhan had no compartments or divisions in her life—she was always an activist.

'The last time I tried to get her to tell me what she was up to she asked if I'd intervene if Amy or May tried to commit suicide. I said of course I would. She said society had decided it had the right to intervene in such cases, whether it meant drugging the suicidal or incarcerating them in institutions. So why were people like herself expected to stand by while humanity slowly but surely committed mass suicide?'

'Intellectually I understand the argument, Bryan, but I can't believe her actions were justified under any circumstances. It begins with blackmail, then where is the line eventually drawn? And who decides?' She shook her head, trying to dislodge the overwhelming feeling of disorientation that had settled around her that afternoon on Siobhan's living room carpet. 'All this time I thought I knew who she was, what she stood for…'

'She loved you, Dunai. She admired the woman you are and the woman she knew you'd become; you can be absolutely certain of that. She did what she had to do and that was between herself and her conscience, but it changes nothing about your relationship with her.'

Dunai felt his arm around her shoulders tense suddenly. 'You aren't going to the police with this?'

She said nothing.

'Dunai?'

'What if she was murdered by one of the people blackmailing her, like Dan Cowley? He was there the night she was killed.'

'I want you to think very carefully about what you're going to do,' Bryan said, and Dunai recognised the slow, patient tone he'd used when teaching her the more complicated aspects of her job, or explaining some statistical axiom.

'Going to the police will destroy Siobhan's reputation and it'll have serious repercussions for STOP. It'll more than likely shut us down. Everything we've worked for, gone. Nothing we do can bring her back, but think about what she would have wanted us to do—go to the police with information about someone who might have murdered her, an action that will most definitely destroy her life's work, or use our energy getting government to adopt the STOP model and bring her life's work to fruition?'

'I know, I know, Bryan. Believe me, I've gone over it again and again; all the scenarios, all the possibilities. It's just all so damn *crazy. Shit!*'

He nodded. 'We're all flawed, Dunai. *I've* felt compelled to do things I'm not proud of—you probably will too one day— but despite this our lives can count for something. We still can make a difference. Siobhan believed this. I believe it. So think long and hard before you potentially destroy all the good we've done in order to right this wrong. If going to the police is eventually what your conscience dictates, I'll be right next to you at that charge desk. Just give me some warning, okay?'

'Of course I will,' Dunai said and reached for his hand.

She tried to think what Siobhan would say if she were here with them and it was as if she could hear her voice in the small room: *Always plan for first prize, Dunai. It's better to aim high and miss than aim low and hit.* No, Bryan was right, she couldn't go to the police. She had to work for first prize, which was finding Siobhan's murderer while keeping her work and reputation intact. After all, it was nothing short of the way her mentor had lived every one of her forty-eight years.

9

It was darker than the inside of a buried coffin when Dunai set out at six the next morning. She was jumpier than a Maasai warrior and she'd questioned her sanity every time she'd woken during the night, which was often. But she'd known all along there was no other way of finding Mr Bojangles. She had to mount her search before the streets began to stir.

She'd prepared as best she could—jeans, running shoes and a meat mallet in her coat pocket. It wasn't comfortable; it weighted her down on one side, but it was comforting. She'd first reached for a knife, then discarded it. She knew she didn't have what it took to stab someone. Bludgeoning she'd tried and it was now her preferred method of self-defence.

She began in Greenmarket Square with a penlight torch in her left hand and the mallet in her right. Finding Mr Bojangles among the street sleepers who were rolled into blankets, plastic, cardboard and newspaper was a bit like trying to guess which gift under the Christmas tree was yours by studying the wrapping.

Passing the torch beam over one group then another, her calls and nudges were ignored or met with curses and a couple of growls from dogs she found sleeping beside the vagrants. She'd never expected this to be an easy task but, having had to resort to this craziness, she was at least going to do a thorough job. If a bundle ignored her, she'd carefully lift the edge of a blanket with her torch or nudge the mass with the toe of her shoe until she got a reaction. Mr Bojangles was nowhere.

Almost every weekday for two years she'd come across the old man in the square, ready to remind her of his need for a morning coffee. Was it coincidence that she couldn't find him, the day after he might have seen Siobhan's killer? But there was no reason to harm him no matter what he'd seen. Nobody would believe him anyway. She'd keep searching.

She headed reluctantly for Cape Town Railway Station, where she'd been told many of the homeless spent the night.

On the Strand Street side of the station, men, women and children were sleeping everywhere. She made her way carefully between them, trying not to stand on limbs or shine her torch in anyone's eyes. Halfway down the ramp she felt eyes boring into her back. She turned slowly and shone her torch in that direction. She was being watched by a young man. His dark face was almost indistinguishable in the darkness but from the whites of his eyes she could see they were wide and alert. She saw a flash of white teeth and her heart froze.

Her fingers tightened around the handle of the mallet. Slowly she pulled it out of her pocket, let it catch the light of her torch beam. The movement wasn't as smooth as she might have liked; she was shaking so much it was a miracle she managed to hold on to either item, but it seemed to work. Although he kept watching her, he made no move and after a minute she backed carefully away and began to make her way down the ramp towards the underground mall that ran beneath Adderley and Strand Street and formed the lower level of the Golden Acre shopping centre.

She was at the bottom of the ramp when something slithered into her path. Dunai stared down in horror at the woman whose legs were missing below the knee, the stumps covered with plastic bags.

'You give me money. Give me, give me,' the woman said, wagging one of her stumps at Dunai.

'I'm looking for Mr Bojangles. He wears a navy blue cap with "I love Cape Town" in red,' she blurted.

The legless woman threw back her head and laughed, her mouth wide open, showing rotten teeth. The laugh was cut off suddenly and she slithered forward with remarkable speed. Dunai jumped back and turned to run. A voice said, 'This way. To the right.'

The words were sober, rational, and she obeyed. As she rounded the corner of the rockery, she came across a woman of about her own age wearing a dark turban, an infant sucking at her breast. This section of ramp in front of the lawns of Cape Town Station wasn't nearly as crowded. There were more children here and many couples, as if this were family quarters. Dunai stopped in front of the turbaned woman just long enough to thank her.

'Wait,' the woman said. Her accent was African, but Dunai couldn't tell if it was Xhosa, Zulu or any of the country's other seven official black languages. Dunai turned but made no move forward.

'I haven't seen the man you call Mr Bojangles since yesterday,' the woman said.

Dunai stepped closer, lowered her voice. 'D'you know where I could look for him? I've looked everywhere. I don't know where else to go.'

The woman shrugged. 'Shelters, day clinics, the processing plant.'

'Processing plant?'

'The morgue. Particularly this time of year.'

Dunai thanked the woman, started to leave, then turned back. 'I wish I had something to give you but I left all my valuables at home.'

The woman smiled, nodded, then turned her attention to her infant, detaching the small mouth from her nipple and shifting the baby to her other breast.

Dunai felt stupid as she made her way up the ramp. Stupid, naïve…and contaminated. Stupid because she'd allowed herself to be chased by a legless woman. Naïve because she'd felt really good about stopping now and then to talk to Mr Bojangles, but the cup of coffee she'd provided nearly every morning for two years sure as hell didn't make her Mother Teresa. And she felt contaminated by the dirt and desperation and misery she'd been forced to brush up against. The words of the nursing mother cut right through her: '…the processing plant. Particularly this time of year.'

The sky over Greenmarket Square was just beginning to lighten at seven-thirty. She'd been walking the streets for an hour and a half, her feet hurt and she was hungry. She did one more circuit of the square before heading for the office.

Carl Lambrecht had another irritating habit: he was a late riser. Dunai, who had never slept past eight o'clock in her life, found this widespread habit inexplicable. It was just after ten when she finally found the safety gate unlocked and Carl in his office.

'I've been waiting all morning to show you something.' Dunai started to rummage in her pockets.

'We playing twenty questions or you going to show me?'

Carl watched as she took folded pages from the right front pocket of her jeans, then the left. She placed the sheets on the desk, then reached under her red body-warmer.

'This looks like it's going to take a while,' Carl said. 'I'll get us some coffee,' and he left the office.

By the time he came back with two steaming cups, she'd smoothed out the pages and placed thirteen neat piles on the desk. She accepted the coffee with a tense, 'Thanks,' took a sip and noted, despite her distraction, that Carl made a really good cup of coffee.

She sat down as he took his seat, then leaned forward as he picked up his mug. Their eyes met over the rim. Dunai stared back, this time with confidence. Unlike their previous encounter, this morning she had the upper hand. She'd swear there was no way he'd expected her to come up with any motive at all, never mind thirteen in two days.

Carl seemed to sense her excitement. He frowned slightly, placed his mug on the desk and began to read the sheets in front of him. She had almost finished her coffee when he said, 'Shit,' and sat back in his chair.

'That's what I thought,' Dunai said. 'And there's more.'

She told him about the wiped computer files and Mr Bojangles. But she kept her encounter with the amazon in the Company Gardens to herself. Until she had some idea of what Siobhan had been involved in she'd keep this information to herself.

'Those files could've made our job a lot easier. Still, this is enough,' he said, picking up one of the sheets. 'It gives Dan Cowley motive *and* places him at the scene.'

'Except he'd left the building by seven-thirty while Siobhan was still alive.'

'He could've come back,' Carl mused.

'But why draw attention to himself by coming to see her if he intended to kill her?'

'*If* he intended to kill her. His visit earlier in the evening could've been a last-ditch attempt to get her to stop blackmailing him and when she refused he felt he had no choice. Since he'd been seen entering the building he couldn't exactly do it then, so he decided to leave making sure somebody saw him, then came back later. Perhaps Siobhan had told him to get out, she had a lot of work to do, and he guessed she'd be working late.'

'The police believe him,' Dunai said. 'He's a religious man, pillar of the community. Without this motive,' she said, motioning towards the stack of papers, 'they have no reason to doubt his story.'

'Exactly,' Carl said, tapping the desk. 'You need to decide if you want to take all this to the police.'

Dunai said nothing. Her reasoning and resolve after the conversation with Bryan the night before were still fresh in her mind. If she took the blackmail notes to the police it would ruin Siobhan's reputation and kill every goal she'd worked towards, and they were so close.

Carl sipped his coffee, watching her over the rim.

'It seems the National Intelligence Agency is encouraging the police to treat Siobhan's murder as a burglary gone wrong,' Dunai reasoned, 'and we still have no idea why that is. What if we rush off to the police with the blackmail motive, only to have them believe Cowley's story anyway? This doesn't change the fact that he was seen leaving the building; the door was locked behind him while Siobhan was still alive.'

'He could've got hold of a key,' Carl said, 'but waited downstairs for someone to let him out so he'd be seen leaving the building.'

Dunai shrugged. 'Maybe we should find that out before we go to the police. Gather more information so we can go to them with something concrete. If we find some definite way of linking him to the crime we might not have to bring out all the blackmail documents and ruin Siobhan's reputation.'

Carl's smile annoyed her. She was probably being too touchy but now was as good a time as any to clear the air.

'You know, when you grin at me like that it's very condescending. I might be using clichés, but all I have right now to draw on are detective novels and TV series.'

Carl held up his hands in a don't-shoot gesture.

'Not this time,' Dunai said, looking pointedly at them. 'So does this mean you'll help me?'

'That was the deal.'

Dunai smiled with relief; Carl didn't return the gesture.

'Don't get too happy,' he said. 'We're not even close. This could take months of hard work and it would have to be handled very carefully. We're talking about card-carrying pillars of the community here. And Dan Cowley might have been telling the truth.'

'Still, it shows these people had a motive.'

'Yes, but, as you pointed out, you still have to find evidence linking them to the crime.'

'So where do we start?' she asked with genuine humility.

'The post-mortem,' Carl said. 'You can't take anything for

granted till you know exactly how she was killed, and till time of death has been confirmed.'

Dunai swallowed hard and resisted the urge to screw her eyes shut against the image that popped into her head.

'The post-mortem's been done,' he said, his voice gentler now. 'I'll find out what's in the report. I don't expect you to go into that. I'll handle it.'

Dunai nodded.

'We'll get the ball rolling once the memorial's over,' Carl said. 'It's tomorrow.'

He nodded. 'I've been asking some questions and it would seem the NIA is unofficially involved.'

'What does that mean—unofficially?'

Carl massaged his unshaven jaw. 'It usually means their involvement is part of an ongoing operation—a delicate one.'

'I still don't understand what that means,' she said, feeling frustrated. 'For all we know, it could be nothing more than something that overlaps one of Siobhan's projects or one of her contacts. It might not even have anything to do with her.'

'First tip, Dunai; this is a line of work that demands enormous patience.'

'You be patient, I'll move things along.'

Carl looked at her, but this time there was no challenge in his gaze; he was assessing her and she felt as if she'd pitched up at a Greenpeace rally in a four-wheel drive, guzzling a whale-meat sandwich.

'Only about twenty per cent of murder cases are ever referred to court,' he said. 'That means out of the average nineteen thousand murders in this country every year, around four thousand get to court, while fifteen thousand go unsolved.'

Dunai sat back in her chair, shocked by what she'd just been told. 'I'll try to be patient,' she said. 'But whoever killed Siobhan's not getting away with it.'

'Another thing—keep looking for Mr Bojangles, but take someone with you next time you decide to do it in the dark. Just keep in mind that, although he might be able to give you some information, he'd be no good as a witness.

'The role of the PI is to gather enough evidence for the police to do their job—to catch the perpetrator and send him to court with solid, backing evidence that'll lead to a conviction. That isn't going to include a schizophrenic vagrant called Mr Bojangles.'

'Point taken,' Dunai said.

'We'll start contacting these suspects day after tomorrow. I'll make copies of these.' He began to collect the sheets.

'I already have,' Dunai said. 'They're in a safe place, separate from the disk.'

Carl smiled slightly as he finished putting the sheets into a pile. 'I think you're catching on.' And this time she decided to take it as a compliment.

10

SIOBHAN'S memorial service was held in Silvermine Nature Reserve. She'd had no close family still alive, other than Philippe, so it was he who scattered her ashes over a small stream, tears sliding down his ebony cheeks. This had been her favourite spot as a child. Now friends and fellow activists lined the banks, paying tribute to her courage, altruism and honesty. Dunai noticed Carl at the edge of the crowd.

Siobhan's body had been brought back to this stream where she'd once been innocent and happy, and Dunai's heart surged with the rightness of it. Siobhan was at peace.

The will was read by Siobhan's lawyer, Graham Harstead, at his office in the city centre. The running and directorship of STOP had been left to Bryan and Philippe. The legalities seemed endless. What little cash she'd had now belonged to various charities. She had left her flat to Philippe, its furniture, appliances and artworks, except the dunai, which was to go to its namesake along with the contents of Siobhan's cupboards and her personal effects. 'Title-deed to the house in Chiappini Street,' Graham continued, 'is to be transferred to Dunai Marks.'

Dunai felt as if she'd been jabbed with a cattle prod. 'But I…' she began, then stopped. Again, this was all wrong. 'The house in Chiappini Street doesn't belong to Siobhan; it's owned by her

friend who lives overseas. She told me he was willing to charge
a low rent for a trustworthy tenant.'

They were all looking at her.

'It made sense,' Dunai said. 'The house's over two hundred
years old…' She looked at Bryan, who also seemed confused but
he shook his head and shrugged at her unasked question.

'You must be mistaken, Dunai. The house has been Siobhan's
since…' Graham rifled through some papers on his desk, then
turned back to them '…since 1994. It's yours now.' He smiled
at her, mistaking her turmoil for surprise at having suddenly become the owner of a house in one of the most sought-after areas
in Cape Town.

As soon as Graham had finished the reading, she excused herself and rushed out of the building. She walked aimlessly through
the streets, trying to make sense of it all.

Yes, she was surprised the house had been left to her but she
was more surprised that Siobhan had lied to her, made up a story
about an overseas friend who was offering a low rent in exchange for someone who'd look after the property. Siobhan had
deliberately downplayed her involvement in Dunai's life. And
what of their meeting? Had that been the happy coincidence
she'd always thought it to be? Now, as she ran through it again,
it seemed ludicrous that, having witnessed her sacking, Siobhan
had rushed into St George's Mall and, without even interviewing her, offered her a job as her assistant—a position that required
enormous sensitivity and discretion.

The more she thought about the last two years, the more she
was pulled back into the past—to the very beginning. She had
been abandoned at St Mark's when she was about a month old.
It had been October 1977. Siobhan would have been twenty-one
then; young—desperate and on the run from the apartheid government's security police. Dunai knew she'd slipped out of the
country and gone into exile in late 1977. Perhaps she'd dumped
her baby at St Mark's before taking off and the statue of the dunai
she'd had all those years before they'd met had been kept as a

reminder of the baby she'd left at an orphanage with nothing but a scrap of paper and the word 'Dunai' scrawled across it.

She couldn't believe she'd never seen it before. It was so damned obvious.

Dunai hurried across Greenmarket Square. Her heart kept pace as she raced into the building and rushed up the stairs.

Philippe was in Siobhan's office, her diary spread out in front of him. His large black hands caressed the pages covered in her handwriting as if he could in this way make contact with the woman he'd loved most of his adult life, who was now out of reach for ever. He looked up as Dunai rushed in and stopped at the desk.

'You okay, Dunai?' he asked, rising from the chair.

'No, I'm not, Philippe,' she said, knowing her voice sounded wobbly.

He came round the desk and eased her gently into one of the visitor's chairs, sat and took her hands in his. 'Tell me,' he said, and the command reminded Dunai that she sat beside one of the world's most formidable activists.

'The house, her personal effects—she had other female friends but she left it all to me, and she lied about the house. I don't believe our meeting was coincidence either. I think she was keeping an eye on me, then intervened just at the right time—when I'd lost my job and had a three-month-old baby to look after.'

Philippe nodded, patted her hand, then let go and sat back in the chair, raising his arms above his head and flexing first biceps then triceps. 'Hmm,' he said.

'So you've also wondered.'

'Not until you said this. There is so much to be dealt with.' He waved his hand towards the desk strewn with administrative detritus.

Dunai felt a moment's guilt but pushed it aside. 'What about her background, Philippe? Her family. Everyone has family. She wasn't adopted, so where are they and why has she always refused to talk about them? She must have told you something.'

Philippe shrugged, then shook his head. 'No, Dunai, she did not do this. We saw so little of each other. When we were together… It was a passionate liaison, and there was always so much to talk about—our work we live for.'

'But didn't you find it strange that you knew nothing about her family? She was your wife, Philippe.'

'Let me explain,' he said. 'When I was a baby, my mother left Benin for Marseilles. Life was hard, poverty-stricken. It was common for people to lose family they left behind. I went back to West Africa in my twenties. Found my mother's father, an old man, but my father was gone a long time. I do not even know what he looks like or if he is alive.'

'I'm sorry, Philippe,' she said, 'but South Africa isn't West Africa. Families don't just disappear here.'

'Not any more,' he said, reminding her of the tyranny of apartheid. 'But you must believe me, she said nothing about them—only that she had changed her family name.'

Dunai shook her head; her hands were bunched into fists. 'What do I do now? I can't ask her. All I want is to know if she was my mother.'

'You are the same height, have the same build,' Philippe said. 'It is possible. Those were troubled times, Dunai—the seventies in South Africa. She has spoken of them to me, but not of her family and not of a baby. I am sorry. I don't know.'

They were silent for a while, then Philippe said, 'But of course you can have a test for DNA.'

Dunai took a moment to digest this, then nodded. 'Where do they do those?'

'Here? Sorry, don't know,' Philippe said, shrugging his massive shoulders.

'I think I know who to ask,' she said, jumping to her feet. She took Philippe's face in her hands and kissed his forehead. 'Thank you,' she said. 'I'm so sorry I've dumped all this on top of your grief.'

'Ah, Dunai,' he said and shook his head.

* * *

Carl was slipping a file into a drawer his back to the door, when she rushed into his office.

'I need some advice.'

'Come right in,' he said wryly, without turning round.

'I need to know where a person can have a DNA test.'

Carl said nothing but his grey eyes contemplated her; she hated that. He was the only person who'd ever made her squirm—other than Siobhan.

'Well?' she said impatiently.

'That depends.'

'What do you mean, "that depends"?'

'Who wants the test done?'

Dunai sighed impatiently. *'Me.'*

Carl was all business when he said, 'Take a seat.' She was about to argue, then thought better of it. Thankfully, he asked no further questions. 'I've got a contact at Wynberg Military Base.' He scribbled a name on a piece of paper and handed it to her. 'He's a pathologist. Ask for him at Two Military Hospital. He'll get you the results quickly.'

Dunai's shoulders sagged with relief. 'Thank you, Carl, I appreciate this. And thanks for coming to Siobhan's memorial.'

Carl nodded.

'I'll see you tomorrow morning at eight,' Dunai said, jumping to her feet and rushing from the office.

11

DUNAI HAD teamed camouflage trousers with a long-sleeved T-shirt. The Punky Fish cardigan had been flung on after Jesse'd wiped his porridge-smeared mouth on her in Barbara's kitchen. She'd been late as it was and hadn't had time to go home to change. The scrapes and bruises on her cheek at least matched her trousers.

'Next time,' Carl said, as she climbed into his four-wheel drive, 'try not to be so obvious.'

'What?'

He turned in his seat and looked pointedly at her trousers, then touched a fingertip to her jaw just below the scrapes and bruises. He ran his finger slowly towards her chin and her body reacted as if he'd struck a match and lit a fuse that sizzled all the way to the bottom of her stomach.

'You look like you're up for your next scrap,' Carl said.

Dunai jerked her head away. It had been a long time since a man had had this sort of physical effect on her. And Carl Lambrecht of all people! They weren't even each other's type. Not that type came into it because Carl was here to help her find Siobhan's killer. It was the only reason she was sitting in this gas-guzzler with him. Attraction was not on the agenda—and definitely not the sort that made you want to do something about it.

'It wasn't intentional,' Dunai said, reaching for her seat belt.

'Ever heard of a guy called Freud?'

'Matter of fact, I have,' she said. 'Skinny guy, glasses. Gets beaten up all the time by the cousins, Chaos and Coincidence.'

She turned her head just in time to catch a flash of amusement in his eyes but there wasn't a trace of humour in his voice when he said, 'We might have to interview suspects today and you never wear combat gear to interviews.'

Once they had left the garage, he said, 'I've got the results of the post-mortem.'

Dunai had turned to look out of the window. Her head spun sharply in his direction.

He shook his head. 'There's nothing in it that'll help us.'

'Can you tell me anyway?'

'All right.' He glanced at her, then looked straight ahead. 'Siobhan died as a result of asphyxia caused by manual strangulation. From bruising of the soft tissue around her neck the assailant wore gloves and from the position of the bruises it's likely her attacker was male.'

'But there were gouges all over her neck.'

'They were downward wounds made by her own nails as she tried to relieve the constriction around her throat.'

Don't think about Siobhan, Dunai told herself, concentrate on the facts. 'What about other evidence? They had a whole team of people dusting light bulbs and anything else they could get their hands on.'

They'd stopped at a traffic light and a group of street children, aged about four to ten, appeared at the driver's window with Coke cans held out for spare change. Carl ferreted under the dashboard, wound down his window and dropped a few coins into the nearest can. The light changed and they drove on.

'In real life forensic investigation doesn't happen the way it does in TV serials,' Carl said. 'There's a shortage of forensic scientists and equipment, laboratories take an average six months to analyse DNA, evidence corrupts easily and results are sometimes inconclusive or open to interpretation.'

'So you're telling me all that prodding and poking was useless. Why send in all those people then?'

'In certain circumstances,' Carl said, 'it can be effective. And it's possible for victims' families to pay for private forensic analysis. It's a fast evolving area of—'

'But it's useless in our case.'

''fraid so. They collected a large number of samples from an office they believe hadn't been cleaned in a while.'

'Siobhan was busy preparing the presentation to government,' Dunai said, feeling the need to defend her. 'She didn't want to be disturbed. All she'd allow our cleaner to do was empty her bin.'

'Well, since the person who killed Siobhan wore gloves and there were no prints on the passage light bulbs that had been tampered with, they'll run the print samples but they don't expect to find anything. They're not even going to try to process the DNA samples.'

'I still don't understand why,' Dunai said, frustration evident in her voice. 'Even if he wore gloves, what about hair and stuff?'

'Hundreds of samples were collected from an office that saw a lot of traffic and hadn't been cleaned for weeks. Techs have nothing to compare the DNA to other than Siobhan, you, Bryan and your cleaning lady, so analysis and cataloguing would take hundreds of hours, cost the taxpayer a bomb and more than likely prove fruitless anyway. DNA forensics is a last resort; solid detective work's the first choice.'

'And DI van Reenen is proving to be as fruitless as the forensic samples.'

'Van Reenen's a good detective,' Carl said, sounding defensive. 'But, like most officers, he's under pressure that's inhuman at times. Way things are, a detective can have forty open murder dockets on his desk at any given time when it's almost impossible to work effectively with more than four. And he works alone, not like in other countries where a team is appointed to a murder case.'

'Thank you for sharing that with me,' Dunai said, giving full vent to her disappointment. 'Now I not only feel a whole lot worse but you've also blown the last shred of faith I had in getting any help from the police.'

'All the more reason to learn whatever you can from me,' Carl said as they turned onto the N2 and headed away from Cape Town's CBD.

Khayelitsha, with its montage of squalid shacks, suburban homes, shopping centres, clinics and brightly painted recreation centres, was South Africa's largest single township, covering some forty-seven square kilometres. It was home to half the city's unemployed and had a notoriously high crime rate. Born of a colonial society's insatiable need for cheap black labour, it defined itself in a decade-old democracy as a place of artists, craftspeople, actors and musicians, criminals, gangs, syndicates and all the people who fitted somewhere in between—the housewives, artisans, blue collar and office workers, students, company directors and entrepreneurial millionaires.

The township had been a second home to Siobhan. She'd spent at least half her time here, and it was in this environment Dunai sensed her, even more than in her flat in Queen Victoria Street.

'This is it,' Dunai said, indicating a large three-storey golden face-brick building behind a precast wall topped with electric wire and CCTVs.

Carl pulled up in front of the wrought iron gates and swiped Dunai's card through a slot beneath the intercom. The gates opened and they drove into the small parking area that fronted the building.

Dunai had a brief chat to the security guard while they waited at the steel security door. There was a loud click, it swung open and they stepped inside.

There were two women seated on chairs in the reception area—one crying softly, the other with a recently stitched gash across her forehead and an eye that was swollen shut. A third woman sat on a sofa, a toddler sleeping on her lap and a young boy pressed to her side, sucking his thumb and staring dead ahead without blinking.

Women were usually never kept waiting at reception but Monday was always a busy day. Rapes and beatings tended to go through the roof at weekends.

Dunai spoke briefly to those staff who could spare a few moments, then led Carl along a passage and unlocked an office two doors down from reception.

Siobhan's office was cramped and messy, stuffed with chairs, books and periodicals, files, folders, a fire extinguisher and first aid kit, and handmade gifts of every description.

'And I thought I was challenged in the housekeeping department,' Carl said, looking around him. 'You take the computer. I'll start with the desk. You got keys for those cabinets?'

Dunai gave them to him. She moved a life-size rooster made of plastic bags off the seat, then turned on the computer.

Just as Siobhan had rarely thrown anything away, she'd hardly ever deleted anything from her computer. Dunai restricted herself to e-mails received in the last month, keeping an eye out for any of their suspects' names. There was nothing. Next she did a network search of folders, files and content containing the word *Ubuntu*. There was one folder of that name and it contained a single e-mail, subject: 'Shame on you'. Dunai opened it.

It was an electronic card featuring Itchy and Scratchy from *The Simpsons*. It said, 'Fool me once, shame on you. Fool me twice…watch out for my tool.' And the demented cat began stabbing the mouse in the eyes, then hacking at his chest with a butcher's knife.

'My God, who sent this?'

Carl bent over her shoulder. 'Someone who is not a poet.'

'This is a death threat.'

'Who's it from?' Carl asked. She was aware that his chest was almost touching her shoulder.

'Info@wcpa.gov.za.'

'Western Cape Provincial Administration,' Carl said, snatching the blackmail list from the desk and searching through the names. 'Here we go. Wayne Daniels, Western Cape Provincial Administration.'

'Sending something like this is a bit stupid, isn't it?'

'Not really,' Carl said. 'It would be difficult to prove it came from him since it wasn't sent from his personal e-mail and, even though it looks like he was threatening her, Siobhan was black-mailing him so it's unlikely she'd have shown it to anyone.'

'But still, why risk something like this when you're planning to murder the person?'

'If at the time you're not planning to murder them. From the wording, it looks as if he was trying to warn her off blackmail-ing him a second time, which from her records we know she had no intention of doing. Or if the murder's made to look like a bur-glary so there's no call for the police to spend hours trawling through someone's computer.'

'So Wayne Daniels joins Dan Cowley on the list of people we definitely want to speak to.' Dunai tried to keep her voice light but she felt sick at the implicit violence in the card that had been aimed at Siobhan.

'First we do preliminary interviews over the phone with everyone on the list. Get alibis, confirm them, then interview the people who don't check out. I'll set up the interviews with Daniels and Cowley, then do a couple of calls to people on the list so you get a feel for how it's done.'

Dunai bombed out on her first call, getting way too heated when Siobhan's name met with a tirade of abuse. Carl was ob-viously angry with her.

'You wanted to learn, so here's a lesson,' he said as she re-placed the receiver. 'Self-control in a situation like that is not op-tional.' He collected the list and headed for the door.

Dunai took her time turning off the computer, locking the of-fice and saying goodbye to the staff.

The lesson continued in the car. 'There's a difference be-tween an interview and an interrogation. You go gently in an interview. The objective is to not only get information but to learn as much about the subject as you can. So you listen and let the subject do the talking.'

'But you were aggressive with one of the people you called.'

'Even if I hadn't known courtesy of Siobhan that the person I was speaking to was from a privileged background, I picked it up from her accent, her speech mannerism. And someone from an affluent background is usually sheltered and less likely to be able to handle social aggression. Sometimes it's good to shake things up a little. But shaking things up is not the same as alienating the subject.'

Dunai said nothing. As much as she hated to admit it, she was impressed.

'Here's a list of reading I want you to do,' he said, coming to a stop at a traffic light and pulling a piece of paper from his pocket. He handed it to her. There were at least ten titles on the page.

'First one I want you to read is *Interview and Interrogation Techniques*.'

Dunai looked away from the sheet to his hands on the steering wheel. Long fingers with a fine covering of light brown hair, short nails showing a few specks of white. She imagined them on her body, cupping her breasts, a thumb rubbing her nipple, sliding across her stomach. Shit! Dunai tore her eyes from the steering wheel and stared out of the window.

'Don't ever do that again,' Carl said and for one horrible moment she thought he'd read her mind. 'If you want to learn, keep quiet, observe and listen,' he said, oblivious to what was going on in the seat beside him.

Dunai let out a slow breath, said nothing. She felt a little chastened, probably because she'd never been very good at self-delusion and she did think she'd treated Carl a little harshly. He wasn't charging for his help and advice and he was taking his role as teacher very seriously. Perhaps there was more to learn from Carl Lambrecht than she'd originally thought.

When she arrived at the office, she asked Philippe if he would call the police and find out what progress they'd made. But his conversation with DI van Reenen was depressingly brief and he shook his head as he replaced the receiver.

'There is nothing new to report. He says evidence is pointing to burglary. In six months two people in this building have lost their keys and another one mugged; so it was not difficult to get inside,' he said sadly.

Dunai glanced over at Bryan, who shook his head, guessing no doubt that she was about to tell Philippe about the blackmail documents. She was also dying to tell them both about Carl's investigation. She felt guilty at keeping something so important to herself but she didn't want to worry them and she didn't want anyone trying to talk her out of it. She'd leave them to concentrate on STOP and the presentation to government, then let them know about the investigation when she and Carl made a breakthrough. Thinking of it this way made her feel a little less guilty.

12

CARL came to fetch Dunai at seven-fifteen the next morning. She was waiting on the stoep wrapped in her dark-blue duffel coat. It was cold but clear with a blue sky and no sign of rain.

Carl's four-wheel drive smelled of fast food and Dunai noticed the wrapper on the dashboard as soon as she climbed in.

'You shouldn't eat that stuff,' she said. 'Even Jesse knows that.'

'I'm a big boy, I can handle it.'

'From those white specks on your nails it looks like you have a zinc deficiency. You should eat pumpkin seeds.'

'Eugh,' Carl said, pulling a face. 'But that's a good observation, Detective Marks, and thank you for your concern.'

'It's not so much you I'm worried about. Fast food companies torture and kill billions of animals every year and enormous herds fart methane gas into the atmosphere, literally blowing a hole in the ozone. Natural habitats are destroyed to produce protein in the most inefficient way possible while global hunger worsens as poor countries use their land to grow fodder to feed the meat-eating habits of those who have more than enough to eat already.'

Carl frowned at her. 'You know, I haven't heard that much hot air expelled in one go since Mr Fourie's hot air balloon was attacked by two black eagles over my uncle's farm in Matroosberg.'

'That's rude,' Dunai said.

'So is criticising someone's eating habits.'

Carl seemed genuinely disgusted with her, which didn't faze her in the least. He didn't say another word till they'd left the city and harbour behind them and were speeding along the incline of the N2. Only then did he bring up the reason for this morning's excursion. 'So what's your research turned up on our primary suspect?' he asked.

'He's a sick bastard.'

'Facts, Dunai.'

'Okay. Dan Cowley's a sick bastard and that's a fact.'

Carl looked at her, his expression indecipherable, then turned back to the road.

Dunai pulled a notebook from her pocket, turned back a few pages and began to read. 'Son of a prominent apartheid judge. Went to two of the most expensive public schools in the country. Was an average student but excelled at team sports. Graduated from the University of Cape Town with a degree in commerce. Made a fortune in property development. Married, two children, a boy and girl, and head of the South African chapter of Men of The Covenant.'

'So what makes him a sick bastard?'

'How much d'you know about Men of The Covenant?'

'A bunch of men who meet in stadiums and hug and kiss a lot.'

'Yet remain resolutely homophobic,' Dunai added. She flipped another page. 'Men of The Covenant is an international organisation that promotes a particularly nasty brand of bigotry with some five million members worldwide. It's built on the belief that chaos in society is caused by rejecting traditional gender roles. They believe women are being allowed to influence men, turning them into sissies and throwing households, communities and entire nations into crisis. Why are you smiling?' Dunai scowled at Carl.

'I can't believe anyone would take this sort of thing seriously.'

'Well, they do. They even encourage men to take back their

place from their wives as leader of their families,' Dunai said, shaking her head and going back to her notepad. 'Consensus is the organisation teaches men to honour their wives and children but uses its narrow interpretation of the Bible to promote racism, homophobia, patriarchalism and misogyny. They publicly state that women were created for men, gays are stark raving mad and abortion is a capital crime. They've even said slavery was re-demptive because it taught black people to be slaves of God.'

'Bunch of kooks,' Carl said.

'Dangerous bunch of kooks,' Dunai added. 'It's been reported that men have been organised into small squads, infiltrating all levels of society—schools, government, even the military, for what they refer to as "war" to fulfil the Bible's prophecy of a great force that will destroy sinners and infidels in the period pre-ceding Armageddon.'

'Siobhan must have loved busting this guy's balls,' Carl said as he took the Bishopscourt turn-off.

'And I'd like to bust what's left of them.'

'Which you'll do under no circumstance.'

Like hell, Dunai thought, but she said nothing.

'Dunai?'

She realised she was clenching her jaw and tried to relax.

'I want you to promise you'll let me handle this; that you'll say or do nothing to jeopardise this interview. Give me your word or I'll leave you in the car.'

'Shit!' Dunai exploded. 'Why don't you take out membership of Men of The Covenant while you're at it?'

Carl said nothing. Dunai sighed. 'Okay, I promise.'

'Thank you. So, to sum up, we know the guy has a need to con-trol and manipulate, and he uses institutionalised rules and regu-lations to do that. He's fearful, intolerant and more than likely has a lifelong pattern of refusing to take responsibility for his actions.

'If he was involved in Siobhan's death, we're going to have to stay calm and non-confrontational if we're going to get him to slip up. You're doing this for Siobhan, Dunai; keep that in mind.'

Dunai had never thought the day would come when she was impressed with Carl Lambrecht, but here it was, and so soon.

Cowley's home was a three-storey mansion of cream paint, stone quoins and Corinthian columns. They were met at the door by a painfully thin woman who introduced herself as Annette Cowley. Her blonde hair was puffed up and blow-dried, and a thick layer of carefully applied make-up gave her the appearance of an American soap star. This was the acolyte, Dunai guessed.

Annette Cowley led them down a wide passageway lined with family photographs—all posed studio portraits. She stopped at a carved oak door, knocked and waited. There was a cheerful call of, 'Come in.'

She opened the door and poked her head inside. 'Dan, honey, Mr Lambrecht's here to see you.'

'Thanks, sweetness. Show him in.'

Dunai'd stuck her finger in her mouth as if she were gagging. She quickly pulled it out as Annette began to step aside to let them through. Carl sent her a warning look and they stepped into Dan Cowley's study.

He came towards them with hand outstretched. He was slightly shorter than Dunai, thin and wiry with brown hair that had begun to recede. His face was broad and strongly boned. A sudden image flashed into her mind of this man in the foyer of their building the night Siobhan was murdered. His palm was moist when he shook Dunai's hand and she pulled away as quickly as she could, fighting the urge to spit on her palm and rub it against her coat.

'Thank you for coming to see me,' he said, taking his seat behind an oversized cherrywood desk. 'Please have a seat.'

Cowley's figure was a silhouette against the light radiating off the white tiles of the terrace and Dunai's eyes watered as sunlight flashed across the surface of his highly polished desk. She wondered if their suspect was trying to wrestle control of the meeting at the outset, not only by placing himself in such a way as to make it difficult for them to see his facial expressions, but by implying that it had been his idea to meet.

Carl was having none of it. 'I don't know how pleased you'll be at the end of the interview,' he said, lowering himself onto a red cushion on one of the ornately carved chairs. 'I've got some difficult questions to ask.'

Cowley nodded. 'I've already spoken to the police—Detective Inspector van Reenen, if I remember correctly. I told him everything I know which, I'm afraid, is precious little.' He shifted in his seat and looked at Dunai. 'So how are you involved in all this, Miss…?'

'*Ms* Marks. I'm Siobhan Craig's protégée.'

Cowley stopped smiling and Carl jumped in. 'For clarity's sake, Mr Cowley, I am correct in assuming you didn't tell the police you were being blackmailed by Siobhan Craig?'

'I really didn't see the necessity.'

'Well, you see, Mr Cowley—' Carl's voice sounded almost lazy and his accent was more pronounced '—that's the thing about police work. When you're the last person to see a victim alive it really isn't up to you to decide what is and isn't necessary; that's the investigating officer's job.'

'Of course,' Cowley conceded, 'but something you must realise is this whole business came as an enormous shock to me. I had to make a split-second judgement call and, since there were several reputations at stake, I decided to keep my own counsel. It was never my intention to deceive.'

'But you do realise, Mr Cowley, you had a motive for killing Siobhan?'

'Although provoked, I didn't respond, Mr Lambrecht, I do assure you.'

'Despite the fact that you must have really hated her for what she put you through?'

Cowley smiled sadly. 'Hate, no. Pity, yes. You see, Mr Lambrecht, I believe that feminists are just frustrated women unable to find the proper male leadership. If a woman were receiving the right kind of attention and leadership she wouldn't want to be liberated.'

Still smiling, he looked over at Dunai as if he actually expected her to agree with him. She opened her mouth but Carl grabbed her hand behind the desk and laced his fingers through her own. She was so taken aback by the feel of his fingers sliding between hers that she clamped her mouth shut.

'So you claim to have harboured no ill feelings towards Siobhan.'

Cowley sat back in his chair. 'The Bible warns, Mr Lambrecht, that the evil among us will be cast down and shattered at the feet of the righteous.'

Carl still held Dunai's hand. She tried to pull away, but he squeezed it gently.

'Mr Cowley, we know that Siobhan was blackmailing you, but we're not sure what she was getting you to do.'

Cowley winced. 'All our activities throughout Khayelitsha had to stop immediately. She told me that if she so much as heard a whisper about Men of The Covenant she'd go public.'

'And if Siobhan went public your reputation would be destroyed, wouldn't it, Mr Cowley? Not to mention what it would do to your father.'

'Oh, I wouldn't go so far as to say destroyed. Damaged, maybe, but not destroyed.'

Carl said nothing. He waited. Dunai watched the man behind the desk squirm and felt a fraction of tension leave her body for the first time since she'd walked into this house.

'I…' Dan Cowley said. 'Men of The Covenant would understand that a son should not be held accountable for the sins of the father.'

'They might,' Carl conceded. 'But what about all those still to be converted? And can you imagine what feminist organisations would do with that sort of ammunition?'

'It was an accident,' Cowley blurted.

The sun had become less fierce outside thanks to a bit of cloud cover and Dunai watched his face redden.

'She was a prostitute. My father thought she was a decent

woman. It was raining. He stopped to offer her a lift. She got into his car, then started clawing at him, propositioning him. He tried to get her out of the car—'

'She was beaten to death.' Carl's voice was like ice. 'I remember the case, Mr Cowley. I'd just joined the police force. The woman turned out to be a domestic worker on her way home from work, not a prostitute. She had four children waiting for her at home.'

'That was a lie!'

Carl raised his voice. 'Your father was a prominent apartheid judge. He had a nickname. What was it? Oh, yes, I remember now—"the hanging judge". The crime was simple enough, but the case never got to court. General consensus was that the security police hushed it—'

'She attacked him! All he did was defend himself—'

'Ah,' Carl said, his voice softening, becoming consolatory. 'But how would it look to others if it ever got out? You know what the media's like. They wouldn't stop till every skeleton had been dug up and every bone picked clean. Your father's still alive, isn't he? Who knows what retribution there'd be?'

The rise and fall of Cowley's chest had quickened. 'I didn't kill Siobhan Craig. As God is my witness, I didn't kill her.'

'Why did you go to see her the night she was killed?'

'You ever been blackmailed, Mr Lambrecht? Well, I can tell you it isn't a pleasant experience. Khayelitsha's the country's fastest growing township. Questions were being asked. Members and committee wanting to know why Men of The Covenant wasn't trying to reach people there.

'I went to ask Siobhan Craig to stop what she was doing. I tried to appeal to her sense of honesty and decency, but she said she was forced to keep people like myself away from communities where the uneducated and poverty-stricken were vulnerable to organisations that handed out money and promises in exchange for adherence to some or other poisoned doctrine that furthered the aims of a select group of individuals.'

'That must have been very difficult for you to hear.'

'Yes, it was,' he said. 'But I didn't kill her, if that's what you think.'

'Where were you the night of the fifteenth, after you'd been to see Siobhan?'

'I went straight to seven o'clock prayer meeting. I was a little late, must have got there round seven-thirty. I was home by ten-thirty.'

'Do prayer meetings usually go on for three and a half hours?'

'The prayer meeting was over at about eight-thirty. I stayed on to discuss business matters with our leaders.'

'Till what time exactly?'

'I'd have left just after ten if I arrived home around ten-thirty.'

'We'll need to verify all this,' Carl said. He let go of Dunai's hand, then pulled a notepad from his pocket. 'I'll need contact numbers for your secretary, the person who ran the prayer meeting and the leaders you met with afterwards, and we'll also need to speak to your wife about your movements on the fifteenth.'

'There's no need for her to know,' he snapped. Then he brought his voice under control. 'She'd only make herself sick with worry.'

'The numbers,' Carl prompted him.

He began with his secretary. As soon as he'd finished, Carl stood. 'Thank you for your time, Mr Cowley.'

'We'll show ourselves out.'

Just before opening the door, Dunai turned back. 'Oh, by the way, Mr Cowley, just so you know. The reason for your all-male conclaves is not one of your arguments for male supremacy possesses even a modicum of intelligence, wisdom or compassion. You are no different from the apartheid government, the Third Reich or any other despot who's ever existed. Goodbye.'

She yanked the door open, stepped into the passage and let out a sigh—boy, that felt good! Even so, she avoided eye contact with Carl as they made their way along the passage.

They met Annette Cowley in the hall and Carl asked her about her husband's movements on the night of the fifteenth. She confirmed what he'd told them but Dunai noticed, as they questioned her, that she began to wring her hands, although she asked no questions.

Once they were in the car Carl repeated Dunai's parting salvo. '"You are no different from the apartheid government, the Third Reich or any other despot who's ever existed",' and he shook his head.

'I know I promised not to say anything, but I promised not to say anything in the interview and the interview was over. You can't honestly have expected me to walk out of there without saying a thing.'

Dunai was startled as Carl smiled broadly at her. 'You have the gift of oration, Dunai Marks. You almost had me in tears there.'

'I was that good, eh?' she asked, grinning back.

'You were that good.'

'Well, never mind me,' Dunai said. 'I thought you were going to have *him* in tears and, let me tell you, that's a sight I'd have paid good money to see.'

She glanced over at Carl and it struck her that he was really quite good-looking when he smiled.

13

DUNAI rushed into the outer office of the Right Reverend Richard Helmsley of the Church of the Province of Southern Africa and slid on the kelim. She righted herself in time to see Carl tip his head back and raise his eyes to the ceiling.

'Can I help you?'

She turned in the direction of the voice. 'I'm with him,' she told the middle-aged woman seated behind a mahogany desk, who gave her a curt nod. Dunai sat beside Carl on one of the upright chairs.

'You're late,' he said, scowling at her.

'And you've shaved this morning,' she countered. 'Congratulations.'

The door to the inner office opened and the bishop of the diocese of Cape Town stood in the doorway dressed in his usual uniform of grey trousers, maroon shirt and dog collar. He was a tall, thin man with pale skin and white hair.

'Mr Lambrecht, Ms Marks, please come through.'

As Dunai passed him he smiled at her. It was a smile that seemed genuine and gentle and she liked him straight away.

He closed the door behind them, then took his seat at his desk.

'Thank you for seeing us, Bishop Helmsley,' Carl began. 'To start, I'd like to ask you why Siobhan chose to blackmail you.'

'Expediency, I think. We met in the mid-seventies. I was young and out of my depth, trying to find shelter for families who'd had their shacks bulldozed, or encouraging victims of poverty and torture, and there were constant visits from the security police. Siobhan was different, a freedom fighter. She always seemed so sure of what she was doing. It was she who helped me through many a crisis.'

'So it was an amicable relationship.'

'I had to turn her down when she wanted to use church grounds to hide items intended for violent ends. I don't think she ever forgave me for that. And she knew, of course, what I'd been at pains to hide for so long. We discussed it once before she went into exile, then I didn't see her for more than a decade. She came to see me when a woman was murdered after an abortion at her clinic. I could see age had done nothing to mellow her.

'She wanted me to instruct parishes in the area that no one was to persecute women visiting her clinics. I would have done this anyway. But she wanted me to request our priests stop speaking out against abortion and that is something my conscience would not allow. It was then she said she'd go public with what I'd been at pains to keep to myself. The decision to ask for our priests' silence was not an easy one, but it was one I made quickly.'

Carl nodded. 'How far would you go, Bishop Helmsley, to keep your homosexuality a secret?'

'As far as my conscience would allow me, Mr Lambrecht— no further.'

The bishop's shoulders lifted, then dropped in a heavy sigh. 'I am a celibate homosexual. I spent much of my energy well into my twenties denying my sexual orientation. When I did accept it, I isolated myself from others as much as I possibly could, physically and emotionally.'

'Why don't you just come out?' Dunai asked, unable to keep quiet any longer. 'The good work you've done is legendary. Let people deal with their own bigotry.'

The bishop smiled. 'Thank you for your compassion, Ms Marks. But there are seventy-five-million Anglicans my decision would affect. The issue of homosexuality is causing the church to teeter on the brink of a major schism. Bishop is turning against bishop; it's tearing families apart. I've spent years weighing up the pros and cons and each time I come to the same conclusion—I must remain silent.'

'And what about Siobhan's silence?' Carl asked. 'You have no alibi for the night she was killed.'

The bishop nodded. 'Siobhan, no less than I, had her struggles, Mr Lambrecht. I saw that the last time we met. It's my hope she's at last found some peace. She spent so much of her life fighting battles that hadn't been hers to fight in the first place. Her courage and determination were at times superhuman. Despite her fire, or perhaps because of it, I loved and admired Siobhan. As far as her tragic death is concerned, if I'd been involved in any way you'd be looking at a man who'd gained the world but lost his soul.'

Dunai waited for Carl's next question. It never came. 'Thank you for your time, Bishop,' he said, standing suddenly.

The bishop nodded and stood up. Dunai got reluctantly to her feet as they started for the door. But, before he could open it, she asked a question that had been lodged in her throat throughout the interview.

'You said you worked with Siobhan in the late seventies; she wasn't by any chance pregnant at some point?'

Bishop Helmsley looked taken aback, then was silent for a moment. 'There were long months that I had no contact with her.' He shook his head. 'No, not that I remember.'

Dunai tried not to let her disappointment show as the bishop said goodbye, then disappeared inside.

Carl drove to Greenmarket Square without saying a word. Dunai was grateful for his silence, concentrating all her energy on keeping the gathering storm in check.

When the lift reached Carl's floor, he took her arm and steered her towards his office. She stood silently as he pushed the safety gate aside and unlocked the door.

'I'll put on coffee,' he said once inside and disappeared. She made her way to his office and stood stock-still in the centre of the room, staring at his cluttered desk, seeing nothing, yet strangely aware of a minute tautness in every muscle.

Carl came back in, stood in front of her. 'Okay, Dunai, what is it?'

She didn't answer.

'That last question; what was that about?' he persisted.

She made a last-ditch grab for control, wanting desperately to keep it together, especially in front of this man, but he kept prodding and poking, his voice barely above a whisper. 'I can't help you if you don't tell me what's going on.'

She knew it was useless trying to contain it. She gave up the struggle and felt her defences crumble like muddy banks before floodwater.

'I think Siobhan was my mother. I think she left me at St Mark's when I was a month old. I was late this morning because I went for that DNA test.' She was trembling and tears began to flow down her cheeks.

'I knew she could be hard as nails for a righteous cause but not this. Maybe she convinced herself she was saving the world so anything was justified. I spent almost every day of the last two years with her and here I am, a week after I spoke to her last, trying to come to terms with a different Siobhan. Now I know all the battles she fought left scar after scar till they twisted her, changed her shape, and I was completely unaware of it.'

Dunai took a deep breath. 'I hate it that she was less than the hero I thought she was, but I also feel guilty because that's probably the reason she felt she couldn't share this with me. She didn't want to destroy my faith in her.'

Dunai was relieved that he offered no pat answers. He put his arms around her and drew her against his chest. She had no idea how long she stood there, but eventually her tears subsided and she became aware of the strength of his arms, the warmth of his body and a need in her own, something close to craving. She was aware of every nuance of his response—the changing tension in the muscles of his arms, his breath against her hair. His chest expanded as he drew in a deep breath, then she felt his hands slide along her arms and he pushed her away.

'Sit,' he said gruffly and strode from the room.

The word was like a trigger that broke a hypnotic spell. She walked to one of the visitor's chairs, sat down and gripped its cream upholstered arms. Could she actually be attracted to him? Of course not! A week ago she'd thought he was a brainless, macho stereotype. She didn't think that any more. He was intelligent, kind, perceptive… 'Holy *shit*,' Dunai said under her breath. 'I'm overwrought. It's understandable.'

'Who're you talking to?' Carl had come back into the room and was carrying two steaming cups of coffee.

'No one,' Dunai mumbled. 'Just myself.'

Carl launched into an analysis of the interview with Bishop Helmsley. Dunai jumped gratefully into the conversation. Half an hour later when she left his office she'd made up her mind that a little delusion wasn't always a bad thing. She was going to pretend that nothing had happened between them, only she had a sneaking suspicion it wasn't going to be as easy as all that.

14

THANDIWE DINGAKE had refused to meet them until Carl had given her an ultimatum: it's us or the police. She'd agreed to speak to them at one o'clock near the fish pond in front of the National Gallery in the Company Gardens.

As they waited, Dunai plied Carl with questions inspired by her steady progress through his list of recommended reading for aspirant private investigators. Neither made any mention of the incident the day before.

At a quarter past one they were beginning to think Ms Dingake had changed her mind when a petite woman somewhere in her early thirties came into view in a dark green short-skirted business suit that showed off a pair of gym-toned legs.

Carl signalled to her with a nod of his head as her eyes swept over them, but she made no move to approach. Instead, she walked slowly around the pond nibbling a sandwich. As she passed by, Carl said, 'Ms Dingake?' She said nothing, but went to throw her sandwich wrapper in a bin, wiped her hands on a serviette in a leisurely manner, threw that away too, then came to sit at the end of the bench.

'Why the need for cloak-and-dagger, Ms Dingake?' Carl asked, bringing his ankle to rest on his knee and draping his arm over the back of the bench.

'Politics is a watchful game, Mr Lambrecht,' she said, staring straight ahead. Her voice was surprisingly strong and husky for so small a woman. It was inflected with just a trace of a Xhosa accent. 'One can never be too careful about the people with whom one is seen.'

'Like Siobhan Craig?'

'Siobhan and I had a deal which anyone in public life knows is utterly essential for survival. You scratch my back, I'll scratch yours, as the cliché goes.'

'Why did you offer to help Siobhan blackmail Wayne Daniels?'

'He needed to be taught a lesson, while Siobhan needed support from local government.'

'So you helped Siobhan set him up.'

'No, I did not, Mr Lambrecht. Wayne Daniels has climbed the political ladder from abject poverty and on every rung he's left a traumatised woman. His reputation for being a ruthless bastard means no one's been willing to touch him. He needed to be taught to keep his hands to himself and Siobhan was willing to give the lesson while getting a little something out of it for herself.'

'And you just happened to have a tape recorder handy when he sexually molested you.'

'That's right, Mr Lambrecht.'

'Why not bring disciplinary action against him?'

'Because, like most abusers, he goes to work on his victim till she's too intimidated to do anything. Systematic verbal abuse, a hand shoved up a skirt or down a blouse, threats of redundancy and violence can be a potent combination. And, like most abusers, he has a sixth sense about his victims' vulnerabilities. You get away with it continuously and what incentive is there to change your technique?'

'There's just one thing that doesn't sit right with me,' Carl said, and when he made no attempt to enlighten them, Thandiwe Dingake said a little irritably, 'What's that?'

'This particular sexual predator just happens to be the Superintendent-General of Social Services and Poverty Alleviation, perhaps the most effective person in aiding Siobhan's pilot project. Correct me if I'm wrong but his department is responsible for welfare services, grants, education and training, not to mention establishing shelters for abused women in partnership with local authorities, private welfare agencies and NGOs like STOP.'

'No need to correct you, Mr Lambrecht—you're right.'

'So Wayne Daniels, who just happens to head up the department most useful to Siobhan, also just happens to be a sexual pervert and open to blackmail?'

'Nothing just happens, Mr Lambrecht.'

'So who was next on Siobhan's list, Ms Dingake? The Minister of Health?'

'Siobhan already had her co-operation.'

'And if she hadn't?'

'You're asking me to speculate. I don't know what Siobhan had in mind.'

'But you do admit to deliberately going after Wayne Daniels.'

'I admit nothing, Mr Lambrecht. But I am dying for you to ask me the most obvious question about him.'

Carl waited a full ten seconds before saying, 'Do you believe he was capable of murdering Siobhan?'

'Was and is,' was her quick response. 'I've been in local politics for twelve years and the corridors of power are crawling with sexist bastards. But I've never seen ruthless ambition in any pervert like I've seen it in Wayne Daniels. He's more than capable. As a matter of fact, I could see him thinking of Siobhan's murder as combining business with pleasure.'

Dunai felt queasy. She'd heard enough. She wanted to tell this woman to shut up. Siobhan would never willingly align herself with this jaded person who reeked of ruthless ambition no less than the man she was slating.

'How did you meet Siobhan?' Carl asked.

'That I will not tell you. It's been a pleasure but the interview's over.' She got to her feet and ran both hands over her skirt. A gold ring on her wedding finger caught the wintry sun. It was a double cross.

'Wait!' Dunai said, getting to her feet. 'Where did you get that ring?'

Thandiwe Dingake made no reply. She turned her back and began to walk away.

Dunai went after her, caught her arm. 'Please. I need to know who gave you that ring. Why do you wear it? What's its significance?'

Thandiwe Dingake brought her face close to Dunai's. 'Get your hand off me right now, Ms Marks. I'm going to walk away without a word from you or you'll never get another thing from me, ever.'

Carl was beside Dunai, his voice barely above a whisper. 'Let her go.'

She had no choice. She had to drop her hand and watch helplessly as another clue walked away.

'*Shit,*' she said, turning her back on the woman's fleeing figure. 'I'm getting to the point where I'm ready to start *beating* the truth out of people.'

If Ms Dingake's eyes had been hostile, Carl's were gun metalgrey. 'We've got fifteen minutes to make our next interview,' he said between clenched teeth and began to walk in the direction of Wale Street. Dunai rushed to keep up with him. He was obviously furious and his pace matched his mood.

'You going to tell me what that was about?' he asked without looking in her direction.

She hesitated. 'Nothing. I just thought I'd seen that ring before.'

Carl's head swivelled in her direction. 'Let me get this straight. You physically manhandle, in a public place, someone I've identified as a valuable source of information and impulsively jeopardise Siobhan's murder investigation because you think you've seen her ring before?'

'Just for the record, *I* was the one who identified Thandiwe Dingake as a valuable source of information.'

'*Shit.*'

'Yes, shit,' Dunai said, allowing her own anger to erupt. 'Go right ahead and be as hard on me as you like. And please don't let it worry you that less than two weeks ago my life was perfectly normal; now I'm trying to track down the killer of someone I loved and thought I knew but has since turned out to be a ruthless blackmailer. Heaven forbid you should cut me any slack at all.'

Carl said nothing, but he did slow his pace as they came to the end of Government Avenue. They headed to St George's Mall, stopped at a café, took a table outside and ordered coffee as they'd been instructed to do.

A small, middle-aged man in a Fabiani suit took the table next to theirs. Wayne Daniels, or Mr Itchy and Scratchy as they'd started calling him, had agreed to meet so long as no one could connect him to the detective.

As the Superintendent-General of Social Services and Poverty Alleviation ordered an espresso, Dunai took the opportunity to cast furtive glances his way. His yellow-brown skin, high cheekbones and almond-shaped eyes marked his Khoi-San ancestry. Several thin but distinct scars criss-crossing his cheeks were evidence of a childhood spent in one of Cape Town's worst ganglands while neatly plucked brows, polished skin and manicured nails were proof of his more recent climb in local politics.

Dunai felt nothing but distaste for him, which she knew was based on Thandiwe Dingake's description of the man.

'So you've spoken to Thandiwe Dingake,' he began, watching casually as a street artist laid out his sketches on the walkway. There was barely a trace left in his voice of the distinct accent he'd no doubt grown up with on the Cape Flats.

'Did you murder Siobhan Craig?' was Carl's response.

Wayne Daniels's head moved just an inch in their direction, then back to the artist. 'I had nothing to do with it.'

'You have your eye on the provincial premiership. You're an ambitious man, Mr Daniels. Siobhan had the power to destroy you. You telling me you didn't have the urge to do something about it?'

'I was born in the worst years of apartheid,' Daniels said, his face and body betraying not the slightest agitation. 'By the time I could walk I'd learned the only real truth about my life—that I was going to have to fight or be destroyed. There is no middle ground in the ganglands of the Cape Flats. Siobhan Craig—' and he actually snorted '—sure as hell wasn't the first person I'd had to deal with who had the power to destroy me.'

'And how did you deal with those threats in the ganglands of the Cape Flats?'

The Superintendent-General smiled. 'Good point, Mr Lambrecht. But I don't use guns or knives myself. My weaponry's a little more sophisticated these days.'

'Siobhan wasn't killed with a gun or a knife,' Carl said. 'So what do you use these days instead of guns and knives, Mr Daniels?'

'Ah, that I can't tell you. Trade secret.'

A woman approached the street artist and bent over slightly to take a closer look at a sketch. Daniels cocked his head in her direction and Dunai was sure she hadn't imagined a sudden alertness, a narrowing of his eyes. She turned her head so she could better watch as his eyes fixed on the woman's backside as she bent lower. Dunai saw him bite down hard on his lower lip. She had to stop herself throwing her hot coffee in his face and crowning him with the cup. He made her want to take a shower with disinfectant and a wire brush.

'Where were you on the night of the fifteenth?' There was ice in Carl's voice.

'At an HIV AIDS charity dinner given by my department.'

'You have a good memory of the night in question.'

'Your questions are predictable. Now it's my turn. What do you intend to do with the information Siobhan left you?'

Carl made the man wait twenty seconds before answering. 'If you're innocent of Siobhan's murder, your other crimes will probably never see the light of day. But if you did kill Siobhan, I'll hand everything over to the police, then put a copy in the mail to every major newspaper in the country.'

'Well, then, I have nothing to worry about,' Daniels said. He took a note from his wallet and placed it beneath his coffee cup.

'I'm not finished with you,' Carl said, leaning back in his seat. His Afrikaans accent was strong.

Daniels glanced at his watch. 'Make it quick, Mr Lambrecht, or I'll have you arrested for attempted murder; you're boring me to death.'

Carl leaned forward, took a sip of coffee, put the mug down, and leaned back in his chair while Dunai's stomach tied itself in all sorts of knots.

'So you're an Itchy and Scratchy fan,' Carl said. 'Why doesn't that surprise me?'

'I'm not a detective, Mr Lambrecht, but I'd think if you want information from people you need to be a bit clearer.'

'How's this for clear? Wayne Daniels is a sleazy sexual predator who was being badly screwed over by a woman who wore tasselled skirts and loafers. You send her a card from a WCPA address: "Fool me once, shame on you. Fool me twice…watch out for my tool" which, far from intimidating her into never blackmailing you again, probably gave her a good laugh. So you had her killed. That clear enough for you?'

Daniels smiled. 'Western Cape Provincial Administration has thousands of employees. I'd think a good percentage of those feel very strongly against abortion. So good luck with that.'

He got to his feet.

'You make all your own cards, Daniels? Maybe send your mother something special for her birthday, Mother's Day? You think she'd like to know what sort of cards you send to other women?'

Daniels's face went deep pink in an instant and he leaned over Carl. 'Go *fuck* yourself,' and he turned and strode up the mall in the direction of Wale Street.

'Well,' Dunai said, 'you two really bonded, didn't you?'

'At least you didn't butt in.'

'I'd have been killed in the crossfire.' She tilted her chin towards the warm wintry sun.

'Thandiwe Dingake was right,' Carl said. 'He is capable of strangling someone. His reaction to that last comment was completely overboard. Makes me think he's got a problem with impulse control—the number one requisite for aspirant criminals.'

Carl stopped as their waitress approached with bill in hand. He took out his wallet and paid for the coffee. When she'd gone, he said, 'As a matter of fact, I have an urge to go over every detail of that man's life.'

'What can I do?' she asked, following as he got to his feet.

'You can find out exactly how long he was at that dinner, when he left, if he stopped anywhere on his way home. I'll show you how to draw up a timeline, who to ask and how to ask without being obvious.'

Carl rubbed a hand over his stubble. They began to walk along the mall.

'But if Wayne Daniels did do it,' Dunai reasoned, 'wouldn't he be taking one hell of a risk? He seems to get his face on TV a lot these days.'

'He would be,' Carl agreed. 'So what would be a logical course of action for someone in his position who wants to commit murder?'

'Hire one of his old gangster friends?'

'That's why we look at the alibi and, if it squares up, which it probably will, we use our contacts on the Cape Flats.'

'We have contacts in the hood?'

'Dunai, on the Cape Flats if you're not an ordinary person trying to get on with your life then you're one of two things—a gangster or an informant.'

She was filled with a sudden foreboding. 'Be careful, okay?'

Carl looked down at her and grinned, and in that moment if she'd had anything sharp on her person she'd have cut out her tongue. Instead, she had to go for diversion. 'D'you know your Afrikaans accent gets stronger when you interview certain people?'

He stopped smiling.

'Is that a stress thing? You did it with Cowley and Daniels.'

Carl hesitated before answering and when he did speak it was with obvious reluctance. 'I do it deliberately. It's a throwback to apartheid. The average person's still intimated when they're questioned by an Afrikaans authority figure in a hostile environment.'

'That's cold,' Dunai said.

'Welcome to the world of crime investigation,' Carl said grimly.

Dunai was exhausted. Apart from the Dingake and Daniels interviews, she'd spent every moment of the day running between STOP's offices and Carl's. It was well after six when she headed home. She was passing the trendy Soviet nightclub when she heard her name called softy from the doorway. She stopped dead in her tracks. A tall, slim woman in a white stole, very short black skirt and white thigh-high boots stood in the almost dark doorway. Dunai hesitated, not knowing how to respond. This time she had no mallet to protect her.

'It's okay, Dunai. I've got information for you. Come closer so I don't have to raise my voice.'

Like hell, Dunai thought. By now she knew better than to ask how the woman knew her name.

'I'm here to help you,' the woman said.

Dunai stepped forward but stayed out of reach. With a swirl of her hand the woman beckoned her closer; again she hesitated until she saw the double cross ring on her wedding finger. Dunai stepped closer.

'You're looking for the vagrant you call Mr Bojangles. Go to Professor Anna Cooper at Valkenberg Hospital; she'll be able to help you.'

The woman turned towards the door.

'Please,' Dunai said, putting a hand out to her, 'tell me what the double cross means.'

'Not now,' she said, stepping inside the club and closing the door behind her.

Dunai tried to go after her but the door wouldn't budge. 'Shit, shit, shit,' she said, banging her fist against the barrier. She waited ten minutes, hoping someone would open, but when they didn't and she began to shiver, she was forced to head home, once again frustrated but with a spark of hope ignited. Professor Anna Cooper, whoever she was, just might be able to help.

15

VALKENBERG HOSPITAL was Cape Town's main state-run mental health facility. Set against a backdrop of fynbos-covered mountains, its once well-tended buildings, lawns and swimming pools were in a state of disrepair. Dunai made her way past boarded-up wards and shivered to think how many desperate or dangerously unstable people had been forced onto the streets.

Following the directions she'd been given, she entered a building that looked as if it still had a pulse. A smiling young secretary immediately ushered her into a large cluttered office full of books, pot plants and sunshine.

Professor Anna Cooper was tall and slim with fine blond hair pulled into a ponytail. The sharpness of her nose and jaw were belied by merry blue eyes that settled comfortably into crinkles whenever she smiled. She came striding across the room, hand extended, dodging piles of books stacked on the carpet.

'Welcome, Dunai,' she said, shaking hands. 'Please come in. Just watch your step; it's a minefield in here. I really should tidy up but then I wouldn't know where to find anything.'

As she led Dunai towards a chair she put an arm around her shoulders and gave them a squeeze. 'I was so sorry to hear about Siobhan. When someone of her enormous energy dies it's not only a personal blow to those who loved her but one to society in general. We so desperately need women like her. Sit here,' she said, letting go of Dunai. She sank into a comfortable visitor's chair of plush russet upholstery; the pair looked like the only items of furniture that had been purchased in the last two decades.

Dunai was feeling a little shell-shocked. The professor was none of the things she'd expected. According to her Internet research that morning, Anna Cooper had been awarded her PhD in her early thirties, she was on almost every psychiatry board in the country and had headed up a UN commission on mental health in war-torn African countries. She was recognised for her ongoing work for the World Health Organisation in studying mental disease in developing nations and had recently been appointed advisor to the Minister of Health.

Dunai had expected an arrogant woman who'd resent her time being wasted in search of a vagrant, or just a brilliantly cold scientific type. Not this warm, smiling woman who was behaving as if this meeting was the most important thing on her agenda that day.

'Thank you for seeing me, Professor Cooper.'

'Oh, not at all. And call me Anna. Let's first get business out of the way. What can I do for you, Dunai?'

'This is probably going to sound strange…' Dunai told her about Mr Bojangles and his schizophrenia; how she thought he might have seen Siobhan's murderer. She told her how he'd disappeared and found herself relating her encounter with the legless woman and the mother and infant.

Anna sat forward, legs crossed, throughout the tale, concentrating on Dunai's face, nodding with absolute seriousness at the mention of Mr Bojangles and her admission that she'd run from a legless woman. Never once did a look of disbelief cross her face and Dunai found herself saying more than she'd intended.

At the end of the tale Anna sat back in her chair, a look of deep compassion on her face. 'Well, Dunai, you've been through a lot, haven't you?'

Dunai nodded.

'My goodness but you've held up tremendously under terrible trauma—well done. Of course we'll help you. I'm going to put word out about Mr Bojangles. If he's passed through any mental health facility we'll find him, and soon. That's very important.'

'Thank you, Anna, I really appreciate it.'

'Oh, not at all. I always get a buzz out of helping.'

Dunai swallowed. 'Anna, how did you meet Siobhan?'

'Oh! She came looking for someone…very much like you are.'

'When was that?'

'Uh…let me see…' Anna frowned. 'Must have been right after she came back from exile. So that would have been the early nineties.'

'Who was she looking for?'

'I really wish I could tell you, Dunai, but I can't. Her visit was confidential. I gave her my word.'

'Is that the only time you saw her?'

'No. Our work brought us into contact from time to time. What a terrible loss…' She shook her head, then clapped her hands once. 'But I don't want you to worry, Dunai. I'm going to do everything I can to help you find Mr Bojangles.'

She sprang to her feet and came around the desk.

Dunai stood up. She was beginning to feel a little irritated with Anna's avoidance of her questions, but she showed none of her annoyance. Anna had assured her she'd help with the search for Mr Bojangles. That was more than she'd started out with this morning and she had no intention of antagonising Anna and perhaps forfeiting her help. So she smiled and thanked her.

'I want you to talk to me about Siobhan's death any time you feel you need to. You don't even have to make an appointment. Just phone and I'll always take your call if I'm available. If I'm not, I'll get back to you as soon as I can.'

Dunai felt both gratitude and confusion at being treated like a favourite niece by this powerful stranger.

'I was stopped in the street yesterday by a woman I'd never seen before,' Dunai said, her heart beating a little faster. 'She told me that you'd be able to help find Mr Bojangles. You don't know who she was, do you?'

'How extraordinary,' Anna said. 'No, I have no idea who that might have been.' She took Dunai's hand and patted it. 'I just wouldn't tell anyone about her. They might think you're crazy.'

Dunai looked quickly at Anna but her pale blue eyes were merry as usual.

Halfway across the room, Anna stopped suddenly, dropped Dunai's hand and said, 'I want to give you something.'

She strode across the room between piles of books till she got to a collection that looked as if it had been stacked on the floor beside a ceramic plant pot for hundreds of years. She bent to retrieve a book from the pile and a gold pendant slipped out of her shirt. Its two melded crosses seemed to wink at Dunai in the weak sunlight coming in through the window.

Anna straightened and came striding back across the room. She looked down quickly when she saw Dunai staring at her chest and slipped the pendant back inside her shirt.

'Where did you get that?' Dunai asked very quietly.

'Oh, it's just something I was given a long time ago. Here, I want to give you this,' she said, handing her a very old brown book with faded gilt edges. 'It's the works of Marcus Aurelius. I think it'll be a great comfort to you.'

Dunai was led from the room, hugged, then left in the outer office with Anna's assurance of assistance and a growing sense of confusion.

She fetched Jesse just before one and took him home for lunch. They were halfway through their sandwiches when there was a knock at the door of the turquoise house.

'No, you stay,' she said as Jesse began to scramble down from his chair at the kitchen table. As usual he ignored her and by the time she opened the door he was standing in front of her, back pressed against her legs.

'Hi,' Carl said, his bulk filling the doorway. Dunai was so taken aback it took her a moment to recover.

'Come in,' she said, placing her hands on Jesse's shoulders and moving them back a couple of paces so he could step inside.

'Who's this?' he asked, looking down at the round-faced boy with the thatch of dark hair and a spattering of freckles across his nose.

'This is my son, Jesse.' She felt his head press against her thighs as he peered up at the man who must seem like a giant to him.

'Hi, Jesse,' Carl said casually.

Jesse smiled shyly but turned away from the stranger and pressed his face against his mother's jeans. Dunai picked him up and he hid his face against her neck.

'I've just spoken to Cowley's prayer meeting leader and his alibi doesn't add up.'

Dunai held her breath. Jesse swivelled his head to peer at Carl.

'Seems he left the meeting at nine, not after ten as he claimed. And, since he arrived home around ten-thirty, there's a missing hour and a half that matches time of death. I think we should pay him a visit.'

'When?'

'He's at his office if we go now.'

Dunai saw her hour with Jesse evaporate and felt guilt and regret.

'I'll take Jesse next door; my neighbour looks after him during the day.'

'I go too,' Jesse said, rearing up and looking at his mother excitedly.

'Not this time, Jes. It's work stuff so you need to stay with Barbara.'

'No, I go too.'

'No arguments, Jes; you're going next door for a nap.'

'Dammit,' the toddler said.

'You shouldn't say that word,' Dunai said.

'Why?'

'It's a shouting word.'

'Dammit!' he shouted at the top of his voice.

'No, Jesse, that's enough,' Dunai warned, setting him on the ground.

Jesse jutted out his bottom lip and she watched with trepidation as it began to quiver.

'Jesse,' Carl said, hunkering down in front of him, 'you know that when you nap, time goes away—it disappears, just like that?' Carl snapped his fingers.

Jesse looked from the fingers to Carl's face. His eyes narrowed and he cocked his head to the side. 'Where it go?'

'Nobody knows,' Carl said. 'It's magic. You close your eyes, go to sleep and, when you open them again, time's gone and your mum's back.'

'And then we'll play some games,' Dunai said, sensing Carl was onto something.

Jesse looked at his mother. 'You read story?'

'You bet.'

'Two,' Jesse bargained.

'Deal,' Dunai said.

'Okay,' Jesse conceded, reaching up and placing a hand on Carl's shoulder. 'I go next door now.'

'Good man,' Carl said, getting to his feet.

Jesse nodded and Dunai grinned. She took him next door while Carl waited in his car.

'You handled Jesse like a pro,' she said, climbing in beside him. 'Where did you learn your technique?'

It was meant as a light-hearted question but Carl didn't answer and she sensed a sudden tension in the car. She glanced sideways and saw the muscles of his jaw bunch.

'I'm sorry,' she said. 'I didn't mean to pry. I was just grateful—'

'I have a daughter,' Carl said, stunning her. For some reason she'd never thought of him as a father. She'd heard he was divorced but the information might not have been accurate. The idea was like a kick in the stomach.

'I hadn't thought…I didn't…I thought I'd heard you were divorced,' Dunai stammered.

'I am,' Carl said, looking sideways at her.

Dunai nodded and looked out of the window and up at the monochrome sky. Carl started the engine and pulled into the street. A couple of minutes passed before he said, 'Charmaine lives with her mother in KwaZulu-Natal.'

Dunai nodded but sensed he'd given her this information only to avoid offending her so she got off the topic. 'We're not heading for the southern suburbs,' she observed. 'We interviewing him at work?'

'Hmm,' Carl said. 'I think it's time Mr Cowley sweated a little.'

They passed the entrance to the Victoria & Alfred Waterfront, a tourist mecca of hotels, marina apartments, restaurants and hundreds of shops built around a working harbour.

Traffic was heavy this time of day and they crawled along Coen Steytler past the hulking, yet strangely unobtrusive Cape Town International Convention Centre and headed north up Heerengracht towards the harbour, Table Bay Boulevard and The Cowley Building.

Carl filled out his details at the security desk and they were issued with security cards. Dunai found herself battling to keep up as he headed across the large reception area towards a row of lifts.

They went up to the twelfth floor and Carl strode into the reception area of the executive suite. He reached the receptionist, rested his knuckles on her desk and leaned towards her. 'I'm Carl Lambrecht; I have business with Mr Cowley. I don't have an appointment but I'm sure he'll see me right away.'

The pretty blonde receptionist half rose, then sat down again, reaching for the telephone without taking her eyes off Carl's face. It took about ten seconds for a corpulent middle-aged woman dressed in a navy suit to appear at the reception desk.

'Mr Lambrecht, we've spoken on the phone. I'm Joyce, Mr Cowley's secretary. Please follow me.'

She led them into a small office with cream walls, oak furniture and a door leading to another office; asked them to take a seat, then slipped through the door to the inner sanctum.

'You're very quiet,' Carl said to Dunai after a moment's silence.

'Ten minutes ago I was hell-bent on getting Jesse to eat a sandwich instead of Coco Pops, now we're about to confront someone who might confess to Siobhan's murder.'

'Bewildering,' Carl said with no conviction at all.

She looked straight ahead at the double doors and kept her voice steady as she said, 'I haven't said anything because I'm trying to talk myself out of killing him if he confesses.'

Carl's head swivelled in her direction. He cocked his head and raised an eyebrow. 'Nice,' he said. 'But I doubt we'll get a confession today; he's got too much to lose.'

The door opened and Joyce ushered them into Cowley's office. Dan Cowley stood behind his desk. This time there was no smile, no handshake. 'What can I do for you, Mr Lambrecht?' He looked at his watch, glanced at his diary, then straightened his tie.

'Your timing of events on the night of the fifteenth doesn't add up.'

'What do you mean?'

Carl moved to within a foot of the desk, forcing Cowley to tilt his head back and look up at him. He sighed as he pulled a notepad from his pocket. 'You told us the prayer meeting ended at about eight-thirty, you stayed on to discuss business till just after ten, then arrived home at ten-thirty.' His Afrikaans accent was pronounced. Dunai's gaze slid to his face; his eyes narrowed. 'You lied to us, Mr Cowley. Why's that?'

Cowley snatched up a pen and rapped it against his diary. 'You know I've had enough of this. I'm busy, I have a business to run and I've already answered your questions.'

'You see, I not only spoke to the prayer meeting leader, who it seems you got to lie for you,' Carl said, ignoring him. 'I also spoke to two others who were at that prayer meeting and both say they saw you drive off just after nine. Since you arrived home around ten-thirty, that leaves you with no alibi from nine till ten-thirty. Ms Craig's time of death was around ten.'

Dunai chose that moment to step up beside Carl.

'I've had enough,' Cowley repeated. His colour deepened and his breathing quickened. 'I'm going to call a guard.'

'You can phone a friend for all I care, Mr Cowley, but I would advise you to co-operate with us. The alternative is an interrogation room at a police station.' The accent was now even stronger. 'So I'll ask you one more time. Where were you between nine and ten-thirty the night of the fifteenth?'

Dan Cowley's chest heaved and his eyes skittered across the room. 'I want her out of here,' he said, jabbing a finger at Dunai.

'She stays,' Carl said.

Dunai smiled at the man with as much venom as she could infuse into her features. She'd never had a physical fight in her life but she remembered how some of the orphans had to be prised apart before doing real damage to each other. She fantasised about launching herself at Cowley and smashing her fists into his face.

Cowley threw his pen onto the desk; it shot across and landed on the floor. Carl took a step forward, towering over him. Suddenly the smaller man's shoulders sagged and he dropped his eyes to the desk.

'I was driving around, okay? Just driving. I didn't know what to do about her. I didn't know how to handle it.'

'How *did* you handle it?'

'I didn't kill her. I told you that. I decided to go to the leadership of Men of The Covenant and tell them about the blackmail. I was nowhere near the city centre and I can prove it.'

He tossed his head and crossed his arms in front of his chest.

'Ten o'clock I stopped at a chemist on Kenilworth Main Road—the one across from the Seven Eleven. I bought headache tablets. The sales girl will remember me. There was a security guard—he'd remember me too.'

'Don't you keep headache tablets at home?' Carl asked.

'What?'

'Ten o'clock you were on your way home,' Carl said. 'Most households keep a supply of painkillers so why not go straight home, take them and go to bed?'

Cowley threw his hands in the air. 'My head was killing me, okay. I didn't want to wait another ten minutes to get home so I stopped at the nearest chemist.'

'You got the receipt?'

'I… There was no reason to keep it.'

'You buy anything else?'

'No.'

'You sure about that?'

'Yes, I'm sure. Look, I've—'

'Did you go into the Seven Eleven?'

'*No!*'

'You needed to take the tablets straight away—how did you swallow them?'

'I keep a bottle of water in the car.'

'So it's just the sales assistant at the chemist who saw you?'

'How many people need to vouch for me before you stop harassing me?'

'Just one would do the trick, Mr Cowley. But one who isn't lying.'

Cowley's hands balled into tight fists at his sides. 'Get out. Just get out. I don't want you in here any more.' But there was little fire left in his voice.

'I need a description of the sales assistant before we leave,' Carl said, pen poised above his notepad.

Cowley mopped the shine from his face with a handkerchief as he gave the description. Carl had been right on the money when he'd predicted there'd be no confession today, but he had made the man sweat.

'You okay?' Carl asked once they were back in the car and heading for the city centre.

Dunai wasn't even close to okay. Until Siobhan's death she'd have sworn she was a pacifist. She'd never raised a hand to any creature in her life, had never committed an act of aggression. But moments ago she could have shredded Cowley's face, then beaten the truth out of him. And when he'd admitted to throttling Siobhan, she'd have kept beating him, and no amount of crying, begging or blood would have stopped her until he was dead—as dead as Siobhan.

Now that the rage had passed Dunai felt shocked and nauseated. She'd never thought she had it in her. She craved a cup of tea and home, her son and her animals and all the personal things that made up her life—and the person she'd been before Siobhan's death.

'Dunai?' Carl prompted. He reached out and touched her hands; they were clutched tightly in her lap.

She forced herself to smile and nod. 'Don't worry, I'm not going to go to pieces again. So what do we do now? About Cowley, I mean.'

Carl didn't answer at first. When he did, his voice was gentle. 'The urge to put a name and face to one's pain can be very strong, Dunai. Perhaps this is too much to ask of you at this stage, but it's important as an investigator to remain impartial. So far, all the evidence against Cowley is circumstantial. He's pathetic, obviously warped on several levels, but I don't know if he's a killer. We need to work on his alibi. I'll interview the sales assistant tonight. You've got Jesse to think about.'

'Thank you,' Dunai said. Yes, she did have a lot more to think about than just her newfound penchant for violence.

That evening, once Jesse was asleep, Dunai went to the computer in the dining-cum-storage room and began trawling the Internet for some reference to the double cross.

Her meeting with Anna Cooper had again left her with more questions and no real answers. She was beginning to feel about the double cross the way Sir Lancelot must have felt about the Holy Grail. If she could just find out what it meant she might discover what Siobhan had been mixed up in.

She tried several search engines, different word combinations. Just after ten she got a hit—a handful of obscure articles she'd almost missed. They'd been typed on an old typewriter and scanned into a research project connected via a series of links to Oxford University's website. They'd been written in the late 1930s by Everett Gethers, a lecturer in anthropology at Oxford University.

Dunai found mention of the double cross in a section titled *Beyond Suffrage: A Global Feminine Voice.* She skimmed the section till she found mention of the double cross, then went back to the beginning of the paragraph to read it in context.

...codex fragments [1, 2 & 3] and correspondence [4 to 12] support the existence of a radical female group formed by a handful of Roman Catholic nuns and mystics working in Greece in the 4th century at a time when Church Fathers put together the canonical version of the Christian Bible. Christianity, with its call for social justice and proclamation that freedom and grace belonged to everyone, had shaken the establishment and given women a powerful new voice. Political expediency dictated that this voice be silenced. Gnostic tradition was banned, references to the female aspect of divinity deleted and women barred from teaching, officiating at religious ceremonies and holding positions of authority and leadership.

During this time high-born and learned women organised into a pressure group, their sole objective being to challenge the church's 'perverse application of Scripture' [13] and institutionalisation of misogyny. The emblem of the double cross [14] is first recorded as a unifying symbol within this group.

The first cross of yellow gold symbolised the organised, male-led church, the second cross melded just to the right of the first was wrought in rose or white gold to symbolise the abiding truth of the divinity of God as represented in the feminine sacred.

The church began a campaign of repression against those wearing the double cross and it is believed that many of the church's foremost activists, teachers and theologians, some men but mostly women, were martyred as part of this group [15]. By the end of the 4th century, the church claimed to have eradicated the heresy.

The resurgence of a group claiming similar ideology is again recorded in the 13th century, in response to official church doctrine that females were failed embryos. The double cross as an adornment is again recorded [16], as is the church's attempts to silence this group [17].

For some time a powerful female movement had been growing with veneration of the Virgin Mary reaching its zenith in the 12th and 13th centuries. Many goddesses, who had enjoyed frequent sexual encounters, had in the ancient religions been called 'virgin', meaning whole unto herself, not under a male's control. The symbol of the double cross again became a popular adornment for adherents to this movement.

At this time a cyclical backlash began against women that would eventually spiral, in the 16th and 17th centuries, into a holocaust of witchcraft trials in which an estimated nine million people, mostly women, were tortured and put to death for the 'constellation of beliefs and practices we have come to recognise as the way of the Goddess.' [18]

'A climate of absolute terror prevailed,' writes 18th century historian, Franz Johannesson [19] 'By the time the witchcraft trials in Salem, Massachusetts took place towards the end of the persecution in 1692 there were villages in Europe with not one woman left alive or, as in the Bishopric of Trier in Germany, two villages left with only a single female inhabitant apiece.'

By this time what some had once called the Sisterhood of the Double Cross had not been seen or heard from in almost a century, except during Martin Luther's reformation in the early 16th century when several letters of correspondence from the Sisterhood of the Double Cross were purportedly received with great empathy by Martin Luther's wife, Katharina von Bora, a former nun [20].

What is of interest to the scholar of anthropology, based on evidence of correspondence from the Sisterhood of the Double Cross surfacing as late as the 16th century, is that the group had in effect become sufficiently organised and proficient to survive several campaigns of severe persecution and had created means by which the torch could be passed to other educated and like-minded women.

It has been noted in recent years that a number of women appointed to positions of power in several areas of public life [21] have been seen to wear the double cross as rings or pendants. Since the beliefs of these women span not only Christianity, but Judaism, atheism and several other global belief systems, it would seem the group is no longer confined to any one religion.

A question for hypothesis is—if the Sisterhood of the Double Cross did survive 1,500 years of relentless persecution, what might the nature of the group in the early 20th century?

One explanation is that the movement, long dormant, has resurfaced and is being carried forward by educated, resolute and powerful women. This theory demands scrutiny. Should the group become a vigorous political pressure group for women worldwide, what is their agenda likely to be in years to come?

Dunai found four other articles written in 1938 and '39, all different versions of the first. She searched the web for further mention of the lecturer's name and found a small obituary. Everett Gethers had been killed in a car crash in October 1939. There was only one other reference that mentioned his study into an organisation of radical feminists. From the reference, it was clear that his studies were subject to some derision prior to his death.

Dunai rubbed her eyes, sat back and stared at her cold pizza. There was almost too much to take in. She'd suspected Siobhan had been caught up in something local, but not this. Not some conspiracy that demanded she believe in a 1,500-year-old persecution that now encompassed a radical group of women drawn from heaven only knew how many countries and religious persuasions.

Dunai had always refused to believe conspiracy theories, but she could not dismiss the evidence of the past week.

Siobhan had left all her personal effects to her, so the double cross pendant was now hers, along with all its secrets and conspiracies, which were still a mystery to her.

She went over what she'd encountered so far. Siobhan's campaign of blackmail to keep her population control project afloat. The double cross worn by the amazon in the Company Gardens who'd told her they'd made sure Siobhan couldn't be implicated and had likely wiped her computer and removed her documents. The same woman who'd told her she was being watched over by a mysterious 'we'. Then there was Thandiwe Dingake, Director of Communications in local government, ready to help Siobhan blackmail a sexual predator. The woman in the doorway of the Soviet Club who'd known of her search for Mr Bojangles. Professor Anna Cooper, probably one of the most influential people in the country, whose work spanned the globe but who was happy to help her find a vagrant. How had all these women been linked to Siobhan, and what was their connection to Dunai now? She needed answers and she had an idea where she might find them.

16

ST MARK'S HOME FOR CHILDREN had been built one hundred and forty years ago on the outskirts of the CBD beside St Mark's Cathedral. Forty years later a school had been added that eventually became St Mark's Primary and Secondary Schools. The collection of square white buildings with their base of rough stonework, sash windows, red Spanish tiles and bell tower had changed little over the years.

Dunai and Jesse arrived just as the bells rang to mark the start of morning tea. As they moved along the passage to the office she could hear the excited chatter of children making their way from Saturday morning sports activities to the dining room for fruit and tea.

'Siseray give cookies,' Jesse said.

'Yes, she probably will,' Dunai said. 'But say hello before you ask for them, okay?'

The first thing Sister Raymunda said when she saw Dunai was, 'You look like a stick insect, little one.' She took both Dunai's hands in hers and kissed her cheek. 'We'll have to do something about that.' She turned her attention to Jesse. 'And who is this handsome young man you've brought with you today?'

Jesse giggled and said, 'You got cookies, Siseray?'

'Well, of course I have. Why don't you come with me and we'll find them.'

'Kitchen, kitchen,' Jesse chanted, and grabbed Sister Raymunda's hand.

'Sit down, little one,' she said to Dunai. 'We'll be back in a jiffy.'

Dunai watched Sister Raymunda in her usual sandals, skirt, golf shirt and cardigan leave the office with Jesse beside her. Her cropped white hair stuck up in front of her black and white habit in at least two places. She had continued to call Dunai 'little one', even though from the age of thirteen she'd exceeded the nun in stature. Now in her early sixties, Sister Raymunda was head and shoulders shorter than her former charge.

'So Dunai, tell me what's been happening,' Sister Finbar said from behind the desk. The nun had been appointed Mother Finbar Dominic Safirey some ten years ago, but Dunai only ever thought of her as Sister Finbar. She had small brown eyes, a high-bridged nose, full mouth and a face that bore a look of implacability. 'Although—wait,' she said, holding up a hand as Dunai opened her mouth. 'We'd better not start without Sister Raymunda.'

So they talked about other things until Sister Raymunda burst into the room, slightly out of breath. 'You haven't started your story yet?'

'No, Sister,' Dunai said, hopping up to take the heavy laden tray from her and putting it on the desk.

'Sit, little one,' Sister Raymunda said, moving towards the tray. 'Jesse's helping Cook make cut-out cookies. The pie's vegetarian,' she said, handing it to her.

'I can't manage anything—'

'No, no, none of that now. Not a word till you've eaten your pie.'

Dunai looked to Sister Finbar who shook her head. 'She's right, Dunai. Next south-easter we'll be looking for you at sea. Eat!'

Being outnumbered, she began to shovel pie into her mouth. She was glad they'd insisted because it was delicious and after the first bite she ate the rest quickly.

'That's better,' Sister Raymunda said as she poured tea for them. Dunai handed back the plate and took her teacup.

Dunai began to talk. Telling the nuns what she could. Leaving out the bits she knew would worry them, which was most of it. She talked more of her grief, of her suspicion that Siobhan might have been her mother and that she'd been for a DNA test. Then she came to the real reason for her visit.

'Have you heard of the Sisterhood of the Double Cross?'

There was silence before Sister Raymunda leaned forward. 'Have a cake, dear.'

'No, please, Sister. This is important. I need to know if you've ever heard of the Sisterhood of the Double Cross.'

'Mother Finbar Dominic Safirey,' Sister Raymunda said, 'I believe this is a question for you.'

Dunai's heart sank. Sisters Raymunda and Finbar had been best friends since childhood and Sister Raymunda only ever used the other's title when something was to be handled officially.

'There have been many women's movements in the Church,' Sister Finbar said in her teacher's voice. 'The Sisterhood of the Double Cross is just one of them.'

'So you have heard of them,' Dunai said, failing to keep relief from her voice.

'Rumours only,' Sister Finbar said and pursed her lips.

'What rumours, Mother?'

'You know, Dunai,' Sister Finbar said, leaning back in her chair, 'I told you this when you pestered us about whether Father Bhengu wore knickers under his cassock. Curiosity is not always a good thing.'

'But I'm asking about a women's movement in the Church.'

'Oh, no, dear,' Sister Raymunda said. 'They haven't been part of the Church for some time now.'

Sister Finbar cast a disapproving glance at her colleague, then looked back at Dunai and sighed. 'Early feminism was led almost entirely by women of faith,' she said, using her teacher's voice again. 'It was often Scripture that was called out at protest marches, from jail cells and meeting places that were surrounded sometimes by mobs of rioting men. Isaiah 58, "Loose the chains

of injustice and untie the cords of the yoke,'" Sister Finbar en-
unciated in a rich alto, '"set the oppressed free and break every
yoke… Then your light will rise in the darkness, and your night
will become like the noonday." Also popular was the call, "Let
justice roll down like water," and Psalm 146, "The Lord who re-
mains faithful forever upholds the cause of the oppressed."'

Sister Raymunda clapped; Dunai kept her eyes on Sister
Finbar's face as she continued.

'But the institutionalised Church became one of the fiercest
opponents of equality for women and last century it caused a split
along religious and secular lines, particularly in the US. Not so
much here; spirituality's always been part of political activism.

'Unfortunately, there has been a tendency in organised religion to use fundamentalist doctrine to justify what divides the
sexes and excludes women. Religion as a political vehicle has
without doubt compromised women's human rights and turned
the religious-secular split into a chasm.'

'So you're saying the Sisterhood of the Double Cross split
from the Church in the last century,' Dunai prompted.

'Something you must understand, Dunai,' Sister Finbar said,
sitting forward and leaning her arms on the desk. 'The Sisterhood
of the Double Cross has always been an urban legend within the
Church. No one seems to know exactly who or what they are and
I personally have never seen proof of their existence. I've only
ever heard rumours.'

'What rumours?'

Dunai's frustration was beginning to turn to anger. As if sensing her escalating mood, Sister Raymunda leaned forward and
patted her hand. 'There were some stories that popped up in the
eighteen-hundreds,' she said in a near whisper. 'Rumours that the
group was not only active but had changed their methods and ideology. There have since been stories of violence and manipula-
tion. Horrible stories.'

'Tell me one,' Dunai said.

Sister Finbar cleared her throat but perhaps Sister Raymunda hadn't heard because she said in a near whisper, 'We heard once about a cardinal. Poisoned. And he was found clutching a double cross. They had to break his fingers to get it out of his hand.'

'Stories, yes,' Sister Finbar said. 'Rumours. What's made you ask about this?'

Dunai had known this question would come up and she had her answer prepared. 'I came across an article on the Internet and thought it was interesting.' She hated lying to them.

'Well,' Sister Finbar said, 'that's all we can tell you. I wouldn't take the rumours too seriously.'

The thought struck Dunai that Sister Finbar might be lying, too.

'I've seen a couple of powerful women wearing the double cross as rings and pendants,' Dunai said, watching Sister Finbar's face carefully.

The Mother Superior nodded. 'It's obvious they've heard about the group and decided to wear the symbol as some sort of statement. Symbols are often recycled. Have a cake, Dunai,' she ordered, shifting in her seat and crossing her legs.

Dunai reached for a cake. 'Tell me, Mother,' she began, 'how can women adhere to organised religion with a clear conscience?'

'Don't talk with your mouth full,' Sister Finbar said absent-mindedly. 'Religious organisations are merely flawed reflections of the principles they hope to embody. It is up to the individual to strive for the values of love and justice at their core. As women, to cut ourselves off from our right to a spiritual home would be like throwing the baby out with the bath water, to use a nasty but apt cliché.'

'But you'll always be second class citizens within an institution that governs almost every aspect of your life.'

'Not always, Dunai, and never in our own eyes.' Sister Finbar uncrossed her legs. 'Let me tell you a story.

'Early seventies, I was invited to a conference in Brazil for religious women. To open proceedings a group of vested priests walked up the aisle to the front of the auditorium singing the opening hymn of the liturgy. The women joined in, but as the priests sang, "I will raise him up", a handful of women sang, "I will raise *them* up". The priests sang again, "I will raise him up", and this time a few more women joined in and sang a little louder, "I will raise them up". Within minutes the refrain had been taken up by a hundred women, then another hundred till the entire gathering of some two thousand female voices were raised in unison, drowning out the priests and soaring heavenward. That gathering gave us the courage to express what we'd known all along in our hearts—that the manmade structure was flawed and that there was no shame in admitting it.'

Before Dunai had a chance to comment, her mobile rang. She recognised Carl's number. 'Sorry, I have to take this,' she said and left the office. 'What is it, Carl?'

'Top of the morning to you too,' he said. 'Our informant has some info for us about Mr Itchy and Scratchy. Where are you?'

'St Mark's.'

'What are you doing there?'

'It's where I grew up.'

'Oh, right… You busy or something?'

'Not any more.'

'Good. This can't wait. I'll fetch you.'

'I'm at Mother Superior's office.'

'You've been a bad girl, have you?'

'Shut up, Carl.' She rang off and went back to the office.

'I need to take care of some business,' she said to the nuns. 'Could I leave Jesse here till I get back?'

'That'll be lovely,' Sister Raymunda said, springing to her feet. 'And, as always, I'll pray that angels will watch over you and keep you safe, little one.'

'Thank you, Sister,' Dunai said. 'And thanks, Sister Finbar, for the info and chat. And I think your story is beautiful and brave.'

Sister Finbar came round the desk and looked intently at her. 'You look after yourself now, Dunai Marks. Heaven help us if those angels ever take a break.'

'They won't,' Dunai said. 'Sister Raymunda won't let them.'

Sister Raymunda laughed her small, breathless laugh and said, 'Always so funny, little one. Come, I'll walk you out.'

They left the main building and stepped out into a clear winter's day of powder-blue sky and golden sunshine. Dunai lifted her face to its warmth and felt for a moment the peace she'd always found at St Mark's.

'They're called *Cerchio di Gaia*.'

'Who is?' Dunai asked, turning to see a resolute look on Sister Raymunda's face.

'The Sisterhood of the Double Cross. That was never their real name. It's *Cerchio di Gaia*—Gaia's Circle.' Dunai stared at the diminutive nun. Sister Raymunda looked stubborn for a moment, then shrugged. 'Promise me you'll come to us if you need help.'

'Always,' Dunai said and kissed both her cheeks.

17

'WHAT did the sales assistant at the chemist say?' Dunai asked as they pulled away in Carl's four-wheel drive, heading for the Victoria and Alfred Waterfront. 'Did she serve Dan Cowley the night of Siobhan's murder?'

'She did,' Carl said. 'But she was extremely nervous, which means one of two things: either she didn't want to get involved or she was paid to provide him with an alibi.'

'And the security guard?'

'Cowley wasn't the only customer that night. There were quite a few. And the guard doesn't remember him. But the sales assistant said he reads magazines while he's on duty so it's unlikely he took note of a customer who didn't seem in the least threatening.'

'Or,' Dunai said, 'he doesn't remember Cowley because he was never there.'

'That's the other possibility.'

'So what do we do now?'

'See if there's a connection between Cowley and the chemist assistant; maybe a member of his congregation or a family friend.'

Carl parked in a bay within the Clock Tower Precinct. Dunai assumed they were meeting the informant in the Clock Tower Centre, but they strode past it to the Nelson Mandela Gateway.

'Where are we going?' Dunai asked.

'Robben Island.'

'Why?'

'Because the ferries are full on a Saturday and you have to book a place days in advance. The informant's bought our tickets, we'll collect them at the last minute and hop on. It'll make it almost impossible for someone to follow us on the spur of the moment.'

'When does the ferry leave?' Dunai asked.

'Twelve.'

'It's quarter to.'

'That's the idea,' Carl said as they strode into the Nelson Mandela Gateway—a triple-storey glass building that housed museum offices, a shop, restaurant and auditorium. Carl collected their tickets and they raced to the sleek Robben Island ferry.

Neither said anything as they glided across the Victoria Basin and out into Table Bay. It was a smooth ride across a calm sea; there was a cool breeze but no wind and the sun shone warmly between wisps of cirrus cloud.

'When do we get to speak to this person and how will he know who we are?' Dunai asked.

'I've used him before,' Carl said. 'He'll approach us.'

Half an hour later they entered Robben Island's Murray Bay Harbour, nothing more than a cement jetty and high blue slate wall. The large tour party walked from the harbour to three waiting buses.

As Dunai and Carl took a seat on one of them she glanced around at her fellow travelers, surreptitiously she thought until Carl put his arm around her shoulders, brought his lips close to her ear and whispered, 'Don't be so obvious.'

'You said it was almost impossible for anyone to follow,' Dunai whispered back.

'Almost,' he whispered. 'But he still needs to make sure. His life depends on it.'

As their guide pointed out sea and water birds, crowned cormorant and night herons, Dunai thought of the forced occupants

of the island and how they must have envied the birds. The van-
quished Xhosa chiefs, the Muslim leaders from the East Indies,
Dutch and British soldiers, lepers, the mentally ill and thousands
of anti-apartheid activists.

She couldn't help but feel moved by this flat, rocky island,
once the summit of an ancient mountain, which had been turned
into the hell-hole of apartheid, designed to crush the spirit, but
had become the foundation of a democracy.

Almost an hour later the three groups, about one hundred and
fifty people, filed into the maximum security prison that had been
built over lepers' graves. She looked at the people around her,
this time more carefully and, as a former prisoner spoke of life
in the dark cement dormitories, Dunai listened with only half an
ear. She was taking note of accents; most of her fellow tourists
were foreigners.

By the time they'd reached the eighty-cell isolation block,
with everyone wanting to stand for a few minutes in the tiny cell
that had been Nelson Mandela's, she had narrowed the South
Africans in the tour party to just five, Carl and herself included.
Out of the three remaining South Africans, two were a middle-
aged couple, white and visiting from upcountry. This left one
Coloured man in his early twenties who had originally been indistinguishable from a group of Malaysians.

After they left the maximum security building they were encouraged to explore the surrounding natural habitat, view the
holy Muslim *kramat* and visit the museum shop on their walk
back to the harbour.

'Want to see the penguins?' Carl asked.

'Yes!' Dunai said, always excited at the prospect of explor-
ing some aspect of the animal kingdom.

They veered off left and followed a path between rocks,
mounds of sand and straggly shrubs and fynbos. The colony of
African penguins ignored them as they passed or stopped to look
at nests or watch their antics, and now and then the air would be
filled with their strange calls that sounded like dog barks.

'I know who it is,' Dunai said as they walked along. 'It's the young skinny guy in jeans and grey sweatshirt.'

'You know, Dunai,' Carl said, 'I think you'd be good to have around in a fire-fight.'

He'd barely finished speaking when the man in the grey sweatshirt approached from behind. There were other people on the path so Carl stopped to let them pass.

'Howzit?' the man in the grey sweatshirt said.

''preciate it,' Carl replied.

''bout a month back, your boy did a *kuier* by Brandon Cupido, maybe about a paper bang but the jury's still out.'

'So there were no lights.'

'Ja, *bra*. That's the way it is. You make a move, better burn up the dance floor.' He brushed past them and continued along the path.

'What the hell was all that about?' Dunai asked, disappointed. The exchange had to be one of the worst anti-climaxes of her life.

'Direct translation,' Carl said, as they began making their way back to the ferry, 'is Wayne Daniels visited Brandon Cupido about a month ago. Seems it might have been about a contract killing, although it hasn't been confirmed. Officially, nobody saw or heard anything so if we want to move on Cupido we'd have to find some pretty damning evidence.'

'Okay,' Dunai said. 'So who is Brandon Cupido?'

'A Cape Flats gang leader known to every police officer in the province. Thirty years ago he was charged a few times but never tried because nobody survived long enough to bring evidence against him. After that even the charges dried up, although he was guilty of just about every crime in the book. There were rumours till about a decade ago that any investigations involving him were window dressing because he'd turned informer for the old government, ratting out anti-apartheid activists in exchange for immunity from prosecution. Apart from being a sadist, he'll do anything for money and he has no conscience, even where his family are concerned.'

They stepped off the path to allow another group to pass, then continued towards the harbour.

'About ten years ago his daughter converted to Islam and turned informer. Before she could pass on anything, she was found in a field in Manenberg. She'd been gang-raped and stabbed seventeen times—one wound for every year she'd been alive. Consensus was her father had ordered the hit.'

'Shit, that's sick.'

Carl was silent for a moment and when he spoke again his voice was grim. 'If Wayne Daniels did ask Brandon Cupido to organise a hit on Siobhan, you and I have just waded into some very dangerous water.'

18

DUNAI had just turned out the light and put her head on the pillow when she saw a shadow move behind the curtain. She lay still and listened, her eyes fixed on the large sash window. Since it was at the front of the house, it was always locked. The shadow appeared again; it looked as if it belonged to a man, and it wasn't a passer-by. Whoever was out there was pacing at her window and it had to be someone who had business with her, but not the sort that required a polite knock at the front door.

Dunai's first thought was Brandon Cupido and it set her heart thundering in her chest. She watched the shadow pass again, then turned slowly onto her back, reached in slow motion for the telephone beside her bed and dialled Bryan's number.

'Hello?'

'Belle, it's Dunai. There's someone on my stoep who's walked past my bedroom window at least three times; I think it's a man. Could you ask Bryan to come over? But tell him to approach with caution.'

'Oh, my…Okay,' Belle said, sounding a little breathless. 'I'll tell Bryan right away.'

'Thanks.'

'Dunai, don't do anything, okay? Don't go out or even look through the curtain.'

'I'm not that brave,' Dunai whispered.

'Hold on a sec.'

She heard Bryan's voice in the background, then Belle's. A moment later she came back on the line.

'He's on his way. D'you want me to stay on the line with you?'

'No, it's okay. I'm going to phone the boys next door. Thanks so much. Sorry to disturb your evening like this.'

'God, of course not, I'm glad you did,' Belle said. 'And get Bryan to let me know as soon as everything's okay.'

'Will do.' Dunai said, 'Bye now,' and hung up.

All the while she watched for the shadow at the window but it didn't appear again. That frightened her even more. Where the hell had he gone? She tried ringing Rory and Gavin.

'Hi. You've reached Rory and Gavin. We're off somewhere having a good time so leave a message and we'll call back.'

'It's me,' she said in a loud whisper. 'It's just gone nine. I need you to come over; someone's prowling outside my window.'

She carefully replaced the receiver, then sat very still listening for any unusual sounds in and around the turquoise house. There was the constant whoosh of traffic on Buitengragt Street, the odd shout or dog bark, then a knock at the front door. Thank God, Dunai thought, Rory and Gavin had got her message.

She pulled on a pair of sweat pants and tiptoed to the front door so she wouldn't wake anyone in the house. She turned on the stoep light, kept the chain on the door, just in case, and opened it.

Dan Cowley stood there. He was wearing a suit and pale blue tie. Dunai started with surprise, then wished she hadn't. She said nothing, but her arms were tensed, ready to slam the door shut if he moved an inch towards her.

'Can I come in, please?' he asked.

She was at first taken aback by the request, then recovered enough to say, 'No, of course not.'

'I'd really like to speak to you.'

'What about?'

The stoep light above his head threw dark shadows under his eyes.

'About Siobhan.'

'What the hell have you got to say to me about Siobhan?' she said, feeling suddenly aggressive.

'I don't want to talk about it out here. Can I come in, please?'

'No.'

'It wasn't easy for me to come here.'

The skin around his jaw looked slack and his face seemed pallid in the harsh yellow light.

Horse appeared beside her and gave a small exploratory bark. Dunai rubbed his neck to reassure him and keep him from waking the rest of the house.

'You're the person who might have murdered Siobhan. How can you even ask me to let you in?'

Dan Cowley looked exhausted. He nodded, then began to turn away.

'Wait!' Dunai said. 'I can't let you in but I want to know what you came here to say.'

He turned back, his eyes sliding from Dunai's face to his feet.

'This has nearly destroyed my life,' he said, so quietly she had to lean forward to catch the rest. 'I haven't only had to live with the blackmail; now the questions you're asking have got the congregation talking. I don't know what will be left of my life when all this is over.' His arms hung at his sides. 'I came to tell you that I've never hurt anyone in my life. I have never physically raised a hand to another human being.' He smiled dejectedly. 'Sometimes I wish I had but I just don't have it in me, you see.'

Dunai had no idea what to say and they stood watching each other till Bryan's blue Citroën roared up to the stoep thirty seconds later. So much for approaching with caution, Dunai mused.

'A friend of mine who's come to check on me,' she explained to Cowley, who had jumped nervously at the sound of brakes and was now half turned towards the pavement.

'What's going on here?' Bryan asked, striding up the steps.

Cowley looked agitated and ran a hand through his hair, which was already dishevelled. He ignored Bryan and turned back to

Dunai. 'I came here to try to make you see that I didn't kill Siobhan. I could never murder another human being, I swear to you.'

Dunai glanced at Bryan, saw shock register on his face, then anxiety settle in its place.

She and Cowley stood staring at the ground while Bryan looked from one to the other. Then Dunai looked him in the eye and said, 'I don't know why I believe you, but I do.'

He nodded, then turned and headed for the steps.

'Mr Cowley?' Dunai called.

He stopped, looked back over his shoulder.

'Perhaps you don't hurt people intentionally but your ideas are prejudiced and they do a lot of damage.'

'I believe I'm doing the right thing, Miss Marks. That's all any of us really have at the end of the day,' and he stepped off the stoep and headed up the street.

'You've got a whole lot of explaining to do,' Bryan said as Dunai slipped off the chain, held Horse by the collar and opened the door for him.

'I'll make us some tea,' she said, playing for time. She headed for the kitchen and, while the kettle boiled, went over exactly what she could tell him and what was better left unsaid.

When they were settled on the sofa, she told him that she'd decided to look into the people Siobhan had blackmailed, but didn't mention Carl's part in it. She didn't want him to feel hurt or slighted because she'd ignored his advice and his offer of referral to a grief counsellor and had instead gone to a private investigator.

'Dan Cowley,' she said, 'was not only being blackmailed by Siobhan but the last person to see her alive; his first alibi didn't check out and the second's suspect. But the person who seems most guilty is Wayne Daniels. He's a local government official who grew up on the Cape Flats with Brandon Cupido, who's a gang leader involved in organised crime,' Dunai explained. 'He was seen going to visit him at his home in Atlantis about a month ago and some think it was to ask Cupido to put a hit out on Siobhan—'

Bryan put his cup down on the coffee table so abruptly its contents almost slopped over the sides.

'You know, Dunai, I expected more from you than this.'

She blinked in surprise.

'You have people who care about you, a son. Tell me how you could have deliberately put yourself in danger like this. Gang leaders, organised crime. *Listen* to yourself. You're not some damned investigator in a detective serial. This is real, Dunai. And you've put yourself in a position where you could actually get killed. You're a mother. Did you even think of Jesse when you started all this?'

Bryan jumped to his feet and Dunai felt a ridiculous urge to burst into tears.

'I had to do it for Siobhan, Bryan. I did think of Jesse. I've done nothing but think of him in all this. But what sort of person would I be if I didn't even try to find who murdered the woman who was like a mother to me? I owe her this, Bryan.'

'No, Dunai,' Bryan said, still on his feet. 'Siobhan would *never* have asked this of you. *Never.*'

She was about to argue when the telephone began to ring. It was Rory. As briefly as she could, she explained what had happened and told him she was fine.

Bryan had sat down again and she went to sit beside him. Neither said anything at first, then he took her hands in his. 'I want you to understand something. I will never get over Siobhan's death as long as I live.' She watched him swallow. 'Please don't make me have to get over yours too. Listen to me, Dunai. Sometimes terrible things happen to us and, as much as we regret or try to undo them, we eventually realise we must put them behind us and get on with living or they eat away at us till there's nothing left of the person we once were. I know this because I've had to do it myself. It's one of the reasons I came to this country. And, as trite as this sounds, there's nothing more important than living a life of service to your community and working at being the sort of person your kids will be proud of one day.

So you see you have to go to the police with this or leave it alone completely. It's just too dangerous. I'm asking you to do this for me, for you, for Jesse, for Belle and Philippe. We're a small family who's already lost one of its members. To lose two…'

Dunai looked at his stricken face and felt torn down the middle. She couldn't bear to hurt him like this but she'd come too far to give up now.

Yesterday she'd lied to Sisters Finbar and Raymunda. Tonight she'd lie to Bryan for the first time.

'I'm sorry I put you through this. I really am. I hadn't realised how dangerous it would be. I'll leave it for a while but if I find that's too difficult to do I'll go to the police.'

'Promise me,' Bryan said.

Dunai swallowed.

'I promise.'

19

IF COWLEY hadn't pitched up on Sunday night they'd probably have come for her then, but as it turned out they had to wait for the following night.

It began with two knocks at the door of her house just after ten.

Horse barked and rushed to the door, Mr Nelson started shouting 'Bosh! Bosh!' and Jesse appeared in the doorway, rubbing his eyes.

Making a mental note to get a peep-hole fitted, Dunai put her mouth to the crack between wall and door and shouted, 'Who is it?'

'We met in the Company Gardens after Siobhan's death.'

'What do you want?'

'You have questions; it's time to find answers to some of them.'

'About the Sisterhood of the Double Cross?'

'Yes.'

'Wait there.' Dunai managed to shut the dog and the parrot in Jesse's room. Her son refused to be shut in with the animals so she told him to stay in the passage. She went back to the door. 'Are you alone?'

'Yes.'

'How do I know you're not here to hurt me?'

There was the briefest pause. 'You've got spirit, Dunai, but you're ill equipped to defend yourself. There've been better opportunities in the last two weeks.'

Dunai still wasn't convinced but she didn't want the woman

to go away. 'Hold on a minute.' She raced to the kitchen, grabbed the mallet, then wasn't sure where to put it. She was in slippers, track pants, a T-shirt and sweatshirt. She put the head of the mallet in the pocket of her track pants, lifted her sweatshirt and placed the handle against her side, keeping it tucked under her arm. The metal felt like ice through her T-shirt. She went to the front door, took a deep breath, opened it, then moved back quickly.

The amazon stepped inside. 'I'll wait for you to dress.'

'Aren't you coming in?'

'No, you're coming with me,' she said in her calm, even voice. Dunai felt slightly breathless. 'That's how it has to be,' the woman said.

Dunai knew that if she really wanted answers she'd have to go. 'I need to make arrangements for my son.'

'You can bring him with you.'

'No,' Dunai said, heading for the passage. 'I need to get dressed, then I'll take him next door.'

'Dunai?'

She turned.

'You won't need the mallet.'

It took her a second to recover. She headed down the passage to Jesse, who for once was exactly where he was meant to be, and took him to her bedroom. While she dressed, she called Barbara, told her she had a work emergency and needed to bring Jesse over.

She grabbed her coat as they left the house. The woman got into a silver Mercedes-Benz while Dunai went to the lavender house and dropped Jesse off.

As soon as she'd climbed into the amazon's car, the woman handed her a pair of sunglasses. 'You need to put these on.'

'You're joking.'

She said nothing, just continued to hold them out till Dunai took them. Once they were on she discovered they were no ordinary sunglasses. The blacked-out lenses were surrounded by a rubbery substance that clung to the skin, forming a type of suction. It would be impossible to sneak a peek without making a production of it.

'You've got nothing to worry about,' the woman said soothingly.

'Please don't say that; it makes me nervous.'

Dunai had memorised the registration number on her way to the car but she wished she could see her watch. If she survived tonight she'd want to know how far they'd travelled. She started counting off the seconds.

'What's the dog's name?' the amazon asked.

'Horse,' Dunai answered.

'Why'd you call a dog Horse?'

'My animals are named after characters in the Pippi Longstocking books.'

'I loved those books,' the amazon said, surprising Dunai, who doubted she'd ever been a child. 'So what's the parrot's name?'

'Mr Nelson.'

'Who was Pippi's monkey.'

'I taught him to say, "Bosh", like Pippi always said.'

'Don't tell me,' the amazon said. 'The cats are Tommy and Annika—Pippi's friends.'

'They are.'

'Those were amazing books,' the woman said, sounding nostalgic.

'They still are. You should read them again—they're hysterical. I think I've appreciated the humour even more as an adult and I still think Pippi's a brilliant role model for girls. I mean, look at you,' she said, turning her head towards the amazon, then feeling a little foolish in the sunglasses. 'I bet you could lift a horse above your head.'

Dunai wasn't sure what the woman's reaction was but it suddenly occurred to her that the questions might have been a ruse to sidetrack her and it had worked; she'd stopped counting without realising it.

'How did you know I had the mallet?'

'Most people don't walk around at home in their sweats with something that size in their pocket.'

'Yes, but how did you know it was a *mallet*?'

'You've been brandishing it all over town recently.'

Dunai was stunned to silence, beginning to doubt the wisdom of her decision to be blinded, put in a car and taken to heaven knew where by an amazon who probably belonged to a dangerous organisation.

The car eventually came to a stop. Dunai was guided across what felt like paving, then through a door and into a building. She was led over wooden floorboards, down a passageway that seemed to go on for ever, round a corner and down another passage; or so she thought.

'You can sit now,' the amazon said, pushing her down gently. She felt herself sink into a soft chair. The sunglasses were removed and she looked quickly around the dim room.

'Wait here,' the woman said, then disappeared through a door to Dunai's left.

She was in a private library, that much was obvious. Cabinets in dark wood stood on a polished floor that was strewn with thick-pile kelims in deep jewel colours. Above the cabinets, bookcases fronted by glass doors rose in two tiers, separated halfway up by a wooden gallery that ran all the way around the room. There was a doorway in the upper gallery and she could see a staircase railing behind it. On a wooden panel above one of the cabinets a row of clocks showed the time in ten of the world's major cities. There was an uncomfortable-looking chair and wooden desk in a corner. Dunai was seated in a brown armchair that formed part of a suite in living room formation.

'Hello, Dunai Marks.'

Dunai turned in the direction of the voice. The face of the woman standing before the closed door was familiar but she couldn't at first place her. Then she realised it was Paula Swanepoel-Higgs, the only female justice in the Constitutional Court.

The woman made her way towards her, took her hand and said, 'Come, Dunai, let's talk.'

'You know me?' Dunai asked.

'In a manner of speaking, yes. Sit,' she commanded and Dunai obeyed.

She studied the woman's face as she took a seat on the opposite side of the coffee table. Dunai had seen her on television, seated alongside her colleagues on the semi-circular bench in the highest court in the country, delivering some judgement that would set a national precedent. Her regular features bore no trace of make-up, which probably made her look younger than she really was. Thick grey hair was combed into a neat bob and she wore a white blouse and velvet suit the colour of blackberries. There was no sign of the double cross but it might have been tucked beneath her blouse.

'I've been looking forward to meeting you for a long time,' she said. Her eyes were bright and a smile tickled the corners of her mouth 'But you have questions. Tonight we'll answer some of them. First question—what is the Sisterhood of the Double Cross?'

'*Cerchio di Gaia.*'

'Yes, you've got that far. But there aren't many who know that name. It's still the Sisterhood of the Double Cross to the conspiracy theorists. It's better that way—more dramatic, less plausible.'

She paused for a moment and Dunai wondered if she was being warned never to use the name *Cerchio di Gaia*.

'Tell me, Dunai. While you and I sit here chatting, do you know what's going on out there?'

'I don't know what you mean.'

The judge glanced towards one of the clocks on the wall.

'Since you walked into this room ten minutes ago, twenty women have been raped—that's just in this country. Another twelve women and children have been sold into slavery across the globe. As we speak, women are performing two-thirds of the world's labour, producing more than half our food, but own only one per cent of assets worldwide. Two out of every three people who can't read the label on a medicine bottle tonight or write a grocery list for tomorrow are women.'

She glanced again at the row of clocks.

'It's just after eight in London, lunch time in Washington. Fewer than twenty per cent of parliamentary and congressional seats are occupied by women, even though we are fifty-one per cent of the population.

'But this is all a bunch of boring statistics, isn't it?' Changing tack suddenly, she leaned forward, picked up a remote control from the coffee table and pointed it at a section of wood panelling.

Two panels slid back to reveal a large plasma screen. Women's faces began to flash across it—bruised, eyes swollen shut, cheek and jawbones smashed, noses flattened and blood running from gashes, knife wounds and split lips.

'The wounds you see are real.'

Dunai looked away.

'We try to collect, as far as possible the name of every woman who is abused—not as a record but as a roll of honour, like the memorial walls for fallen soldiers. But we had some technical difficulties with this presentation,' she went on.

'To give a better idea of the reality of the situation, we'd have to flash thousands of superimposed images every second, which would have made it impossible to watch. So we had to settle for one face per second.'

Dunai glanced again at the screen and, in an attempt to block out the damage, looked at the eyes, which was a mistake. The shock, misery and pain were worse than the wounds. She had to look away again.

'Women's and human rights organisations,' the judge said, 'in order not to alienate men and to avoid being accused of hysterics, or sometimes simply in deference to the tenets of report-writing, make statements like, "The abuse of women and girls is endemic in most societies around the world." Fact is, there is a war being waged against women—the most bloody, long-standing conflict on the planet.'

Dunai felt something stir in her chest—anger, a deep desire for this not to be so. 'But it's crime,' she said. 'Males are as much victims as females.'

'No, Dunai, they are not. The majority of violent criminals are male—ninety-seven per cent—and the majority of victims are female.'

'It's still crime, not a conspiracy,' Dunai said, feeling angry and not managing to disguise it. 'What possible reason could there be for waging war against women?'

'Same reason for any war. To attain or retain social, economic and political power.'

Dunai realised she'd scooted forward in her seat; she sat back.

'And yes, Dunai, there is a conspiracy.'

Dunai shook her head, not because she had an argument but because it was all too bloody horrifying for words.

'What do you think conspiracy is?' the judge asked. 'A group of silver-haired men meeting clandestinely around a mahogany table?' She shook her head. 'There is a conspiracy by default and it's far more dangerous than the Hollywood type because it's almost impossible to fight.'

She paused and Dunai waited, dreading what was to come.

'The conspiracy by default is the billions of messages generated in everyday life that shape people and the societies in which they live. Think about this, Dunai. What happens if fifty-one per cent or sixty per cent of those messages are negative or degrading?

'What occurs is rape and murder, domestic violence, bride slayings and mail order brides, honour killings, acid disfiguration, sexual harassment, lower paid jobs and unequal sharing of chores, exclusion from golf clubs, social clubs and certain positions in corporations and religious groups. Female circumcision, denial of access to education and medical care. Forced labour, sex slavery, retail therapy, eating disorders and addiction to plastic surgery.

'That's conspiracy by default. And when does a rise in the frequency of negative messages become dangerous for women? Does rape increase when there's a ten per cent rise in discriminatory messages—is it perhaps a five per cent increase, or as low as two? Who keeps a check on these balances and, when a bias occurs, who attempts a counterbalance? That, Dunai, is one of *Cerchio di Gaia*'s many tasks.'

A large ginger cat walked towards them, stopped a couple of feet away and looked suspiciously at Dunai.

'Friend, not foe, Ginger,' the judge said. As if it understood, the cat looked away from Dunai, continued towards the other woman and hopped onto her lap.

'Still,' Dunai said, not managing to keep incredulity from her voice, 'the average man doesn't get up in the morning, button his trousers and go off to wage war against women.'

Justice Swanepoel-Higgs smiled. 'Not consciously. But you see, Dunai, all wars are based on ideology, and the ideals that began this war were developed a long time ago. The war continues so long as our way of thinking about gender is never challenged.'

She kept stroking the cat. 'The root of the problem is the belief that we are defined by our biology. Men are dominant, competitive, aggressive and have large sexual appetites. Women are passive, dependent, emotional, irrational and masochist, with contradicting qualities of modesty and seductiveness. These are gender beliefs that are lived out every day by men and women as if they were a natural or real aspect of our identity when they are not. And it is within these beliefs that violence against women is rooted.

'So, even if we know rape and domestic violence are wrong, we still believe rape is the extreme consequence of men's sexual appetite and women become victims because they are passive, unable to fight back effectively, or contradictory, sending out conflicting sexual messages, like saying no when they really mean yes.'

She again pointed the remote at the plasma screen. The battered, flashing faces disappeared, replaced by a sepia-coloured screen with what looked like footage from a security camera. The date and time—22.45—were displayed at the bottom of the screen.

It showed a garage, petrol pumps clearly visible in the foreground. A woman carrying a grocery bag was walking towards a car in a bay at the top of the screen. Dunai's eyes flicked to the left, where five men had appeared. They moved quickly towards the woman and surrounded her in seconds, one man grabbing her neck, another punching her in the stomach.

The woman was frogmarched to the side of a building, visible just to the left of the screen,. and slammed back against the wall. Her head whipped from side to side and, even though she was such a small figure, Dunai was sure she could see her chest heaving with panic, her eyes bulging with fear as they ripped at her clothes, one man using a knife to slice through her skirt.

Dunai couldn't stand to see any more. She covered her face with her hands and swallowed against the nausea that had risen to her throat. A tinny male voice with a hint of excitement said from far away, 'She's asking for it. You can see it, man.'

'…short skirt,' said another voice that sounded lazy, disinterested. 'Girl out for smokes alone this time of night's begging for a fuck.'

Dunai looked up, but not at the screen. 'Please turn it off.'

The judge switched again to the battered faces. Dunai stared at the ginger cat.

'That rape went on for twenty minutes,' she said. 'And, while it was happening, forty other women in this country were going through something similar. Recreational gang rape is now so common it's called jack-rolling. Eleven per cent of fifteen- to nineteen-year-old boys surveyed thought it was "cool" or "just a game" and eight in ten adult males believe women are raped because they've asked for it in some way or simply failed to protect themselves effectively.

'That was surveillance footage, by the way.' She flicked her hand towards the screen. 'And those voices at the end belong to police officers who were suspended with full pay and later reinstated. The footage was not permissible in court and three of the rapists were acquitted. The other two received sentences of five and seven years, one serving eighteen months, the other two and a half years.'

Dunai felt angry, at whom she wasn't entirely sure, but she channelled her anger into sarcasm and directed it at the judge. 'I worked for Siobhan long enough to know that women are being abused out there. And I do read the papers and watch the news from time to time.'

'Hmm,' the judge said, her blue eyes glittering in the dim light. 'But are you aware that it is not only women who suffer as a result of this belief that we are defined by our biology? Men are victims of patriarchy, too.'

Dunai's brain attempted a U-turn. She stared at the woman in the dark velvet suit.

'Ah, I see I've at last surprised you,' she said, smiling broadly for the first time. 'You see, Dunai, *Cerchio di Gaia* does not prescribe a naïve and romanticised idea of feminism that teaches that men are by nature sexual brutes and women gentle, submissive and nurturing creatures. We're too far down the road for that, and that path leads right back to gender stereotyping anyway. Did you know, for instance, that in so-called first world countries men are increasingly becoming victims of domestic violence?'

Dunai shook her head in bewilderment.

The judge nodded. 'The statistics are alarming. And again, were you aware that seventy per cent of children who are murdered in their homes in the US are murdered by their mothers?'

Dunai automatically opened her mouth to protest, then shut it.

'Men too suffer as a result of biological stereotyping. Just the mention of a man beaten by his wife is usually met with a laugh or at the very least a smile. In Canada, despite the number of men abused by their wives and partners, there is not one shelter for battered men. I think in the entire US there are perhaps one or two. The only course for these men, if they don't want to get friends and extended family involved, which most don't, is to request a jail cell for protection, but they may not take their children with them and must leave them behind with a dangerously violent partner. And on many statute books across the globe, including this country, the law refuses to recognise that males can be raped. The assumption, based on gender stereotyping, is that the male is so strong, resolute and authoritative that if sex is forced upon him, he must be a closet homosexual or have allowed it to happen. Such a man may bring charges of sexual assault but most never do; they remain silent. And children are still placed with mothers who may be wholly unsuitable rather than with a responsible and loving father. This state of affairs is a direct result of naïve patriarchal systems based on gender stereotyping. It must go, Dunai. Primarily for the sake of our daughters, but also for our sons.'

Dunai thought of Jesse then, but fought to push the image from her mind. Her heart was hammering as if her life were in danger. She just couldn't absorb any more. She desperately wanted to leave this room and go home, pick Jesse up off Barbara's sofa and carry him back to his bed.

'Why have you brought me here?'

The judge nodded. 'Most of the violence against women, and men for that matter, will stop only when patriarchal social and political structures are dismantled and this is *Cerchio di Gaia*'s over-arching objective. We work towards this across the globe in myriad different ways. You have a part to play.'

The dubiousness Dunai felt must have shown on her face because Justice Swanepoel-Higgs said, 'Not as far-fetched as it may sound, Dunai. Even those who are not sympathetic to our cause are beginning to realise that power-based patriarchal structures are rapidly degenerating and placing the enlightened progression of our species in jeopardy.

'We are a patient group. Generations have passed who never hoped to see the extinction of patriarchy in their lifetime, and I certainly don't expect to see it in mine, but it will come, Dunai. Of that we intend to make absolutely certain.'

She glanced briefly towards the flashing images on the screen.

'I've spoken of the ideology behind the group but we are quite practical in how we go about our business. Are you familiar with the notion of critical mass?'

Dunai shook her head.

'In physics, critical mass is the minimum amount of radioactive material necessary to produce a nuclear reaction. Once critical mass has been reached the process becomes self-sustaining.'

Dunai felt herself begin to scowl and tried to rein in her growing impatience.

'Illustrations of critical mass are found in everyday life—in fashion, the survival and extinction of species, in language systems, racial integration, political movements and even panic behaviour.

'Based on critical mass, sociologists ask the question—how many people are necessary to adopt a new practice, product or belief system before it becomes a chain reaction that in time persuades most people to adopt that particular practice or product?

'Social change happens when critical mass occurs but you see, Dunai, numbers alone are not enough. In physics, the size of the nuclear reaction and when it happens depends on the concentration and purity of the radioactive material used in the geometry of the surrounding reaction system. For us, this means that the concentration and purity of the actions of women and supportive men will determine the size of the reaction. In other words, just how pure and irreversible liberation will be when it eventuality does become self-sustaining.'

Dunai stored this information away for consideration at some later stage because for now she had more personal questions that were burning a hole in her gut.

'I still don't know why you're interested in me,' she prompted.

The judge glanced down at Ginger, who was nodding off in her lap, then again met Dunai's gaze.

'There are four areas of critical importance to us—politics, the judiciary, media and education. To win a war, one must fight many battles—some large and glorious, others small and seemingly insignificant. This we encourage our members across the world to do, no matter how scarce their tools or how small their platform.

'Siobhan's battle has been her STOP clinics, which have both media pull and are an educational tool. She believed once the model was adopted by government it would have sufficient backing and resources and, if developed to its full potential, could become an important vehicle and rallying point for female activism and a means of reaching into homes and communities across southern Africa.

'The groundwork has been done and, much to our regret, Siobhan is gone, but we'd like to safeguard her work and her aims.'

'You want me to take up where Siobhan left off.'

The judge nodded. 'STOP clinics may be just one very small endeavour in the many that make up the body of work of the South African circle, and to lose them might seem of little importance in the immediate sense but, as the saying goes, "Of such accumulated setbacks were battles lost", and we have no intention of losing this battle, Dunai.'

'I've heard *Cerchio di Gaia* is a violent organisation. Was Siobhan told to blackmail people?'

'Every person is encouraged to follow her conscience, Dunai.' The voice was low and melodious and she continued to stroke the cat. 'We are joined by a common ideology, an unbreakable loyalty, but we are not a dictatorship and it will not help to think of our circle as possessing a patriarchal system of hierarchy. We rather place a matriarchal emphasis on relationships and connectedness. Unfortunately, for the time being, the nature of the conflict continues to generate casualties. As Nelson Mandela has put it, it is always the oppressor, not the oppressed, who dictates the form of the struggle.'

'So extreme times call for extreme measures?' Dunai asked.

'Circumstances dictate measures. Each situation is unique, as are our adherents. Take for instance, the couple in the green Valiant.'

Dunai's breath caught in her throat.

'We'd prefer not to infringe on a person's privacy, but following Siobhan's death we had no idea what sort of danger you were in. That meant following you to keep watch. If we hadn't, you might have been raped or murdered in that tunnel.'

Dunai felt herself being drawn in; she clung desperately to her objectivity.

'Siobhan was blackmailing a priest, a genuinely good man. I don't believe she'd ever do that of her own accord.'

Justice Swanepoel-Higgs looked at her kindly, a hint of sadness softening her features. 'I see you are struggling with a lot of things. You're still young and idealistic, but I want you to keep in mind when judging Siobhan that those who wage war against the worst social crises often become wearier and more desperate as time goes by.'

'So you believe the end justifies the means?'

'Not always, no.'

'Do you know who killed Siobhan?'

'No. But we intend to find out, one way or another. You are one way, Dunai. You and Carl Lambrecht have made excellent progress in a very short time.'

'Why aren't you investigating Siobhan's murder yourself? Your resources have to be far greater than mine.'

'We don't have supernatural abilities. We failed to protect Siobhan. Resources are sometimes a poor comparison to the passion and focus of one motivated individual. And you moved quickly, Dunai; approaching Carl Lambrecht the same day. It was a good move; he has an excellent track-record and we believe this, coupled with your passion and deeper knowledge of Siobhan, is the best way to bring her murderer to justice.'

'You'd also prefer a woman who was close to Siobhan and loved her to look into her life rather than the police, who might come across sensitive information and demand explanations.'

The judge smiled slightly and nodded. 'There is the circle to think about. Siobhan would have been the first to understand that. You know she always believed you'd eventually become part of the circle and, from what we've seen in recent weeks, I believe you'd be a valuable addition.'

'Blackmailing people?'

'We're not the mob, Dunai. We are of all religions, all nationalities and we come from all walks of life. You underestimate our work and our results.'

There was silence in the room except for the cat's purring. Dunai tried again. 'You said Siobhan always believed I'd become part of the group—was she my mother?'

The judge sighed and smiled sadly. 'Yes, she was.'

Dunai felt the room fade away. The word *mother* seemed to spiral, plunge and soar in her mind as her heart thudded to the irregular pulsing of this single word.

Justice Swanepoel-Higgs waited patiently. When Dunai still did not speak after a time, she said, 'You've been deeply traumatised in the last two weeks, yet you've shown remarkable fortitude. Still, it's too much for anyone to assimilate in such a short time, no matter who they are. You need time to adjust to the reality of our existence.'

The room swung back into focus. 'What I need is more information,' Dunai said, aware that her voice had increased in pitch and volume. 'How can you ask me to continue where Siobhan left off when I know nothing about the group, have no idea what I'd be getting myself into?'

'Dunai, please understand our situation,' she said. 'Our survival has been dependent on our invisibility. I need to be very careful of what I reveal to you. Just bringing you here tonight was a risk. Siobhan didn't think you were ready, but her death has caused a reaction in your life that's a bit like a premature birth. All I can say to you now is that, as part of the circle, you would be entitled to certain information, but not as an outsider.'

'I can't make a decision now,' Dunai said.

The judge nodded. 'I've given you what information I can; now it's done.'

She placed the cat on the floor.

'I want you to consider what we've talked about. You are being given an opportunity to make your life really count for something. "Making a difference" is a cliché; we can make it a reality for you. Think about it, Dunai.'

Justice Swanepoel-Higgs got to her feet; Dunai followed.

'It's been good to finally meet you, even in these tragic circumstances,' she said. 'Here is my card.' She took it from her pocket and handed it to Dunai. 'I'm certain we'll speak again.'

Dunai automatically reached for the card then stood unmoving as the judge disappeared with cat in tow the same way she'd come. The amazon returned to the room and proffered the sunglasses. Dunai silently put them on and allowed herself to be led to the car.

20

HER escort saw her safely inside her house, then disappeared back to wherever she'd come from. It was just gone midnight.

Dunai went next door, lifted Jesse from Barbara's sofa and took him home; he didn't stir. Once he was tucked in bed, she sat beside him, watching him sleep. Then she took a shower, made some camomile tea and sat on the sofa.

What dominated her thoughts was the knowledge that Siobhan had been—*was*—her mother. Every childhood fantasy had centred around a woman who, having been forced to give her up, would one day, out of the blue, stride into the orphanage, lift her into her arms and carry her home. The woman's face had always been in shadow or blurred by light streaming in through a window. Not any more. Dunai closed her eyes and conjured Siobhan. Studying her again in this new light, her skin had been like Jesse's–pale with faint gold freckles scattered over the bridge of the nose, like her own. Siobhan's eyes, hazel in colour and al-mond-shaped, had been different from Dunai's, nose and lips her been thinner, but the women's height and lanky build were the same and there was a similarity to the shape of chin and jaw. Tears squeezed out the corners of Dunai's eyes and trickled over high cheekbones that were nothing like her mother's.

Her face was replaced in Dunai's mind by a scene—the first time she'd polished the dunai in Siobhan's flat. They'd been chatting away but at some point Siobhan had stopped talking.

Dunai had looked up to see her sitting on the sofa, legs drawn up beneath her and her eyes fixed on Dunai, an expression on her face she didn't recognise.

'You all right?' Dunai had asked.

'Damn glare in here's making my eyes water,' she'd said and jumped up to draw the voile curtains.

There were other things, like the watch Siobhan had given her for her last birthday, with the mother-of-pearl face. Dunai stared at it lying on the coffee table.

When the judge had told her Siobhan was her mother, Dunai had been stunned and upset; now she was relieved and filled with quiet rage. How could Siobhan have been around her almost every day for two years and have said nothing? Why hadn't she told her? She'd had no right to do that. Dunai wept again for her and everything that was now lost for ever; so much more than she'd suspected two weeks ago.

'...she always believed you'd eventually become part of the circle.' Dunai heard the judge's words again. 'Siobhan didn't think you were ready, but her death has caused a reaction in your life that's a bit like a premature birth.'

Whether sane or insane, Justice Swanepoel-Higgs, Professor Anna Cooper, even Thandiwe Dingake, were enormously influential people and heaven only knew how many other powerful and seemingly insignificant women had found an ideological home with *Cerchio di Gaia*. And now she was being asked to join the group, continue Siobhan's work, allow STOP to be used for the group's aims. Perhaps she'd be forced to do this behind Philippe's and Bryan's back, the way Siobhan had done.

Dunai thought of the group's antithesis—Wayne Daniels, Dan Cowley. Two men representative of millions just like them. To believe she was working towards the eventual eradication of their influence from society would undoubtedly give her life higher meaning, but what of men like Bishop Helmsley? And could she ignore the violence Sister Raymunda had hinted at and the dangerous fanaticism she sensed lay beneath *Cerchio di Gaia*'s surface?

Dunai was also aware that she was clinging stubbornly to the belief that the world around her really wasn't at war with itself, so no drastic action was required of her.

She wasn't a team player. She'd always prided herself on that, had always been fiercely independent. It left her free to follow her conscience. Would she be able to retain that independence within the group? The judge had assured her she would. But surely she couldn't remain untainted by their fanaticism. She thought of how she'd blindly hero-worshipped Siobhan. How long would it be before fitting in and pleasing the group became more important and far more powerful than following her conscience?

The judge had admitted that the circle, as she called it, was not above using violence to further its aims. This dilemma Dunai now wrestled with was not entirely new to her. Her first seventeen years had been lived under the apartheid regime while being brought up in a multi-racial Roman Catholic orphanage opposed to the government's human rights abuses. This meant her ideology had developed into what was then called 'white liberalism'.

She'd been six when the armed wing of the ANC, moulded by Nelson Mandela who years later would be awarded the Nobel Peace Prize, launched its first car-bomb attack, killing more than a dozen and injuring a hundred or so more. And she had been eight years old when the ANC announced that 'soft' targets were no longer off limits. Six months later, and two days before Christmas, a bomb had exploded in a shopping mall, killing five people and injuring sixty. One of the dead had been a two-year-old boy whose bright blue eyes Dunai could still see staring at her from the front page of a newspaper.

Terrorists—it was a word that had become part of everyday South Africa, an expression that for Dunai had come to represent a group of invisible monsters who skulked amongst ordinary people in everyday places, planning acts of unspeakable evil, then executing them without conscience. She'd feared and despised them till the daughter of one of the cleaning staff at the

orphanage had told her how the police had bashed down her
aunt's door in the middle of the night and dragged her to a police station. They'd beaten her. When she'd refused to give up
the names of her comrades they'd brought a tape recorder to her
and played back her baby daughter's screams of agony. They said
they'd only dislocated the infant's shoulder, nothing permanent,
nothing that couldn't be fixed, and that was where they'd leave
it if she gave them the information they were looking for.

'But they didn't really hurt the baby,' Dunai remembered saying. 'It was a trick, wasn't it?'

But the girl had looked steadily at her and shaken her head.
'When they let Aunty go, she found baby at the Red Cross
Hospital. Her shoulder was put back and strapped in a bandage.'

Then, Dunai had no longer known who the real monsters
were and tonight she experienced the same feeling.

She remembered a quote from her last year of school when
they'd just begun to rewrite the history textbooks. Oliver Tambo,
President of the ANC, a former maths and science teacher whose
character was dominated by an exceedingly gentle nature, had
eventually said, 'If I had been approached by an ANC unit and
asked whether they could go and plant a bomb in a supermarket,
I would have said, "Of course not." But when our units are faced
with what is happening all around them, it is understandable…'

Dunai had known and met many liberal white South Africans
during apartheid, including the nuns, who had been called *kaf-
fir boeties*. And she knew only too well that those who hadn't
joined the armed struggle came to occupy a no-man's land,
trapped between loathing of the fascist government's brutality
and aversion to the freedom movement's violent retaliation.
These confused citizens had compensated by being especially
charitable to the black and Coloured people they'd come into
contact with, telling themselves there was nothing they could do
to influence such a brutal regime, whereas they could make a difference in individuals' lives. But the fact was that history had
proved that if it weren't for the violence people like Siobhan had

embraced, a number of black people would be living in tiny, solid brick houses built by their kindly white employers, their children's school fees paid and just enough on the table, but apartheid would still be raging, its casualties mounting daily, costing eventually hundreds of thousands, perhaps even millions of lives.

Dunai had come to only one conclusion by the time the first democratic elections were held, and that was that the debate about violence versus pacifism remained academic until an individual or those close to them were threatened in a very real way. Peaceable, well-adjusted individuals would almost always cross the line if the push was personal enough.

The decision to resort to violence seemed to have been an easy one for Siobhan—she'd become a soldier because that was what it took to win the war. Her decision to join *Cerchio di Gaia* had probably been equally straightforward.

Dunai realised now why Siobhan had often encouraged her to think about which way she'd have gone if apartheid had continued. But, much to her mentor's chagrin, the only verdict Dunai had ever reached was, 'It's one thing to abhor a violently oppressive regime, another to blow up children in a shopping mall.' And she knew the debate well enough to know that the question of whether to join *Cerchio di Gaia* would present no easy answer.

Nelson Mandela had once said, 'The time comes…when there remain only two choices: submit or fight… We shall not submit and we have no choice but to hit back by all means within our power in defence of our people, our future and our freedom…' And, as the history of Dunai's country had proved perhaps more than any other, was that today's terrorist was tomorrow's freedom fighter. How would history remember *Cerchio di Gaia*? And how would she think back on her own decision to submit rather than fight?

Perhaps if she'd been forced to listen to Jesse's screams as his arm was torn from its socket she'd have found some dark place inside herself that was capable of blowing the enemy's child to pieces. Perhaps such terrible trauma, violent and personal, drove one insane, allowing extreme retaliation to be excused by the uninvolved and explained by the mind doctors. But Dunai had no such excuse for joining what she suspected was a dangerous organisation.

Round and round her thoughts went like a hamster on a wheel; no matter what spin she put on it, she was unable to reach a conclusion. It was three in the morning when she forced herself to go to bed, but she hardly slept at all.

21

DUNAI was early into work, which was why she was alone when the call came through from DI van Reenen at eight o'clock to say they'd recovered the coffee and fax machines stolen from the office. She had almost forgotten about the police and that they continued to pursue the burglary line of enquiry, as she believed they'd been instructed to do by the National Intelligence Agency.

'Where did you find them?' she asked.

'Atlantis. Just around the corner from the police station in an industrial tip.'

'But why would anyone go to the trouble of stealing a coffee and fax machine, then throw them away?'

'Because, Ms Marks, they were broken,' the detective said, sounding exhausted as usual. 'They were obviously damaged during or after the burglary.'

'Who found them?' Dunai asked.

'An old man who goes through the tips on refuse day and sees what he can salvage. It's not that unusual on the Cape Flats. When he saw the STOP stickers on both items he remembered hearing on the news that a woman had been murdered in a burglary at STOP's offices and he took the items to Atlantis Police Station.'

'Does this help your investigation at all?' She knew it did hers.

'We'll make enquiries about the theft syndicates in the area.

I told your colleague, Mr Baobi, that two people in your building lost their keys and another was mugged two weeks before
the burglary. The guy who was mugged lives in Atlantis but
he genuinely was attacked. He reported it at the police station.
A case was opened but no one's been apprehended; he didn't
get a good look at his assailant. Also, he wasn't working in
the building when the burglary took place. He'd quit a week
before.'

'Can you remember what company he worked for?' Dunai
tried to keep the question as casual as possible.

'Can't remember the company's name offhand,' van Reenen
said. 'But it's a small risk assessment firm on the first floor.'

'Oh, right,' Dunai said, her brain working furiously. 'Okay,
well thanks for letting us know, I appreciate it.'

As soon as she'd rung off, she jumped up from her desk and
went towards the door but remembered it was too early for Carl
to be in the office. So she went back to her desk and dialled his
mobile. It rang for some time before a groggy voice said, 'Yes?'

Dunai's brow furrowed. 'You still sleeping?'

'Yes, Dunai, I'm still sleeping.'

'It's ten past eight,' she said.

'What do you want?'

She told him about DI van Reenen's call.

'We have a link now,' she said when she'd finished. 'Daniels
wants Siobhan killed so he goes to gangster Cupido, who lives
in Atlantis on the Cape Flats. Someone who works in the building and just happens to live in Atlantis is conveniently mugged
and his keys to the building stolen. Same guy quits his job and
a week later Siobhan is murdered in what looks like a burglary.
Two weeks later, two broken items from the so-called burglary
turn up in an industrial tip in Atlantis where Cupido lives. There
are just too many coincidences.'

'Okay,' Carl said, sounding less groggy. 'I'll get hold of the
guy's address. I want you to talk to his former colleagues. Try
to find out what he's up to now.'

'Will do,' Dunai said, feeling more positive than she had in a long while. 'And, by the way, I had a visit from Dan Cowley on Sunday night.'

'You what?' Carl said, sounding alert now.

Dunai told him about the encounter.

'And d'you believe he didn't kill Siobhan?' Carl asked at the end of her tale.

'I dislike that man so much I'd really like him to be guilty, but yes, I did believe him.'

'Well, that's good,' Carl said. 'Even though we haven't eliminated him from the suspect list, it at least means you're keeping an open mind.'

'Doing my best,' Dunai said. 'Oh, and I'm sorry I woke you.'

'No, you aren't,' Carl said and hung up.

She took the stairs to the first floor.

The receptionist was large, coffee-coloured and had been born without a volume control button.

After the usual pleasantries Dunai told her STOP was looking for an office messenger.

'Can't help you,' she boomed. 'Ours quit couple of weeks ago. Only worked here a month, not even, then pissed off.'

'Oh, yes,' Dunai said, leaning casually on the counter. 'What was his name again?'

'Jerome Plaatjies. Hardly ever talked. Never stopped for a chat. Was one of the most geeky brothers I've ever met in my life. Always had his nose in a book, you know what I mean? Studying through UNISA or something—business, I think.'

'I don't think I remember what he looked like,' Dunai said, looking up at the ceiling and twirling a piece of hair between her fingers.

'Tall, skinny guy with glasses,' she said. 'Looks like he'd fall through his own poop-hole.'

'Oh, okay,' Dunai said, 'I think I remember. So where'd he go?'

'Last I heard he works for a medical supply company in Darling Street—Castle side of the Grand Parade. Don't know what it's called. So, what's the latest with the investigation? The police got anyone yet?'

'No,' Dunai said, beginning to edge away from the desk.

'Useless bunch of arse-wipes,' she said, and the phone began to ring.

Dunai silently thanked Sister Raymunda's angels, waved at the receptionist, then exited the office as quickly as she could.

22

THE Grand Parade was the city's oldest square and its earliest commercial centre. Over the years it had been the site of public floggings and executions, a burial site and a military parade ground. More recently it had reverted to a market place. Its fifteen minutes of fame had played out to a watching world on 11 February 1990, when thousands had gathered to celebrate the release of Nelson Mandela, who had made his first public address in twenty-seven years from the balcony of City Hall that fronted the parade.

Now, at eight-ten on a winter's morning, vendors were setting up for the day, hurrying to fasten tarpaulins over the metal frames of their stalls to protect their wares from the steady drizzle.

Dunai unfurled her umbrella as soft drizzle turned to cold needles of rain. Huddled against a brick kiosk, she tried to sink deeper into her coat, protect herself from gusts of wind that felt as if they were straight off the Antarctic.

Carl arrived ten minutes later, hands thrust deep into the pockets of his suede jacket. He looked as if he hadn't yet woken properly.

'What else did you find out about Jerome Plaatjies?' he asked.

'Just that he was a quiet person, kept to himself. He's studying through UNISA. And he quit his job suddenly. There he is,' Dunai said, straightening. 'Guy with the glasses, in the navy blue windbreaker, rucksack over his shoulder.'

Carl and Dunai had positioned themselves in this spot because they'd guessed that if Jerome really did work in Darling Street, on the Castle side of the Grand Parade, he'd have to walk diagonally across the Parade and there was only one entrance from the railway station—a narrow walkway near the brick kiosks. It had been a good guess.

Dunai wasn't sure when they should approach him. She waited for Carl's lead.

The young man had almost passed them when Carl, with Dunai close behind, moved forward and fell into step with him.

'Jerome Plaatjies?'

Far from slowing down, Jerome picked up the pace.

'I'm a private investigator,' Carl said. 'My colleague and I are investigating Siobhan Craig's murder and we'd like to speak to you about that.'

Jerome stopped suddenly, looked stunned, then glanced nervously around him. 'I don't know anything,' he said.

He was Carl's height but about a third of his width. His skin was the colour of brown paper, the eyes behind the glasses almost black. His hair was black, straight and short.

'Look, Jerome,' Carl said, 'why don't we get out of the open, okay?'

He began to walk back to the brick kiosks, towards a row of benches under bare-branched trees. Here they'd be out of view of most of the Parade.

Jerome hesitated for just a second before following them.

'I'm really sorry about Siobhan but I don't know anything,' he said quietly.

'D'you know you live a street up from Brandon Cupido?' Carl asked. His voice was unconfrontational, soft even, and there was barely a trace of Afrikaans accent.

Jerome bobbed his head but said nothing.

'A couple of days ago some of the stuff stolen from Siobhan's office was found in a tip two blocks from where you live.'

Jerome wiped a hand across his mouth. 'There's a lot of criminals in Atlantis; it's a bad place.'

Carl nodded. 'Okay, Jerome,' he said. 'This is what I think happened—two possible scenarios. Cupido is asked to put a hit on Siobhan Craig. She's working on a government project so her murder could draw attention at several levels and he needs to put a bit more planning into this murder than he usually does.

'I looked into your background. You matriculated last year; did well but you still couldn't find a job. So there you are, young guy living a street up from Cupido. No criminal record, no history of involvement in gang activity. You're conscientious, worked hard at school, just started studying for a business degree and you live at home with your mother and two younger sisters who are still in high school.'

Jerome was watching Carl closely.

'Cupido finds a job opening in the building Siobhan works in and puts you forward for it. Once you've settled in you're told to keep an eye on Siobhan's movements and hand over to Cupido the set of keys you've been given to the building. Only your conscience doesn't allow you to do this so they're taken from you forcefully. You realise this could make you look like a suspect in whatever Cupido's planning so you go to the police with your fresh injuries and lay a mugging charge. But you can't give any details about your attackers because you didn't see them clearly. You've realised Cupido set you up in that job for his own reasons so you leave quickly and find other employment.'

Jerome was staring at Carl as if riveted by the story. Carl waited. Jerome glanced around, stooped even lower by hunching his shoulders and stared at his shoes.

'I'm sorry,' he said. 'All I want to do is get my mother and my sisters out of that place. My mother goes to work, my sisters go to school, even that's a risk. But they never go anywhere else. There's the normal criminals but it's the gangs that are bad. They gang rape girls as an initiation; you hear about it every week. Everyone's afraid.'

His eyes were large behind his glasses. 'I'll get them out soon. If I don't they'll be killed or raped. I'm telling you, man, you don't win going up against people like Brandon Cupido. That's how I kept out of the gangs growing up. I stayed at home as much as I could. I learnt to run fast and if they caught me I let them beat me up and didn't say anything but I didn't join them either; I still did my own thing. Now I've got a job, I'm studying. I'll get my mom and sisters out. It won't be long now.'

'What job are you doing?' Carl asked.

'Messenger,' Jerome said, his features becoming animated. 'But someone's going on maternity leave in three months and they've said I can work in her place as a data capturer.'

'You got a mobile number?' Carl asked.

'I told you, man, I can't tell you anything.' Jerome sounded desperate.

'It's so I can call you if I hear about a better job,' Carl said.

Jerome hesitated for a second, then said, 'You got a piece of paper?'

Carl took a notebook and pen from his pocket and took down the number, which Jerome repeated twice.

'I'm sorry I can't help,' he said. 'I really am but I've got to stay alive, you know.'

'Yes, I know,' Carl said. 'You better get going; you'll be late for work.'

'Thanks, man,' Jerome said, dipping his head and taking a couple of steps back, as if he were kowtowing.

When he'd gone Dunai said, 'My God, that was horrible. I feel so sorry for that poor guy. And it was a waste of time, wasn't it? We got absolutely nothing out of him.'

'Maybe not,' Carl said. 'His body language pretty much confirmed the scenario I put to him and that means we're beginning to put together a clearer picture of what led to Siobhan's murder. It's always easier to find evidence if you know where to look.'

Dunai felt a bit better.

'It was nice of you to offer to keep an eye out for better work for him.'

'He'd come in handy as an informant if he felt more secure,' Carl said.

'That more of your apartheid training?' Dunai asked, not bothering to keep the disgust from her voice.

Carl half turned towards her, opened his mouth, then closed it and stormed off.

23

SATURDAY morning started out well enough with not one portentous sign of what the afternoon would bring. Dunai and Jesse had brunch at the Larsens', and she told Bryan she'd decided to set up her stall in Greenmarket Square. It was what she'd done every alternate Saturday before Siobhan's death and it seemed important to do something normal again.

Bryan seemed really pleased and Dunai knew he'd taken her suggestion as a sign that she'd decided not to pursue the investigation any further and that she was beginning to put Siobhan's death behind her. She didn't have the heart to tell him that nothing could be further from the truth. Also, she hadn't worked out how to tell him that Siobhan was her mother without trotting out all that business about *Cerchio di Gaia*. She needed to think up a plausible story.

Jesse had always spent the afternoon with Siobhan when Dunai set up her stall. Now he stayed with the Larsens while Bryan took her back to Chiappini Street to choose some stock. He then helped her set up her stall between a man selling toys and objects made from recycled material and a woman offering jewellery and ornaments of wire and beads.

Dunai loved the camaraderie between the stall owners—the way they'd chat to each other and move their folding chairs to follow the shade in summer, the sun in winter. But today the companionship wasn't there.

The seller of recycled goods on her left sounded foreign, Nigerian perhaps, and, although friendly enough, communication was strained between them and they gave up after a while. The black woman, about Dunai's age, selling wire and beadwork, seemed disinclined to talk. Dunai had shown some interest in her wares but she'd turned her face away and walked to the front of her stall, where she stood in the sunshine, oil glistening in her tight curls and the smell of coconut hovering in the air.

The weather held and Dunai was selling well, but paranoia had set in—the kind that caused her eyes to keep straying towards the wire and beadwork woman on her right.

She couldn't get Dan Cowley or Wayne Daniels out of her head. Cowley was becoming increasingly agitated as she and Carl dug deeper into his life, but she was more inclined to believe that Daniels and Cupido had been responsible for Siobhan's murder. She wondered how Cupido had managed to get that job in the building for Jerome Plaatjies. Perhaps the receptionist or someone else who worked there was in the gangster's pay. Dunai hated the idea that she might be working in the building with a Cupido spy. And if she were right on this score, how long would it be before Cupido got wind of their enquiries?

She nearly missed the small black hand that reached up, right under her nose, and grabbed the porcelain figurine of the Holy Mother.

'Hey!' Dunai shouted, already rounding the table.

The boy, about eleven years old, in summer sandals, blue tracksuit pants and a filthy brown jersey too small for him, darted along the row of stalls. Dunai ran after him, glad she was wearing running shoes. No doubt the boy was cold and hungry—she'd give him money when she caught him—but he couldn't have her figurine.

She chased him to the edge of the market, to a line of trees about a metre behind the tarpaulin walls of the last row of stalls, and stopped. The narrow lane was empty. He was probably hiding behind one of the trees so she began to creep along slowly. But it wasn't a child who stepped out in front of her as she passed a large plane tree.

The man was tall and thin with light brown skin, scarred cheeks and eyes as cold and black as a fish on ice. His mouth was unusually wide, with lips the colour of raw flesh and his face so narrow it all seemed to come to a point at forehead, nose, mouth and chin without the benefit of a jaw or cheekbones. His resemblance to a tuna fish was uncanny.

His large right hand, covered with short, linear gang tattoos, gripped the base of the twenty-centimetre figurine of the Holy Mother and slapped it with some force into the palm of his left hand.

Dunai froze for just a second before turning to run, but felt herself being hauled backwards by the hood of her red tracksuit top. He grabbed her arm and spun her to face him. Then he stepped up close and brought his mouth to within an inch of her face; his breath had the fetid, sour smell of rotten meat.

'Mr Cupido sends greetings from the Cape Flats,' he breathed in her face. 'He has a story for you.' He paused for effect. 'Mr Cupido bought two Dobermanns a while back, paid a lot for them, training and stuff. But dogs run all over the streets of the Flats, so whenever some bitch comes sniffing around, he blows its brains out. Can't tell you how many he's shot. You see, *bitch,* here's the thing. Mr Cupido always protects what's his.'

His fingers tightened like steel clamps around the tender flesh of her upper arm and Dunai's knees threatened to buckle under the searing pain. Almost of its own accord, her untended left arm shot upwards, the heel of her hand slamming into the underside of his chin. His teeth snapped together, his head shot back and Dunai half expected him to collapse at her feet but he didn't. His head tipped slowly back to its starting position and this time there was a strange luminosity in those dead black eyes. Rage, Dunai thought, and began to claw at the fingers around her arm, feeling slivers of skin give way beneath her nails.

A movement to her left caught her eye and she stopped clawing for a second, turning her head towards the danger. He had the statue of the Holy Mother raised in his right hand, ready to strike.

'Twitch a muscle and I'll cut you.'

Dunai couldn't at first place the woman's Xhosa-accented voice, but she recognised the smell of coconut oil. The seller of wire and beadwork was much shorter than Dunai's attacker and remained hidden behind his back.

'Bring your arm down,' she instructed, 'very slowly. Let go of her and step back.'

He hesitated, then arched his back slightly and winced.

'I'm serious,' the woman said. 'Don't make me cut you more.'

Dunai's breath came out in a rush as the painful clamp around her arm fell away. She stepped back, rubbing at the band of pain. Now she was really angry. 'You're a sick, insane lunatic, you know that? Give me my statue,' she said, reaching out and grabbing it from the man. She noticed a whole lot of bloody furrows along his left hand where she'd raked him. That made her feel better.

'You come stand with me.'

A hand shot out from behind the man's back and beckoned to her. She obeyed, stepping around the man and going to stand beside her rescuer. The woman's eyes were narrowed almost to slits and there was a deepening of colour on her chocolate-brown cheeks. She held a short knife to the man's back. 'We're going to walk to the end of the row,' she said. At the man's split-second delay she pushed the knife a centimetre forward. He winced and arched his back but this time began to move forward.

'You're a dead woman,' he ground out.

She said nothing, only advanced the knife by another fraction, causing the man to swear under his breath, but he directed no more comments to either woman.

They reached the end of the row and moved back into the thick of the market. When they were once again surrounded by stalls and shoppers, the seller of beadwork said, 'Get lost, you rubbish *tsotsi*,' jabbing him once more in the back. Then she turned quickly and strode away. Dunai followed close on her heels, glancing over her shoulder just once, but the man was gone.

She waved away Dunai's thanks. 'I grew up in Guguletu township. I know how to deal with these types,' was all she would say.

'Can you at least tell me your name?' Dunai asked irritably.

'Thandi,' was all she said.

When they got back to their stalls, Thandi handed a packet of cigarettes to the Nigerian selling recycled goods—he'd been looking after the women's stalls in their absence—then went to stand once again in the sunshine in silence.

Of course Dunai wondered if Thandi was part of *Cerchio di Gaia*. She looked for some sign of the double cross but could see only a gold chain just visible above the neckline of her brown T-shirt.

Dunai replaced the Holy Mother figurine, then stared down at her hands; they still trembled. She resisted the urge to pack up her goods, phone Bryan and ask him to fetch her.

So Brandon Cupido had his informants too. He knew she was asking questions and it could only be the receptionist on the first floor who'd got word to him; otherwise Carl would have been mentioned too. Ms Boom Box was the only interview Dunai had done on her own.

She believed she had no choice now but to ask Carl to proceed more cautiously, perhaps back off for a while until the gangster was no longer watching them so closely. Siobhan would never have expected her to risk her own life—or Jesse's.

Dunai called Carl on her new mobile. Since he'd stormed from the Grand Parade on Wednesday, things had been a little stilted between them. She didn't particularly want to speak to him now but this was a call she had to make.

She told him about the message from Brandon Cupido but declined his offer of safe passage home, although his obvious concern pleased her. She promised him she'd be especially careful but she was determined not to run today, particularly in the light of her fellow stall-owner's courage. Just as she was finishing the call, her battery died—she kept forgetting to charge it. Dunai set po-faced Thandi to look after her stall and headed across the square to her office block.

Standing in the deserted foyer, she tried not to think of the last time she'd been here alone. She put the adrenalin coursing through her body to good use by taking the stairs, two at a time. At the top, she forced herself to slow to a brisk walk. She reached the end of the passage, swung into the toilet block, strode to a cubicle and locked herself inside.

When she emerged she was still alert but definitely calmer. She washed her hands, went to the outer door and raised her hand to push it open, then froze. She was sure she'd heard footfalls in the passage outside. She remained stock-still, palm against the pneumatic door; there was no handle. Nobody worked up here except STOP employees and it wasn't Bryan or Philippe out there. Had Fishface come back to finish his story?

'Dunai Marks. I'd like to speak to you, please.' It was a man's voice—definitely not Fishface.

Again she saw Siobhan's murdered body in all its grisly detail and anger flew in the face of fear. 'Who the hell are you?' she shouted. 'I'm not letting you in.' She felt the man push the door and she pushed back, putting all her weight behind it as the pressure increased from the other side.

'I'm an agent with the National Intelligence Agency. I had an appointment with Siobhan Craig but she was killed the night before our meeting.'

Dunai's arms and shoulders were trembling. 'How do I know you're telling the truth?'

'You can't keep pushing this door for ever and there's no one else on this floor,' the voice said calmly. 'You have no choice but to believe me.'

Dunai thought she'd be more inclined to open the door and believe him if she had a weapon in her hand. She looked around but everything was fixed to a goddamn wall, literally nailed down. Except the bins used to dispose of sanitary towels. It was worth a try.

'Look, I'm going to keep—' She sprang back and threw herself across the room to the nearest cubicle. The main door crashed against the wall, there was a slapping sound like hands connecting with floor tiles and the word, 'Shit.' She grabbed a bin from the cubicle, stepped out, spun round and raised it as best she could.

She recognised the man immediately. He was the charcoal suit on the stairwell who'd been talking to DI van Reenen the morning after Siobhan was killed. Thick, dark brown hair had flopped over his forehead. For an instant there was surprise in his brown eyes, then he grinned at her. 'What do you plan to do with that?' he asked. 'Gross me to death?'

The 'ha' that escaped her was half sob, half laugh. She dropped the bin to the floor and sat on it, arms dangling at her sides.

He brushed hair from his eyes, straightened his shirt collar and pulled at the cuffs of his dark brown suit. 'I see you remember me from the stairwell,' he said, holding his hand out to her. 'Jacob,' he said.

Dunai looked at his hand, then sprang up from the bin and shoved him so hard he was forced to take a step back. 'You could have waited in the passage for me, or outside,' she said. 'You've got a sick sense of humour.'

'Oh, there's nothing funny about any of this,' he said, the proffered hand dropping to his side. He stared at her and his scrutiny made her want to shove him again. He was handsome, his features perfect and bland.

'What do you want from me?' she asked.

His eyes narrowed, then he turned abruptly and went to a basin where he began to wash his hands. 'You been approached by *Cerchio di Gaia*?'

Dunai was stunned but still managed to say, 'Who?'

'*Cerchio di Gaia*.'

'I don't know what you're talking about.'

'Oh, I think you do,' he said conversationally.

'You said you were due to meet Siobhan the day after she was killed,' Dunai countered, moving towards the basin. 'What was the meeting about?'

He looked up and their eyes met in the mirror. 'You first,' he said.

'I don't know anything about…whatever name you said. I have absolutely no idea what this is about.'

'Don't play dumb, Dunai. It doesn't suit you. Intelligence is in the eyes and they never lie.'

She forced herself to hold his gaze. He turned, reached for a paper towel and began to dry his hands.

'Siobhan knew we were investigating her and her circle of special friends. She called me the evening of the fifteenth, just after seven, a few hours before she was killed. She said she had information that would be of great interest to me.'

The bewilderment on Dunai's face was genuine. Again the agent's eyes narrowed as he studied her for a full thirty seconds. The only movement from Dunai was a shrug of the shoulders.

'If you don't already have a connection with *Cerchio di Gaia*, they will contact you,' the agent said in clipped tones, 'particularly in the light of Siobhan's death. We have information, Dunai, facts about your birth that would be of interest to you. But you and I have to establish a relationship first and we do that with an exchange of information—you bring me facts about *Cerchio di Gaia* and I give you facts about your birth. That sound reasonable to you?'

She was silent for a moment, then said, 'No, Jacob, it does not. It sounds like the ranting of a crazy person. Give me something about my birth and if it checks out I'll know you're legit and I'll see what I can do.'

Jacob smiled at her and nodded. 'You're a natural.' He scrunched the paper towel and slam dunked it into the bin. 'Unfortunately, it doesn't work like that. You're trying to put the cart before the horse. It's horse then cart.'

'Why are you so interested in this *Cerchio*…whatever?' Dunai asked.

Jacob turned back and smiled at her. The effect on his already beautiful face was devastating. He stepped towards her and the smile was gone. 'They're fanatics, Dunai, but not just any fanatics. They've got money and power and lots of it, and that makes them very dangerous.'

'Don't tell me this is some post nine-eleven thing.'

'You got a computer I can use? I want to show you something,' he said, changing tack suddenly.

'What?'

'Computer, Dunai.'

24

JACOB pulled up a chair beside Dunai's, his thigh almost touching hers, making her feel decidedly uncomfortable.

He inserted a CD into the drive and his arm brushed Dunai's stomach as he reached for her mouse and clicked on an icon of a pink disk that had appeared on the screen, then he sat back in his chair as the file opened in PowerPoint. Dunai moved the mouse to his side of the keyboard.

The logo of the National Intelligence Agency appeared on the first slide—a black, brown and cream eye within protective brackets and, below, the words *Ito la lushaka* (Venda, meaning Eye of the Nation).

The second slide was completely unexpected; Dunai felt a jolt run through her body.

There was an elderly man, almost bald, in a four-poster bed draped with heavy brocade. It was difficult to tell what he'd looked like in life because his body was stiff and twisted, hands frozen like claws and face horribly contorted.

The next slide—a man in torn, bloody robes, lay on the ground surrounded by rocks and stones. His entire body was bloodied and his face so flattened it was unrecognisable as human.

The slide changed again. A fat man was propped against a wall, legs spread in front of him on the cement floor. His mouth was agape and filled with blood and his hands had been severed and placed on the floor between his legs.

Dunai lifted her eyes above the screen and focused on the red beaded flowers and blue vase in the bookcase. 'Please turn it off,' she said quietly.

She heard Jacob click the mouse. 'Sorry about all the gore,' he said. 'Did you pick up anything in the images?'

Dunai's head swung towards him and she looked at him as if he were mad. 'I don't know who or what you—'

'Try not to look at the bodies,' he said quickly. 'Look at what's around them.'

Dunai heard the mouse click again. She forced her eyes back to the screen.

'This is a cardinal,' Jacob said of the old man lying twisted in the four-poster bed. 'He was poisoned.' He skipped several slides. The screen showed a hand—blue-grey, fingers like claws—and lying on the palm was a gold double cross. This, Dunai realised, was what Sister Raymunda had told her about— one of the rumours they'd heard about the methods of the Sisterhood of the Double Cross.

'This sheik was stoned to death. Look how the stones have been arranged beside him.'

Dunai saw stones placed to form a double cross.

Jacob skipped to the fat man on the cement floor. 'Head of an organised crime syndicate in the UK, ran a string of brothels and was believed to be involved in sex trafficking. As you can see, his hands were severed and his tongue cut out. But look at the blood spatter near his feet.'

Dunai again saw the double cross.

'Media mogul in the US,' Jacob said of a man lying on a Persian rug, legs spread apart, arms neatly at his sides, his eyes gouged out. 'He used to publish many of the porn titles in the US, owned websites and DVD outlets. You won't see a symbol in this picture. The afternoon of his death, while police were still processing the scene, there was an entry in the obituaries. Other than his name, it said only, "Take up your cross and follow me. Again I say take up your cross and follow me." The message had

been e-mailed to the obituary department from the newspaper ed-
itor's computer but she was ruled out as a suspect because she'd
never met the victim and she had an alibi and no motive.'

A thin blond man lying face down appeared on the screen. His
knees were drawn up beneath him so his backside stuck up in
the air. Protruding from his anus was a large red vibrator; a line
of blood trickled towards his genitals.

'This businessman ran at least forty paedophile websites out
of Switzerland. A number of photographs were taken of him
lying face down, legs together, arms perpendicular to the body.
They were posted on the websites using some sophisticated password security known only within the paedophile ring. When the
series of photographs are superimposed, you can see the body
has been moved around a point to form a double cross.'

He brought up another screen and there it was—legs and arms
positioned in the shape of the double cross.

Jacob sat back, elbow on the arm of the chair, his chin resting against the heel of his hand.

'A number of intelligence agencies around the world have suspected the existence of a radical feminist organisation for a while
now. They began to collate and cross reference material and built
a list of possible members. But investigating a group with no bor-
ders, no common language, culture or religion poses a unique set
of problems for intelligence agencies. Also, the organisation of
the group isn't based on any known method or structure.
Members seem to act quite independently of one another but pos-
sess unshakeable loyalty to the group and a sense of common
purpose.'

He leaned forward and brought up a slide. The screen split
into quarters. Top left, a masked woman exiting a stairwell.
Bottom left, a woman draped in a burka leaving a building via a
revolving door. Right top and bottom, two pictures of the same
woman—Caucasian, tanned, brown hair and eyes, unremarkable
features, neither too big nor too small.

'Intelligence agencies picked up the two images on the left

from concealed security cameras. This woman was seen leaving the locations of two murders and was tagged as a *Cerchio di Gaia* enforcer. But the images were useless because her face was completely concealed on both occasions. Then advances in technology meant technicians were able to use certain feature reference points beneath the mask to create an Identikit. The woman was identified—those are the images on the right—and put under surveillance. Until two months ago, that is, when she disappeared.

'Around that time the CIA sent a red flag to the SA Secret Service. This woman—' Jacob tapped the screen '—met with a South African who'd been tagged as an ANC operative by Western intelligence agencies when the ANC was still listed as a terrorist organisation. She'd received training in Mozambique and the Soviet Union and her specialities were intelligence and arms smuggling.

'The South African was Siobhan Craig and the Americans were particularly interested because their intel on her hadn't been updated for a while and they believed there could be a connection between *Cerchio di Gaia* and the South African government. Our agencies let them know that of course there was no longer any direct link between Siobhan and our government. She was still put under surveillance as a possible member of *Cerchio di Gaia*.

'Siobhan and our unmasked terrorist must have realised they were being watched because a month after their meeting the terrorist disappears and Siobhan contacts the NIA to say she has information for us.'

Dunai hadn't realised she was wiggling her leg until Jacob looked pointedly at her knee, inches from his own. She stopped and sat up straighter.

Jacob turned slightly in his chair. 'Our only hope of stopping this group is to get inside,' he said softly. 'We need to place a person who they're interested in recruiting, but someone they haven't yet indoctrinated. We believe that person is you, Dunai.'

'Why is the government interested in adopting the STOP

model if they believe Siobhan was part of a terrorist group?' Dunai thought her voice sounded stiff and constricted.

'*Cerchio di Gaia* has powerful women in their ranks and that extends to government.'

'These people who were killed,' Dunai said, flicking her hand at the screen, 'were child pornographers, heads of crime syndicates, involved in human trafficking.'

'What you see here is vigilante justice,' Jacob said, leaning towards her, 'and vigilantes always get it wrong somewhere along the line and then innocent people die. What follows is anarchy and then no one's safe—not you, not your son.'

'I don't see any anarchy here.'

'Because this is just a fraction of the sum. We know enough about some of the more powerful women in their ranks to know they're not interested in merely meting out justice to the odd paedophile. What they're after is something far bigger than all that—a new world order.'

'Organised crime, human trafficking, pornography, paedophiles,' said Dunai. 'Perhaps a new world order is exactly what we need.'

'Governments may bumble along, Dunai, but at least there is a certain transparency. They are visible, operate within parameters and their intentions are more or less predictable. Imagine this group getting into power—an organisation that adheres to a certain ideology but does not subject itself to the norms of society or the laws of any country. One that has no stated objective and thrives on obscurity. Couple this with the certainty that their leaders are no less susceptible to corruption than any other politician and such a group getting into power is a frightening prospect.'

Dunai's head began to throb. She was being pulled in two opposing directions and she had no idea which was the right path to take.

'Dunai,' Jacob said, touching her arm, 'I want you to think about something else.'

She didn't move.

'If you can find what information Siobhan was about to give me the morning she was killed, you'll probably find who murdered her.'

Dunai looked at Jacob then.

'For instance,' he said, looking at her with compassion, 'what if she'd decided to turn informer and *Cerchio di Gaia* had her killed?'

Dunai blinked. 'You told DI van Reenen to make Siobhan's murder look like a botched burglary,' she accused.

'We need to contain any information about *Cerchio di Gaia* that might surface in the course of the investigation.'

'And has it?' Dunai asked.

'Not even close,' Jacob said.

'You know I'm doing my own investigation,' Dunai said, 'and now you want the same from me.'

'We're hoping for more from you,' Jacob said. 'Something else you need to know, Dunai. The attack on you in the walk-through the night after Siobhan's murder was staged, as was the couple in the green Valiant who came to your rescue. It was a tactic used by *Cerchio di Gaia* to soften you up, make you feel valued by them and protected.'

Dunai shook her head.

Jacob's voice was gentle when he said, 'If you were to hang around outside the couple's house in Stadzicht Street you'd see the man who attacked you. At least you'd know his voice, recognise his height and build. He's a member of the extended family.'

Dunai remembered the terror she'd felt in the walk-through and she'd really been hurt. Her back had bothered her for a week after and her cheek had only just healed. They'd also stolen her bag, taken her personal belongings.

Justice Swanepoel-Higgs had admitted their involvement. But she'd told only half the truth. Dunai felt sick and she wanted to get up from this chair and run—but where to?

'Okay, Dunai,' Jacob said, 'I'm going to leave now. Give you a chance to think about this.' He reached into a pocket. 'Here's my card; call me when you've decided what to do. You have the chance to either turn your involvement into something that will benefit the relatively secure society you enjoy today, or make an already insecure world a far more dangerous place. Whether you step up or not is your choice. Please make this decision wisely.'

25

THE phone rang in the turquoise house at five past eleven on Wednesday night. Dunai struggled to consciousness, then groped for the receiver beside the bed. 'Hello,' she croaked.

'Sorry to wake you, Dunai. It's Anna Cooper. We've found Mr Bojangles.'

'No, that's fine,' Dunai said, her brain still chugging from subconscious to ground level .

'It's late and it's cold, Dunai, but it would be good to come through to Groote Schuur tonight if you can.'

'I don't have a car. I'll get a taxi,' she said, pulling her feet out from under Horse.

'Oh, don't do that,' Anna said. 'I'll send my driver. Could you be ready in ten?'

'Yes,' Dunai said, feeling suddenly cautious.

'Good for you,' Anna said. 'See you soon.' And the line went dead.

Dunai replaced the receiver and sat there for a full minute before ringing Barbara, apologising profusely. She got herself ready and took Jesse next door. He didn't stir and she prayed he wouldn't wake before she came back for him.

She returned to the house and waited in the living room. She felt terrible. What sort of mother kept bundling her son off to her neighbour in the middle of the night? She hoped Barbara didn't feel she was being taken advantage of. She'd find a way to make it up to her. She'd had no choice. Anna might have found Mr Bojangles. In a very short while it was possible she'd know who'd killed Siobhan.

She stroked Horse's head and felt comforted in small measure by the rhythmic movement. When the knock came at the door, to her surprise, he didn't bark.

'Who is it?' Dunai called at the door.

'Professor Cooper's driver,' said a female voice.

As they drove away from the turquoise house, Dunai realised she hadn't given her address to Anna Cooper, yet the professor had known exactly where to send her driver. Even stranger was that the realisation of the peculiarity of it no longer shocked Dunai or caused the slightest alarm. Had her mind begun to acclimatise to *Cerchio di Gaia*'s shadowy presence in her life? That thought alone was enough to cause a new type of panic.

Ten minutes later, the car came to a stop in a reserved parking space at Groote Schuur. The hospital had been built almost a century ago at the foot of Devil's Peak in Observatory, just outside the City of Cape Town. It had been made famous some six decades later by Dr Christiaan Barnard, who performed the first human heart transplant in one of its many operating theatres.

The driver took Dunai to an entrance where Anna waited. The professor greeted her with a kiss on the cheek and led her across the empty foyer to a lift.

'I really didn't want to disturb you,' she said. 'Mr Bojangles is back on his meds but he's suffered severe respiratory failure and he isn't responding to medication. That's why I've got you out on such a miserable night.'

The lift doors opened and Dunai followed Anna to the entrance of the intensive care unit. 'Is he going to be okay?'

'I'm afraid I don't know the answer to that.'

Anna opened the swing door and padded across the floor to the nurses' station, where she introduced Dunai. Then she led her across the large room to the third bed on the right.

'I'll leave the two of you. If you need me, speak to one of the nurses and they'll page me.' Anna reached for her hand and squeezed it. 'You're a brave woman,' she said, then strode from the room.

Mr Bojangles looked very different in his hospital bed, but there was no mistaking him, even with his skin shaved and scrubbed clean. Dunai had never seen him without his dark blue cap; his hair was woolly and grey. There was also no mistaking that he was seriously ill. His cheeks were sunken and his dark skin was a couple of shades lighter than she remembered; it looked paper-thin and just as dry. The rise and fall of his chest beneath the hospital gown was exaggerated and erratic. A thin tube ran into each nostril and an IV into his arm. His heart played its own rhythm on the monitor above his head.

Dunai stood by the bed undecided, not wanting to disturb his sleep but desperate to ask her question. She very carefully lifted his gnarled hand and placed it in her palm, ashamed that the thought of their fingers touching had once repulsed her. As soon as she sat down on the chair beside the bed his eyes fluttered open.

'Mr Bojangles?' She leaned closer, kept her voice low. 'It's Dunai. I've come to visit you.'

'Where am I?' His voice was wheezy and very faint.

'You're at Groote Schuur.'

He squinted at her and frowned. 'The president's residence?'

Dunai smiled. 'No, the hospital.'

He nodded slightly. 'Won't give me coffee.'

'That's okay,' she said, wrapping both hands around his. 'As soon as you're out, I'll give you more coffee than you'll be able to drink.'

'Hmph,' he said, then coughed.

Dunai patted his hand. 'I'm sorry it's taken so long for me to visit but I didn't know where you were. I had to track you down first.'

'S'okay.'

'I'm going to leave you to rest, Mr Bojangles, but first I need to ask you a question.'

The old man tried to focus on her face.

'The last morning I saw you in the square, you said you'd had a bad night. That there'd been goings-on and that you'd seen the devil come out of the building where I work. Can you remember what the devil looked like?'

When he said nothing, she tried again. 'It must have been the day you started to feel sick or just before that because no one saw you afterwards.'

The old man stared ahead blankly, then, to Dunai's relief, something came alive in his eyes and he nodded.

'Mr Bojangles? Can you remember?'

'Off the meds,' he rasped.

Dunai could barely hear what he said. She leaned closer. 'What do you remember, Mr Bojangles?'

He frowned. 'Mind plays tricks off the meds. See terrible things.'

'But what did you see, Mr Bojangles?'

He seemed to look far into the distance, then fixed his eyes on her. 'Back on my meds. Better now.'

'I know you are, Mr Bojangles, but that night you thought you saw the devil something bad happened in our building and I think you might really have seen something.'

'No devil,' he rasped, becoming agitated. 'Was sick. Only man, maybe not. I see things off the meds.'

'Can you tell me what the man looked like?'

He shook his head. 'Imagined it,' he said. 'First devil in black, red eyes.' He kept his eyes fixed on her face. 'Then one that works with you—American. He brings food sometimes. I was hungry. Eaten nothing.' Mr Bojangles's chest heaved. 'Thought American bring me something to eat.' His head moved slightly from side to side. 'Wasn't him, though. Was a black bird, very big. Flew away.'

Dunai felt as if her heart had stopped being a throbbing, living thing and had during Mr Bojangles's tortured speech become a heavy, sticky mass that was slowly sinking.

The old man began to cough. 'It's okay,' she said, patting his hand, trying to soothe him. 'Sleep now.'

Dunai felt terrible. Not only had Mr Bojangles's information been useless but she'd caused the old man enormous distress. She sat at his bed, holding his hand, feeling utterly useless. What had she been thinking? Carl had warned her about this. She'd pinned her hopes on a schizophrenic vagrant who'd been off his medication and was in the early stages of respiratory failure. Stupid, stupid, stupid, Dunai told herself.

'Good person.'

Dunai leaned forward as Mr Bojangles spoke.

'Good person,' he said again.

'Who is?' she asked.

'You. Dunai.'

His hand, still encased in hers, tightened a little. She lifted it to her lips and kissed it. 'Sleep, Mr Bojangles. I'm going to stay with you as long as I can.'

'Good person,' the old man said, closing his eyes.

Dunai felt like a fake. Tears rolled down her cheeks and she swiped at them with the back of her hand. Images flashed into her mind. Her anger towards Siobhán. Worrying Bryan half to death. Antagonising Carl. Feeling absolute hatred for Dan Cowley. Manhandling Thandiwe Dingake in public. Lying to Sisters Finbar and Raymunda. Keeping *Cerchio di Gaia* a secret and not wanting to help the NIA.

But all this paled into insignificance beside her failure to find justice for Siobhán. Mr Bojangles was wrong, poor man. She definitely wasn't a good person. Still clutching the old man's hand, she leaned forward and placed her cheek against the blanket.

'Dunai?'

She sat up, looked around.

'You fell asleep, poor thing,' Anna said, rubbing her back. 'Did you get the information you were looking for?'

Dunai shook her head. 'He didn't see anything. Or at least he saw a lot of things, but none of them were real.'

It was Anna's turn to nod. 'Well, at least you tried. And he's had a visit from a friend.'

'Not much of a friend, I'm afraid.'

Anna smiled sadly. 'You must be exhausted. Come, let's get you home.'

'I don't want to leave him,' she said, pushing dark hair from her eyes.

'He's comfortable, Dunai. Well cared for. And he's just been given some heavy pain medication so he'll sleep for a long time. He isn't aware right now of who's here and who isn't.'

Anna helped her to her feet.

'I feel like I'm abandoning him.'

'You're not, Dunai. You've been his only visitor since he was brought here. You care about him and you'll take that home with you. That isn't abandonment.'

'Will he be okay?'

'Eventually we're all okay, Dunai. If death is release from un-bearable pain and constant fear and sickness then it's a type of healing too, isn't it?'

Dunai let go of Mr Bojangles's hand and allowed Anna to lead her away.

26

DUNAI had been expecting the call, only not so soon. And, even though she'd braced herself for the news, it didn't make it any easier when Anna said, 'He died just before four this morning, poor man.'

She didn't tell Anna she wished she'd stayed just another four hours, then at least he wouldn't have been alone.

'What'll they do with his body?' she asked.

'He'll get a state cremation,' Anna answered.

'I'd like to put something towards a proper burial—a plot and all that.'

'Why don't you let me take care of it? I'll let you know the details in a few days and then maybe you can arrange a small funeral for him.'

'Thank you, Anna.'

'Don't mention it. And, Dunai, I do want you to remember he was peaceful when he died. Not in any pain at all. It's a better end than most homeless people have.'

'I know. It's just that there seems to have been too much death around lately.'

Bryan and Philippe had stopped what they were doing and were staring at her across Bryan's desk where they'd been working.

'Why don't you come in to see me?' Anna said. 'Soon. Nothing formal, just a chat.'

'I'll call,' Dunai said, feeling suddenly drained. 'Set something up.'

'I'd like that very much,' Anna said. 'Don't wait too long, okay?'

Bryan and Philippe wanted to know what had happened as soon as she put the phone down. She told them about Mr Bojangles but left out the real reason she'd been searching for him.

'Ah, but this is too *much*,' Philippe said, jumping to his feet as if he intended to take on the world and all its unfairness.

'Jeez, Dunai,' Bryan said, shaking his head. 'I always felt kinda sorry for the old man. You should've called me last night. I would have taken you to see him.'

Dunai didn't want to talk about it now. She'd have to when she told Carl. He'd called earlier, asking to see her, and she'd promised to stop by his office on her way home for lunch.

Bryan and Philippe were still watching her. 'Let's not talk about it now,' Dunai said. They both nodded and looked a little relieved, she thought.

'Since the date's set to make the presentation to government on Friday next week,' Bryan said, putting on a cheery voice, 'I think we should treat ourselves to dinner afterwards. What do you say?'

'I say, good idea,' Philippe said.

'We deserve it,' Dunai agreed.

'I'll make reservations,' Bryan said. 'Where's my diary?'

'You left it on my desk.' Dunai got up to take it to him, then went to the kitchen next door to put on the kettle. She felt exhausted and knew there was a limit to how long she could keep going under so much stress while not eating properly and with too little sleep.

When she returned to the office, Bryan said, 'Belle's just told me she's cooked a soya cottage pie for you and Jes.'

'Oh, you didn't call her and get her to make it especially for me, did you?'

'Not at all,' Bryan said indignantly. 'We've been planning this for months.'

Dunai went over to him, threw her arms around his neck and

kissed the top of his head. 'Thank you, Bryan. You're the best,
you know that? Besides Philippe, of course.'

Bryan cleared his throat and tried to make light of it. Philippe
was all misty-eyed and not in the least ashamed.

'I'll fetch the cottage pie when I'm done here and drop it off
for you,' Bryan said, all business again.

Dunai made coffee for them, then headed for the toilet block.
As she emerged from the cubicle she looked around quickly. It
had become her habit ever since the encounter with Jacob—and
she was being careful after her brush with Fishface.

She washed her hands and glanced at herself in the mirror.
Again she asked herself why Siobhan would contact the NIA. 'If
you can find what information Siobhan was about to give me the
morning she was killed, you'll probably find who murdered her,'
Jacob had said.

The call had come through to him just after seven, which
meant Siobhan had waited for them to leave so she could speak
to the agent without being overheard. But Bryan had returned to
the office for his diary and Cowley had been on his way up to
confront her. Had he heard the conversation? Was that what had
prompted him to murder her? They already knew Siobhan had
dug into Cowley's life, but she might have found something far
more damning than an incident involving his father some twenty
years before.

And Bryan had seen and heard none of this. He must have
missed it by seconds. But what if he hadn't? Siobhan might still
be alive if he'd just stopped to listen to her conversation and
stayed around a little longer. But he would have been in a hurry,
racing upstairs, grabbing his diary and rushing back down, probably not even bothering to wait for the lift.

A jolt of shock ran the length of Dunai's body as if she'd run
smack into a glass wall she'd had absolutely no idea was there.
Her hands hovered beneath the running tap and she stared un-
seeing at her reflection as a sequence of events ran through her
mind in slow, excruciating detail.

She was again in the dim stillness of the passage the morning she'd found Siobhan's body. She remembered walking back to the office with Bryan after the technicians had arrived. She'd turned on the light, then gone to draw back the blinds. The square had been covered by fog and she'd turned away and walked to her desk. She remembered Bryan saying, 'Here, let me take that,' and she'd realised she was still holding the biscuit tin. She'd handed it to him and he'd pushed a diary out of the way and put the tin on the desk in front of her.

Only it hadn't been her diary he'd moved that morning. She remembered very clearly taking hers out of her drawer later that day. She was sure of it. It was a mix-up that happened often enough; they all had the same type of diary. Sometimes when a call came through and she wasn't in the office, Bryan would transfer the caller to her phone so he could check his diary against her desk planner, then he'd accidentally leave it on her desk. It had happened again this morning.

If there'd been a diary on her desk the morning of Siobhan's murder, and it hadn't been her own, it could only have been Bryan's. She remembered him opening his arms to her in the passage that morning, drawing her against his chest. He hadn't had a diary with him.

Dunai realised her breath was coming in short gasps and it made her feel light-headed. She focused on her face in the mirror. 'Don't do this to yourself, Dunai. Just think,' she told herself. 'There has to be a logical explanation.' And there was.

For all his perfectionism, Bryan was easily distracted when he had a lot on his plate, which he'd had with the government presentation just weeks away. He might have been sidetracked by a call on his mobile and come straight back down again without his diary. By the time he'd once again reached the foyer and realised his mistake he'd probably decided to leave it rather than make a second trip upstairs. But she heard Mr Bojangles's voice. 'First devil in black, red eyes. Then one that works with you—American.'

Dunai bent over the basin, splashed cold water on her face. She straightened, stood there not moving, water dripping onto her denim jacket. And this time she wished she wasn't alone in the toilet block. Any other presence would have been a comfort just then. But it was Carl's face that came to mind. He was the person she'd tell.

But would it all sound crazy? She hoped so. She hadn't thought through the implications; couldn't bring herself to do it. She'd far rather believe she was losing her mind. Grief did that sometimes. She reached for a paper towel, wiped her face, threw it in the bin and moved towards the door. She was being paranoid again.

She went to the office, told Bryan and Philippe she was taking an early lunch and would be back by two, then stopped by Carl's office.

'You want coffee?' he asked over his shoulder as he led her through the empty reception area.

'No, thanks,' she said. 'I'm on my way home.'

He went to sit behind his desk and Dunai took her usual visitor's chair, the one closest to the door. The irony of this had not escaped her. She still felt uncomfortable around him. But she was beginning to understand why.

Carl emanated remarkable strength. Unfortunately, it was coupled with an edginess, and he never looked at her the way others did—his light grey eyes seemed to have the intensity of a mind-reader. Add to this the chemistry between them and she was left with a mix that both excited and appalled her. She shifted in her chair; he leaned back, looked at her and his brows rose slightly.

'You wanted to speak to me,' Dunai prompted.

'Cupdio is the most likely suspect in Siobhan's murder but the police don't know about the link to Wayne Daniels and Daniels's link to Siobhan. If they did, they'd be able to go after him with the sort of clout and resources we don't have. They might even convince Jerome Plaatjies to testify in exchange for witness protection for himself and his family. It'd be one way of getting his mother and sisters out of Atlantis.' Carl paused. 'Time's come for you to decide whether to take what we've found to van Reenen. I'd advise you to do that.'

'But it would destroy Siobhan's reputation,' Dunai admitted, 'and the presentation to government... The model works but they'll never use it to draft policy if they know about the blackmail. Can I think about it?'

Carl nodded. 'Don't take too long.'

There was silence in the room. Carl was the first to break it. 'Anything else you want to tell me?'

'Well, there's been no sign of Fishface; I'm being vigilant and I'm still going to report Cupido to the SPCA for shooting dogs. And I tracked down Mr Bojangles. He was at Groote Schuur. I went to see him last night, but he didn't know what he saw the night Siobhan was murdered. First he thought it was the devil, then Bryan because he gives him food sometimes and he was hungry that night. Then it wasn't Bryan; it was a big black bird that flew away. You did warn me,' she said, placing her palms against the edge of the desk and pushing backwards so her upper body was at arm's length.

'Still,' he said, 'it's a pity.'

'He died this morning—respiratory failure.'

'How did you find him?'

'A friend of mine who works at the hospital put word out that I was looking for him.'

Carl said nothing. He kept staring at her as if he were searching for something in her eyes, just like the damn NIA agent had done.

'There's something else,' she said, 'but it's a bit crazy.'

'Okay.'

She told him about Bryan and the diary but hated herself for doing it; every word felt like a betrayal. 'He probably got sidetracked on his way up. I've seen him do it before. I just don't understand why he didn't mention it to me or DI van Reenen. And then there's Mr Bojangles, who thought he saw Bryan the night Siobhan was murdered.'

Carl was staring at her and even the hardened former detective looked a little shocked.

'I know,' Dunai said, 'it's crazy. Once you start to think like an investigator you see something sinister in almost everything. Also, I'm probably only thinking like this because I thought I knew Siobhan really well, then found out I didn't. I know Bryan isn't involved in any of this. There's been absolutely nothing suspicious about his behaviour since Siobhan's death and I've known him for two years, professionally and personally. Matter of fact, I shouldn't have said anything. It's stupid. That morning of Siobhan's murder was chaotic; he probably didn't think forgetting his diary for the second time was that important. And, as much as I feel compassion for Mr Bojangles, he was schizophrenic and off his medication.'

'Still, it's worth looking into,' Carl said, but he didn't sound that interested. 'I'm going to Stellenbosch for the long weekend; I'll look into it when I get back. You got a photo of him?'

Dunai tore her eyes from the overnight bag beside the desk and rummaged in her bag. She pulled out a maroon album the size of a pocket diary and found a photograph of Bryan. He and Siobhan were clinging to each other, laughing, hair sodden, life-jackets still in place after they'd rafted on the Hex River. They'd gone camping about six months ago and spent three days in the grape-producing valley, making their way along the forty kilometre river, surrounded by rugged mountains—Bryan, Belle and the girls, Siobhan, Dunai and Jesse, and a guide. Dunai had taken the photograph on the last day of the trip and they'd all agreed that night around the fire that it had been three wonderful days.

'All we're doing is covering our bases,' Carl said, as if sensing her reluctance to give up the photograph. 'It's what any good investigator would do.'

Dunai nodded and handed it over. He took it but kept staring at her.

'Anything else?' he asked.

She frowned. 'No, why?'

Carl's demeanour changed. He broke eye contact, shook his head and began shuffling folders on his desk. Dunai felt as if she'd failed some sort of test and was being dismissed.

'I was wondering if there was any more info on Dan Cowley,' she asked, reluctant to leave just yet. 'Anything new about the woman at the chemist?'

Carl didn't look at her. 'No. But I'll let you know if something comes up, as I expect you to do with me.'

Dunai's stomach flipped. Had he found out about *Cerchio di Gaia*? It was unlikely if even the NIA were desperate for information. She couldn't contemplate telling him anything about the group till she'd figured out her own course of action and whether she could trust him with the information or not.

'Carl, is something wrong?'

'Not on my side.'

'See you around, then.'

'See you around,' he echoed, then began reading a file.

As she left the office she wondered if he simply wasn't interested any more. He'd advised her to go to the police with what they'd uncovered so far. That way he'd be able to hand everything over to someone else—be done with her and the investigation. Dunai didn't want that. And she didn't want to risk Siobhan's memory and reputation either. But if they continued investigating with limited resources they'd risk losing her murderer. She couldn't live with that. And, by continuing to dig herself, she knew it wouldn't be long before she became too much of a threat and Siobhan's murderer came after her. There was a good chance Jesse too would be in harm's way.

She thought of Brandon Cupido's threat and the way he'd had his own daughter murdered. Perhaps she had no choice after all but to go to the police.

Bryan left the office just after three; he and Belle were taking the girls to spend the long weekend at a friend's holiday apartment on Hout Bay beach. Dunai was relieved that he'd gone.

Throughout the afternoon her eyes had wandered across the office, coming to rest on his face, searching for something in the familiar features that she might have missed before. And on several occasions Bryan had looked up to find her watching him, and he'd smiled and all she'd seen was the Bryan she'd come to know so well over the years.

Philippe left the building around four and soon after Dunai's mobile rang. The deep timbre of Carl's voice sent a *frisson* of pleasure through her.

'Where are you?' he asked, without greeting.

'At the office.'

'You alone?' Words that made her heart beat faster.

Her voice was slightly breathy as she said, 'Yes.'

'Go to the fax machine,' he instructed, which was the last thing she'd expected. 'I thought you'd gone home,' he said as she made her way across the office.

Dunai thought she heard a hint of accusation in his words. 'I did, but only for lunch and to settle Jesse for a nap.'

'I'm sending something through,' he said. 'I sent it to your home fax first.'

'Where are you?' Dunai asked. 'Couldn't you have brought it to me?'

'I'm in a chemist outside Stellenbosch. It coming through yet?'

'Yes,' Dunai told him as the fax machine finished chugging out a page. She caught it before it landed in the wire basket. Carl was saying something but she'd stopped listening. She heard nothing, saw nothing except the photograph in front of her. Her eyes travelled from the photographs to the heading: 'FBI's Most Wanted' and back again. The photo on the left was of a young man with pale blue eyes, largish nose and thick brown hair. The photograph on the right was an aged composite of the picture on the left and Bryan Larsen stared back at her.

27

'DUNAI?' Carl's voice had the crackle, ebb and flow of a bad mobile connection. 'Dunai,' he said again and, although the connection was good this time, she heard nothing of what he said. She wasn't thinking of Bryan, or betrayal and deception either.

She was back in the maternity ward at the Vincent Pallotti, Jesse's father clutching her hand and looking at her as if she were some sort of alien species. Sister Finbar hanging on to her right hand. Sister Raymunda fluttering somewhere near her head, dabbing her face, saying, 'You're doing beautifully, little one.' She'd been in labour for sixteen hours, without drugs of any kind as far as she could remember, but about half an hour before Jesse was born a strange anxiety came over her. It blocked everything out except the pain, and it was this: how much agony could a person bear before something gave out—physically, psychologically? It gnawed at her until Jesse slipped into the world and the white-hot pain disappeared.

But for months after she'd watched herself closely, trying to find where and how that pain had altered the fabric of who she was, because it had. No one else knew, but she did. It had made her more anxious, careful, as if she'd faced her mortality and become somehow heightened to the fragility of life.

Now she felt all these things again, not as emotions, as she had done then, but as knowledge this time. Perhaps this was unique to her, the result of her mysterious physiology and the unique make-up of her mind, or it might have been as old as life itself.

The fax machine was on a small table beside the filing cabinet. She leaned against it and felt the coldness of the metal through her denim jacket. She slid towards the floor till her buttocks rested on her heels.

'Dunai! Talk to me!'

'I'm here,' she said, eyes drawn back to the sheet resting on her thighs.

'I know this is…shock…' Carl said, the connection breaking up '…you can't go to piece…Dunai?'

'This is Bryan,' Dunai said in the same tone she used when pointing to a picture and telling Jesse, 'This is a cow,' or 'this is a sheep.'

'…you sitting down?' Carl asked.

Dunai frowned, looked away from the page, glanced around the office. 'Yes.'

'I want you to get up, get that great big padded coat of yours and put it on.'

Dunai struggled to her feet and started towards the coat stand beside the door, dropping the fax on her desk as she went—she was glad to be rid of it. 'It's a duffel coat.'

'Whatever,' Carl said, then the connection broke up again.

'What?'

'Put it on!' he shouted.

'I am,' Dunai said, putting her arms in one at a time while hanging on to the mobile. It felt hot against her ear.

'Now get out of there.'

'My bag,' Dunai said.

'Well, get it…get out of there.' Dunai went back to her desk, picked up her bag and started for the door.

'D'you have the fax?'

'No.'

'Shit!' Carl said. 'Get it. Put it in your coat or your…'

Dunai went back to her desk, folded the sheet and slipped it into her coat pocket.

'D'you have somewhere to go where he can't get to you?' Carl shouted. There was a lot of noise in the background. A car door slammed, then it was quiet again.

'St Mark's.'

'Go there,' Carl instructed. 'Don't stop to do anything…St Mark's. I'm in the car, on my way back to Cape Town…traffic's heavy…about two hours.'

Dunai had her keys out. She opened the door and stepped into the passage and, as she did so, she had the odd feeling of waking up, not suddenly, but as if she were coming out of a deep sleep. She pulled the door shut and locked it.

'I've got to get Jesse.'

'No,' Carl said. 'Listen to me. Call Barbara…to St Mark's.'

'What?'

'*Call Barbara.* Tell her to keep Jesse…not open the door to anyone except me. Go to St Mark's…I'll bring him to you.'

'Okay.' But Dunai had no intention of going without her son; she just didn't want to waste time arguing. 'I'll call Barbara,' she said, rang off and started down the passage, punching in Barbara's number as she walked. Her mobile beeped once loudly and the screen went blank.

'Oh, shit,' Dunai said, stopping dead. 'Shit, shit, *shit.*'

It was then she remembered the meal Bryan had promised to drop off after work. How could she have forgotten? And when? When had he said he would bring it over? He was going to finish at the office, he'd said, then fetch it from home and bring it to her. He'd left at three; it was now four-twenty so he'd either dropped it off already or was on his way to her house now. Either way, she'd never get there before he did.

Don't panic, she told herself. Bryan had no idea she knew his secret. Then again, Dunai knew he'd take one look at her and know. She realised now what Carl had known instinctively—her

only sure way of staying safe till the police had questioned Bryan
was to avoid him completely.

Dunai ran for the office, dropping her mobile into her bag and
grabbing her keys as she went. She had to call Barbara—tell her
not to answer the door to Bryan. She opened the door, rushed for
the phone but Barbara's line was busy. *'No!'* Dunai slammed
down the receiver. Perhaps she'd dialled the wrong number. She
snatched it up again, dialled carefully but it was still engaged.
Her eyes moved from the wall clock's second hand to the rain
drumming against the window-pane. She tried once more at four-
thirty, then rushed for the door. She'd wasted ten minutes. She'd
have been home by now if she'd opted to run rather than call.

Outside, the wind blew and the light was dim and concrete-
grey. The square was almost deserted except for some late office
workers hurrying home in the pouring rain.

She began to run. The rain plastered her hair to her face and
the cold numbed her fingers and toes. She kept her fear in check
by thinking out a plan of action. She'd get to Barbara, tell her
what had happened and make sure they were locked in. Then
she'd call a taxi and let Sister Finbar know they were on their
way. Carl could pack a suitcase when he arrived and bring it to
St Mark's. She just had to keep reminding herself that Bryan had
no idea she knew about the FBI photofits. Everything was going
to be okay.

She had just reached Chiappini Street when she saw a red
Toyota Conquest very like Barbara's heading away from her towards Church Street. It couldn't be her neighbour, of course; Dunai
still had to fetch Jesse. She squinted at the licence plate through
the driving rain and very nearly stumbled again. It *was* Barbara's
car. She began to run as fast as she could, her cheeks on fire despite the freezing rain that lashed her face. 'Wait!' she screamed.
'Wait!' The car kept moving. If only her damn legs would move
faster. Why was Barbara driving away? Was something wrong with
Jesse? 'Stop!' Dunai screamed, arms waving wildly above her
head, but the car turned right into Church Street and disappeared.

Dunai stopped, chest heaving. Barbara wouldn't just take off like that. She'd have left a note. Maybe one of the boys was sick, which could be why the line had been engaged. Perhaps she was on her way to the doctor but hadn't been able to get hold of Dunai because she was on her way home and her mobile was out of commission. Or it might not be Barbara at all; maybe her husband had borrowed the Toyota.

Dunai knocked on the door of the lavender house. No answer. She pounded on the door; again no response. So she fumbled in her bag for the keys and unlocked the door, her fingers clumsy with cold.

The lights were out and it was almost dark inside. She turned on the living room light, then reached for the piece of paper propped against the phone on the side table:

Bryan brought a meal over for you so fetched Jesse and took him next door. We've got an early start, heading out to Mum for weekend. Enjoy it. Love Barbara.

28

DUNAI'S first reaction was abject terror, then she reminded herself it was Bryan waiting next door for her, with Jesse and a meal prepared by Belle. Carl didn't know Bryan, she did, and she should have kept quiet about her crazy notion of forgotten diaries and deathbed ramblings. Bryan was not a monster. The FBI document was an Identikit of how they thought some criminal named Jeffrey Stappleton had aged over a twenty-year period. There was some resemblance to Bryan but it was not an exact match. It was people like Wayne Daniels who'd ordered the hit on Siobhan, and Brandon Cupido who'd organised her murder who were monsters. Bryan didn't come close.

Dunai felt calmer. She picked up the phone and called Carl. 'Where are you?' he said as soon as he heard her voice.

'I'm at Barbara's—'

'I told you to go to St Mark's,' he said harshly. 'Take Jesse and go.'

'I can't,' Dunai said. 'He's next door with Bryan.'

'He's *what?*'

Dunai explained what had happened but it made no difference to Carl. 'I want you to get out of there,' he said. 'Go to St Mark's now. I'll bring Jesse to you.'

'I'm not leaving him, Carl, and what'll Bryan do if I don't come home? He'll probably take Jesse with him. In any case, we don't even know if it is *Bryan* in that photograph. I mean this is

Bryan we're talking about. He's one of the kindest people I know. I think we're overreacting.'

'*Overreacting,*' Carl exploded.

Dunai blinked with surprise. She'd expected an ex-detective to be a lot calmer in a situation like this.

'Now you listen to me, woman,' he said. 'You do *not* go anywhere *near* that man on your own, do you hear me?'

'Excuse me,' Dunai said, surprise and adrenalin morphing into anger. 'Bryan has been like a father to me. I know him and I know his family, and right now he's completely unaware of all this craziness, waiting next door for me with my son and a meal he's been good enough to—'

'Dunai, please listen to me,' Carl interrupted and she was taken aback by the pleading note in his voice. 'I know you love Bryan and, yes, we could be wrong. But just for a minute think of what could happen if we're right. This is one fucker of a shock and, unless you go next door and give an Academy Award performance, Bryan is going to know something's wrong. And if he knows you as well as he does and is as clever as I think he is, then how long d'you think it'll be before he gets it out of you?'

'I'll do it for my son,' Dunai said. 'I have to.'

'Goddamn traffic,' Carl said through clenched teeth. 'Shit!' It sounded as if he'd hit the steering wheel. 'I'm going to call the police.'

'No! Please, Carl, don't do that till we know for sure. My God, what if we're wrong? I don't want to think what we'd put Bryan and his family through, and based on what? Right now all we have is a neurotic suspicion about his diary, the deathbed ramblings of a schizophrenic vagrant and an aged photofit that bears a passing resemblance to him.

'Look, what I'll do is call a taxi, go next door, make some excuse, send Bryan home quickly, then go to St Mark's with Jesse till we've sorted this out as discreetly as possible. '

'I'm still not happy about you going next door on your own.'

'Well, I'm going. Call me as soon as you get back to Cape

Town or come straight to St Mark's. I'll see you there.' Dunai didn't wait for a response. She called the taxi company she always used and asked for a driver to be outside her house in fifteen minutes. Then, before she could think about it too much, she locked up the lavender house and went next door.

'Boy, something smells nice,' she said loudly to cover her nervousness as she stepped into the living room.

'Bosh!' Mr Nelson screamed and she jumped nervously.

'That would be me,' Bryan said, getting to his feet. He and Jesse had been colouring in at the coffee table.

Horse rushed to greet her but she couldn't see the cats anywhere. Jesse looked up and smiled at her and she had to fight the urge to rush over to him.

'And what have the two of you been up to?' she asked. Jesse held the book up sideways. It was a large fish he was colouring in red. 'You've found Nemo,' Dunai said. 'Well done!' Turning towards Bryan, she noticed he was watching her with head cocked to the side. Her heart beat a little faster.

'You okay?' he asked.

'Oh, yes,' Dunai said, casting around for some reason why she seemed about to break out the pom-poms. 'I nearly had major organ failure when I turned into Chiappini and saw Barbara drive away. I thought something might have happened to Jes. I actually ran up the street after them, but then I went next door and got her note.'

She still had her bag over her shoulder. Do exactly what you'd normally do, she told herself. So she went to the narrow lime-washed table against the wall and dumped her bag on it as she always did.

'I didn't see your car anywhere,' she said, picking up a pile of mail Bryan must have placed on the table.

'It's in the side street,' he said, coming towards her. 'The place was parked up when I got here. Looked like the entire neighbourhood was getting ready to go away for the long weekend. I saw Rory and Gavin drive off.'

'They're not going away,' Dunai said a little too quickly. She kept her back to him, supposedly sifting through her mail. Take a deep breath, she told herself. 'They've probably gone shopping.' She forced herself to put down the mail, turn and meet Bryan's gaze. All she saw was the usual gentleness and concern, and the band of tension that was squeezing her chest eased a little. She smiled, reached out and grasped his hand.

'Let me get you a towel,' Bryan said. 'You're dripping.' And he strode across the room and disappeared down the passage.

It took Dunai seconds to realise she had the opportunity to take Jesse and get out. She had just reached the coffee table when Bryan came back up the passage with a towel in his hand. He handed it to her and she began to automatically rub at her hair.

'You want me to make you a cup of tea?' he asked.

'No, no,' Dunai said, her broken heart shattering just a little more. 'We're all set here. Go home to Belle and the girls and thank her for the meal, Bryan. It was really good of her to do this. She's done so much for us; you both have.'

'Will do,' Bryan said, still holding her hand. 'And, speaking of meals, you'd better come with me to the kitchen. I've got strict instructions from Belle.'

At the mention of the world 'kitchen' Horse leapt forward with a bark and headed in that direction. 'Bosh!' Mr Nelson shouted, fluttering from his perch and following the trail.

As Dunai allowed herself to be led to the kitchen, she glanced surreptitiously at her watch. Ten minutes had passed since she'd phoned for a taxi. She had five minutes to get rid of Bryan before it arrived.

He took her to a tray on the counter that held several bowls and dishes.

'Soya cottage pie,' he said. Horse danced around them and Mr Nelson fluttered to the counter and dipped forward to peer at each item as Bryan said, 'Salad, bread rolls and a lemon pudding.'

'Bosh!' Mr Nelson said.

'Cottage pie can be heated in the microwave, but the pudding has to go into a one hundred and eighty degree oven for twenty minutes to cook properly and get it crisp on top.'

'Your wife is a saint,' Dunai said, trying to keep her voice light. 'Now, off you go—get home to her.'

'Santa Bella,' Bryan said, bending to pat Horse, who was pressing against his legs. 'Life plods along until one day you find this one amazing person and then everything falls into place. It'll happen to you too one day—wedding bells, another baby, the lot. Mark my words.'

'Horse is neutered, Bryan.'

Bryan stopped ruffling Horse's coat and stood up, grinning. 'You know who I'm talking about, Dunai Marks.'

'One amazing person. That's all it takes,' Dunai said, dumping the towel on the counter and moving towards the kitchen door. She wasn't going to get rid of him before the taxi arrived. What was she going to say—that she and Jesse were going somewhere for the weekend? But then why hadn't she packed a bag for them and of course she'd have mentioned this before. Perhaps she should say they were spending the night at St Mark's. But she never did that and if anything did go wrong she'd have given her hiding place away.

Dunai gave a startled jolt as a car horn sounded close by. Bryan looked at her and frowned. She could feel the blood pulsing at her temples and her legs felt stiff as she forced herself to begin feeding the animals as if nothing were wrong. A hooter sounded again. She knew it was the taxi at her front door…Bryan set the dial on the oven. Two more impatient honks from outside.

'Oh, for heaven's sake,' Dunai said, striding from the kitchen. 'Let me see what all this hooting's about.'

If she got Jesse outside, they could jump into the taxi and head for St Mark's. She reached her son without looking back to see where Bryan was, and stooped to pick him up.

'I colour in,' Jesse said, squirming away from her.

'You can colour in when we get back. We won't be a minute,' she said in a low voice.

'No, I colour,' Jesse said as she tried to pick him up. He went stiff as a board and Dunai swore she'd never have another child as long as she lived.

'Everything okay?' Bryan asked.

Dunai spun towards him. He stood at the entrance to the kitchen, leaning against the door jamb.

'No, fine,' she said, her voice sounding a little breathless. She turned back to her son, took hold of his arm. 'Come, Jes,' she said firmly. 'Let's see who's hooting like that outside our house.' She knew she sounded ridiculous but there was a reason they gave out Oscars.

'You don't have to disturb him,' Bryan said, walking towards the front door. He turned on the stoep light. 'I'll see who it is.' He opened the door just a crack. 'It's a taxi,' he said, and opened the door wider.

Dunai stared out into heavy slanting rain illuminated by the stoep light, and nothing but blackness beyond, as if the entire universe had narrowed to the size of one small turquoise house.

'I think Barbara might have called it,' she said, starting towards Bryan.

There was no saliva in her mouth; her tongue seemed stuck to her palate. She forced it to the bottom of her mouth and managed to squeeze out a little moisture. 'Her husband's car was in for a service and she had some problems with her Toyota. She might have called a taxi to take them to her mum for the weekend. She must have forgotten to cancel it. I'll explain to the driver.'

'Don't go out in this weather,' Bryan said, taking his coat from the stand beside the door. 'I'll sort it out.'

Horse had come out of the kitchen and made as if to follow Bryan. Dunai automatically closed the door to keep him inside. That was when it occurred to her to lock Bryan out. But it was such a crazy thing to do. He wasn't behaving strangely. If it was a mistake, how could she face him again? Then again, if Bryan did have something to hide, what would he conclude when the driver insisted the call had been placed by Dunai Marks?

She looked at the empty keyhole and felt a mixture of fear and relief. She'd been so thrown when she'd arrived home she'd unlocked the door and closed it behind her without locking it again. She'd slipped the keys into her bag, which of course she never did. They were always left in the door. Shit! Then again, there was more than one door out of the house.

Dunai rushed to the coffee table and grabbed Jesse. 'If you don't do what I tell you, you're going to get hurt, Jes,' she told him as he began to protest. She hoisted him onto her hip. 'Don't make a sound, do you hear me?'

Jesse looked up at her with eyes round with surprise and his mouth hung open. She resisted the urge to apologise.

She still had Barbara's house keys in her coat pocket and that brought to her attention another mistake she'd made; she'd kept her wet coat on. Stupid, stupid, stupid, Dunai thought as she rushed into the kitchen. Her plan was to go out of the back door and into Barbara's house, where she'd lock herself and Jesse till Carl arrived. And if she was wrong about Bryan she'd make up some excuse, she decided. A nervous breakdown wouldn't be out of the question.

She took Barbara's back door key out of her pocket and moved it to the hand propped under Jesse's bum. She heard the front door open, moved quickly towards the windowsill above the sink and reached behind the African violets.

'You looking for this?'

Dunai spun round to see Bryan standing just inside the kitchen door, holding up the back door key.

29

IT WAS then she knew, of course. There were no more doubts as he slipped the key into his coat pocket. Her loyalty to Bryan had been a fatal mistake. Not fatal, no. Dunai forced herself to think optimistically; mistakes could be fixed. She'd been born with the odds against her; she was a fighter, and this time she had a lot more than herself to fight for. Her arm tightened around Jesse.

'Why don't you let Jesse go back to his colouring?' Bryan said.

Dunai shook her head. Jesse looked from his mother to Bryan and back again.

'Let him go, Dunai. You and I have things to talk about and I know you don't want him getting caught in the middle of it.'

Dunai clung to her son for another precious second, and it took her greatest act of will-power to loosen her arm from around him and let him slide off her hip to the floor. 'You can colour in, Jes,' she said, her voice cracking. Jesse looked up at his mother quizzically. She smiled at him but her lip trembled so she bit down on it, nodded and bent to place a hand on his back and give him a gentle push towards the door. Her eyes followed him as he walked past Bryan into the living room.

Then she turned her attention back to Bryan, took a deep breath and tried to keep her voice steady. 'So what do you want to talk to me about, Bryan?'

He regarded her for a moment; it was impossible to guess what he was thinking. He shook his head and reached into a coat pocket. 'How about this?' he said, unfolding a sheet of paper and holding it up. It said 'FBI's Most Wanted' and the aged photograph of Bryan looked back at her.

Dunai realised what had happened. Carl had mentioned when he'd faxed the composite to her office that he'd first thought she was at home and had faxed it to her there. Bryan must have gone into the dining-cum-storeroom for some reason and seen it lying there.

'You look like you've seen a ghost,' he said.

His face swam in front of her. She thought she was going to faint. Can't, she told herself—stay on your feet. She leaned back, was aware of the kitchen counter cutting into her forearm as she pressed hard against its edge, but she felt no pain.

'There was a covering note,' Bryan was saying. '"On my way back to Cape Town, Carl." You asked Carl Lambrecht to investigate me? Why?'

She noticed a slight trembling in the hand that held the sheet.

'I didn't,' Dunai said, her voice almost inaudible. 'We were investigating Siobhan's death, then I remembered your diary on my desk that morning. You didn't fetch it the way you said you had.'

'Who else has seen this?' Bryan asked, indicating the paper with a twitch of his head, and for a moment Dunai believed he was innocent of the charges on the sheet, that it was a case of mistaken identity.

'Only Carl has,' she said, offering up one last gesture of loyalty to Bryan but still thinking of her own safety and Jesse's. 'I've spoken to him and he's on his way here.' Dunai had the sickening thought that he might go straight to St Mark's when he got back to Cape Town, as she'd told him to do.

Bryan said nothing. Both stood stock-still. Then, very slowly, Bryan looked from Dunai to the sheet in his hand, then back at her again. 'You've jumped to conclusions, haven't you?' he said, and she stared at him, unable to speak or move as he came towards her. 'You know the truth of who I am.'

'No,' she said, never taking her eyes off him. She took a couple of steps to the left. 'I know Bryan Larsen. You're Jeffrey Stappleton.'

'*No!* Yes. I was then. But I put that behind me, Dunai. Please just hear what I have to say. That's all I'm asking.'

She kept staring at him, relieved he wanted to talk, terrified of the moment when all pretence would be over.

She tried to swallow, but her throat was as dry as a saltpan.

'I told you I've done things I'm not proud of, but you see I could either let them destroy me or put them in the past and do everything in my power to make a difference to the people I love and the community around me. And I've done that, Dunai. I *am* doing that.'

She watched him take a deep breath.

'Late seventies, at university I was an idealist, wanted to change things really badly, but I found that all the protests of the sixties and seventies had changed nothing because rock always crushes paper. That's the reality of the world.

'I found an ideological home with the Student Liberation Army. We believed we were living in drastic times—times that forced us to become rock instead of paper.'

Dunai took another couple of steps to the left. Bryan turned slightly to keep her in his sights.

'I built a pipe bomb in 1980 that killed four people. Only three of us escaped arrest. I went to Zambia, where Bryan Larsen was born. I knew no one, owned nothing that couldn't fit into a small overnight bag. But I began work as a statistician for a humanitarian organization—threw every ounce of energy into making other people's lives better. I hated what I'd been forced to do. I'm not a violent man, you know that, and I have made restitution. I still am putting things right, Dunai. Please don't take that away from me now.'

Bryan shook his head, folded the sheet and slipped it into his pocket. He wiped a hand across his forehead; he was sweating.

'I came to South Africa in eighty-seven. I knew I'd be safe here. It was during apartheid and, although I hated the regime I was forced to live under, it meant the country was isolated; there was enormous suspicion and very little co-operation between the South African and American authorities.

'I met Siobhan at a conference in ninety-eight and she offered me a job. Then I met Belle and she changed my life for ever. Amy, May—I couldn't live without them, Dunai. They mean everything to me. And you too—you and Jesse are part of my family, just like Amy and May.'

'Don't say that,' Dunai said, tears sliding down her cheeks. 'Don't you *dare* say that.'

Bryan came towards her, arms outstretched to comfort her like he'd done so many times before.

'Don't!' Dunai put her hand up to stop him.

Tears slid down Bryan's cheeks. 'I'm the person you've always known, Dunai. You know me. I love my family. I've tried desperately to put the past behind me. To spend my life in service to others—'

'Siobhan.' The name tore from her lips like a keen. '*Siobhan*, Bryan. Oh, God. Please tell me you didn't. Please tell me you didn't murder her.'

'Of course I didn't.'

'Don't lie to me,' Dunai shouted. 'I know you did. You went up to get your diary and heard her talking to the NIA. That's why you forgot your diary again. And Mr Bojangles saw you. He told me before he died but I didn't believe him. *Again* I didn't believe him.'

'Dunai, listen to me. I had no choice. You know Siobhan wasn't who you thought she was.' Bryan was speaking quickly now. 'You didn't know her like I did. I had no choice. Please, Dunai, believe me. I had no choice. She was going to betray me, betray our friendship. She'd eaten meals in my home, played with my children. She knew my history.'

'No.' Dunai shook her head.

'Yes, Dunai. Even Belle doesn't know but Siobhan did. She found out soon after I started working with her. But she said she knew what had driven me to do it. That I'd tried to make amends. Said we'd all been forced to do things we thought we'd never have to do, but it would always stay between us. Then one day she decided to give me up. After so many years, she was going to betray me to the NIA.'

Bryan reached into his pocket and pulled out his gloves.

'She thought I'd left for the day but I went back up for my diary. She had her back to the door and I heard what she was saying. First I didn't believe the information she was going to give to the NIA involved me in any way, then she looked up and saw me and from the look on her face I knew. I heard the lift doors opening; it must have been Dan Cowley. So I left. But I came back. I had no choice. I couldn't lose everything. I had to choose between Siobhan and my family. It was the last thing I wanted to do, but that's what it came down to.'

'But Brandon Cupido,' Dunai said, confused. 'They found some of the things taken from Siobhan's office in a bin in Atlantis.'

'The night Cowley came to see you, you told me the evidence was pointing to a hired gang leader in Atlantis, so that's where I dumped the fax and coffee machine I'd taken the night... I'd intended it to look like a burglary.'

Bryan finished pulling on his gloves. Dunai tried to back away from him but she was already pressed against the counter. They'd changed positions now. Slowly she'd manoeuvred so she was closer to the kitchen door and he near the back door. She had to get out. Get to the living room, grab Jesse and get out— the front door was unlocked.

'What you need to understand, Dunai, is that Siobhan would've betrayed you too if it had served her purposes,' Bryan said. 'And she'd have lost no sleep over it. That's the sort of person she was.'

'*You killed her,*' Dunai shouted, pointing a finger at him. 'You killed her, Bryan. You *killed* her.'

Horse lifted his head from his water bowl and looked questioningly from Dunai to Bryan. The cats had shot up onto the top of the cupboard. Mr Nelson shouted, 'Bosh!'

Bryan took a step towards her. She cast around for a weapon

but all the utensils were on the other side of the kitchen. With the counter at her back, she began to move sideways.

'Dunai, you're not like Siobhan; you wouldn't betray me.'

'You murdered her,' Dunai said, her voice quiet now. She kept facing him as she took two quick steps out of the kitchen.

'Mummy?' she heard behind her, but didn't turn.

'Don't make me do this,' Bryan said. 'Please don't make me do this.'

'Carl's on his way,' Dunai said, desperate for more time.

Bryan nodded. 'And I'll be waiting for him when he arrives.' He took his eyes off her for a second, reached back and pulled the kitchen door shut behind him.

Dunai glanced quickly over her shoulder. Jesse was standing at the coffee table, crayon in hand, the colouring book forgotten on the table in front of him.

'Go to your room *now*,' she shouted at him. She turned back to face the threat in front of her, not knowing if Jesse had listened to her. Horse barked once from inside the kitchen and she wasn't sure if she was relieved he'd be out of whatever was about to happen, or if she now felt completely unprotected.

Bryan took a step towards her; she tried to avoid him but he caught her sleeve and pulled her back towards him.

'Bryan, *no*!' she screamed as he reached for her throat.

Horse began to bark in the kitchen. She felt Bryan's hands close around her throat. Terrible pain shot through her as his thumbs pressed against her windpipe. Then even the pain was eclipsed by a desperate need for oxygen. She began to claw at his hands, but he was wearing gloves and it made no difference. She tried to reach for his face, get at his eyes, but he pulled his head back and she couldn't reach. She had the sensation of slipping beneath water. She felt confused. His face seemed less substantial now, as if she really were looking up at him from under water. Jesse. She had to stay conscious—get to Jesse.

There was a thud from somewhere in the house and Horse's barking got closer till she thought her head would burst with the sound. Bryan looked down suddenly and cried, 'No, Horse.' Dunai heard a low, menacing growl. 'Leave, Horse,' Bryan shouted. His grip loosened around her throat. She still couldn't get enough air into her lungs; she was sure she was going to pass out. Where was Jesse?

Then Bryan cried out and let go of her. She sucked in a deep rasping breath and bent forward, thinking she was going to be sick. She saw Bryan's leg was bleeding and he was focused on Horse, who was growling. She knew she should try to move away from him but she couldn't; it was as if her arms and legs were filled with lead. Horse made another dart towards Bryan but he kicked out at him. The dog's scream of pain cut right through her, then everything went black.

It took her seconds to realise she hadn't fainted; the lights had gone out. She had to get away from Bryan, but her head throbbed and she was disorientated. Move, do something, she told herself.

She thought of Bryan's hands around her throat; saw Siobhan's face in front of her—the shrivelled blue-grey lips, the livid bruises around her throat. Bryan had done that.

And when he was finished with her, would he hurt Jesse? Jesse had seen him. Jesse was a witness. Dunai almost sobbed aloud but instinct told her if she made a sound she'd die.

'Mummy?'

Oh, God, Dunai thought, Jesse must have left the living room when she'd shouted at him but hadn't gone to his bedroom; he was somewhere in the passage behind her. She had to reach him, get him into her bedroom, they could lock the door, call Carl. They'd be safe there.

She forced herself to stand stock-still. Where was Bryan? She thought she heard something. Was it the whisper of fabric, perhaps his trousers as he moved? She put a hand to her throat.

'Bosh!'

She almost screamed as Mr Nelson shrieked from the kitchen. She thought she heard a sudden intake of breath but it had come from behind her. Bryan had been in front of her. She'd taken a step back, thinking she was moving away from him towards Jesse. But what if he'd anticipated her move and stepped behind her?

'Mummy?'

She didn't dare answer.

'Is dark, Mummy. I scared,' and Jesse began to sob.

Dunai wanted to scream then, not in terror but in rage. She wanted to rip and claw at the threat that stood between her and her son. But she had to survive, use her head. She forced herself to stay frozen to the spot. She could hear Horse's shallow breathing and had to staunch the panic it brought. Her body was pumped with adrenalin; everything in her screamed for movement. She had to do something. Couldn't just stand there. What if the lights came on again? She took a step back.

'Dunai,' she heard a woman whisper beside her. She spun in shock just as her arm was caught in a firm grip. 'This cannibal has planted his last potato,' the voice said.

It was so low as to be almost inaudible, particularly over Jesse's sobs. The tone was calm and even, and if it weren't for the grip on her arm she'd have thought she'd gone mad and the voice had come from inside her head. But she recognised the voice of the amazon in the Company Gardens and from the trip to meet the judge when, blindfolded in the car, they'd talked about their mutual childhood hero. Now it was one of Pippi Longstocking's lines she'd chosen to convey not only who she was but also her intentions.

'Dunai?' This time it was Bryan's voice.

Had he heard the whispers? Dunai hoped so; it would confuse the hell out of him.

'Go to the spare room window. I'll get Jesse,' the amazon said.

Everything rational in her brain urged her to obey, but she was a mother and to abandon her son to a relative stranger in such a dangerous situation went against her instinct and it was this part that won over all others.

Dunai moved away from the amazon to where she thought Jesse was waiting for her; his sobs were louder now. She had every intention of grabbing him and running for the spare room but what happened next seemed to play out in a parallel universe with a different time system. It occurred in just seconds but each movement had slowed to a fraction of its normal speed.

She took a step back, felt herself come to a stop against Bryan's chest. She tried to scream but too quickly his hands were around her bruised throat. She clawed at his gloved fingers but they kept squeezing. Her eyes frantically scanned the darkness. Oh, God, where was the amazon? Had she gone to get Jesse, thinking Dunai was waiting for her? She was going to die just metres away as they waited for her in the dark.

Dunai saw a change in the quality of blackness just off to Bryan's right—darkness that seemed a little denser, or perhaps she was losing consciousness. Then, just as she could make out the outline of Bryan's face, she saw a fist swing towards his right temple. She heard the impact, felt his hands fall from her throat.

'What's...' he said, his voice strangled as he staggered back.

It took Dunai a while to realise that the hammering was coming not from inside her head, but from the front door. She thought she heard someone shout but there was a loud rushing sound in her ears as if she'd cupped a seashell to either side of her head. Jesse was still crying.

Then the front door of her house exploded inwards. Beams of light zigzagged across the room like drunken fireflies. Horse let out a loud menacing bark, then screamed in pain. Dunai heard someone shout her name, then Bryan's. She chose that moment to drop to the carpet. There was more shouting but she paid no attention to the words. She began to crawl frantically towards the passage. Torch beams lurched towards her in the darkness, then swung away again.

She reached Horse, put her hand out to touch him. Jesse rushed towards her from the passage and she caught him as he flung himself into her arms. She could feel his heart hammering against her chest. Several voices began to shout all at once.

Dunai knelt beside Horse, her weeping son cradled against her chest. She twisted her head to see what was going on behind her, saw a split second played out in slow time.

Bryan coming towards her, voices shouting, 'Move away from her. Stop!' There was an explosion. Dunai flinched. Horse raised his head, tried to get up, cried out in pain. She tried to keep him down with one hand, terrified of what damage he was doing every time he tried to get up. She pressed Jesse against her chest, curling her body around him, her other hand pressed against his ear. There was more shouting. Then her ears seemed to shatter in a series of explosions that lit up the room.

She tried to crouch lower, her head twisted to the left. She watched as Bryan's body stopped suddenly, then staggered backwards as if he'd run at full speed into an invisible force field. He was looking down at her, shock on his face, tears on his cheeks. She saw ink blots appear on his shirt—one, two, three of them. He reached out towards her as he crumpled to the ground, coming to rest on his back, one leg caught awkwardly beneath him. She watched the ink blots spread outwards, their edges joining together till they covered his shirt.

Dunai felt herself being lifted but she clung to Jesse, who was now silent in her arms although she could feel him trembling from head to toe. She looked up to see Carl's face above her. He was talking but she couldn't hear what he was saying. She looked back to where Bryan lay, but Carl placed his palm against her cheek and brought her eyes back to his face. His skin looked cold and pale but his eyes blazed. Even now his eyes blazed. She watched his lips as he spoke and thought she heard the words, 'You hurt?' but they sounded far away, coming at her down a long, empty tunnel.

She shook her head, then reached up and pulled his hand away from her cheek so she could see Bryan again. Philippe was kneeling beside him. His huge bulk bent over the figure on the carpet. Tears ran down his cheeks, he was shaking his head and his lips moved.

Two uniformed police officers, a man and woman, were trying to pull Philippe to his feet; he wouldn't budge. She looked above their heads, saw DI van Reenen coming towards her.

Paramedics appeared, knelt beside Bryan. One of them reached across his chest and took hold of Philippe's arm, gripping it as he spoke. Philippe staggered to his feet and the paramedics went to work on Bryan, blocking her view of him.

Carl reached for her and Jesse and pulled them against his chest. She clung to him for a moment, then lifted herself so she could see over his shoulder as they carried Bryan out on a stretcher. They'd covered him with a thermal blanket. That was good, Dunai thought. No body bag—he wasn't dead, then. The stretcher exited the turquoise house, then Rory and Gavin were running towards her. A uniformed policeman came in after them; he was agitated, his arm raised, finger pointing.

Dunai loosened her grip on her son. She looked down at him. His eyes were enormous, his mouth open.

'I've got you, Jes. It's okay.' He began to wail. 'You're fine, Jes. It's over. You're safe. I'll never let anyone hurt you. Not ever, I promise. You're safe now, okay?'

Rory knelt beside her.

'The animals,' Dunai said, her voice echoing in her ears. 'Horse is hurt.'

She grabbed Carl's hand, looked imploringly at him, thinking she might have difficulty in getting him out of the house in all this chaos. She needed to make him understand.

'Please, Carl. I need to get him to a vet. And the others?' Dunai looked wildly around, staggered to her feet. Carl was at her side, supporting her weight.

They found Tommy, Annika and Mr Nelson on top of a kitchen cupboard, pressing themselves to the wall. Gavin went inside and closed the door. Carl stayed with Horse while she went to get a blanket. He eased the dog onto it while Dunai tried to reassure him whenever he cried in pain. Then they each took two corners and carried him outside. Into absolute chaos. Sirens wailed, lights flashed, radios crackled, neighbours watched from the pavement. Another police car arrived, a second ambulance. And Philippe sat alone on the stoep, head in his hands.

They placed Horse carefully on the stoep as Carl went to speak to Philippe. DI van Reenen came out to join them. He argued with Carl, then seemed to relent. It was decided Philippe would take Horse to the Cape Animal Medical Centre in Kenilworth.

They placed Horse on the back seat of Siobhan's old Renault and Philippe jumped into the driver's seat. 'Phone me as soon as you get to the clinic,' Dunai said. She watched them take off down Chiappini Street. For a split second she searched the crowd for Bryan's face, then she remembered.

30

DUNAI refused the sedating syringe but allowed a paramedic to clean her smashed and bleeding nails and dress her throat wound. He told her she needed to have X-rays and a scan but she assured him she'd get it done the next day.

Carl had taken charge of activity inside the turquoise house, locating a locksmith to replace the broken lock on the front door and moving restlessly from room to room till the last police officer, scene-of-crime technician and journalist had left.

Philippe called to say Horse had three broken ribs and was being kept overnight for observation and pain treatment.

Carl made a cup of tea for Dunai and brought it to her on the sofa. Jesse slept against her chest, wrapped in his Winnie the Pooh blanket, the cats were curled against her hip and Mr Nelson had perched on the arm of the sofa. She drank the tea at Carl's instruction but tasted nothing. He took her cup back to the kitchen, turned out the lights and sat beside her, reaching for her hand; she let him take it.

In the darkness she saw flashes of gunfire, bullets slamming into Bryan's chest, saw blood well from his wounds and spread across his chest, eating his shirt till there was nothing left. And she watched his face—every flicker, every twitch, every changing emotion—as he fell to the carpet again and again.

The images had little effect at first. Ever since she had placed Horse into the car, she'd experienced a strange stillness, as if her heart had stopped beating. But, with no warning at all, she felt a jolt in her chest, as if her heart had started again, only this time it seemed too large for its cavity, its rhythm unnaturally strong. She imagined blood rushing to her temples, her fingertips, too much too soon, her veins and arteries dilating to accommodate the flow. She heard it pounding in her ears like waves dashing against rock. Her nostrils flared and she could smell the hot metal of bullet casings or blood perhaps. She began to shiver and sweat and her skin itched.

She let go of Carl's hand, laid Jesse on the sofa, walked to the bathroom and undressed without turning on the light. The rain had cleared and a full moon shone through the windows, covering her skin with greyish light. She reached into the shower to turn on the taps and a smell rose from her body that reminded her of the smell of Mr Bojangles's blanket—ice, old sweat, fear and confusion.

She stepped into the shower, closed the door and moved under the water before it had heated properly. She turned up the hot water, rubbed lemon-scented soap into a sponge and pressed it to her throat; the pain brought tears to her eyes. Avoiding the dressing, she scrubbed her skin but, no matter how hard she tried, she couldn't get rid of the smell that kept seeping from her pores.

She worked the taps again—less cold, more hot. Steam rose around her. She grabbed the soap, rubbed it into the sponge, scrubbed harder this time—stomach, thighs, reaching down to her legs, and still she smelled of blood and fear. The sponge dropped from her hand. Carl stood in front of her, water running over his T-shirt, down his jeans.

She turned her back on him but he reached around and tried to take the soap. She pressed it against her stomach. Some part of her knew she'd snapped, but there was another part that had to scrub away the smell of blood and Bryan's hands around her throat.

'Dunai?'

She didn't move.

'Dunai, look at me.'

She kept her back to him.

With his hands on her shoulders, Carl turned her to face him.

'I smell of blood,' she said, pressing the soap to her chest. 'I need to wash it off.'

'You smell of lemons,' he said.

Dunai shook her head. 'No, it's definitely blood.'

Carl placed a hand on either side of her face and tilted her chin towards him but she kept her eyes fixed on his throat.

'You've just survived a terrible trauma,' he said. 'This is your mind's way of dealing with it. But you're safe, Dunai. Jesse's safe. And I swear it's going to be okay.'

He took the soap from her, retrieved the sponge and put them in the shower caddy. Dunai placed her palms against his chest and rested her forehead there. His hands slipped to her arms and she thought he was going to push her away again like he'd done in his office that day. She closed her eyes, embarrassed at the thought.

'No, look at me.'

She opened them. He was looking down at her and for a while she lost herself in eyes the colour of storm clouds. She watched a drop of water hover at the tip of an eyelash. Then he blinked and it fell.

'Maybe it'll never be okay again.' The thought broke her heart. She moved forward till their bodies were pressed together. His fingers slipped into her hair.

'Somehow it always manages to be okay again,' he said.

She shifted against him and he dipped his head. She stood on tiptoe to kiss him, roughly at first, their tongues thrusting and swirling about as if frantic to find each other. But eventually they slowed as her tongue dipped in, found his and withdrew, while his lips brushed feather-light against her mouth.

His lips left her mouth and whispered in her ear, 'I'll be here, Dunai, when it is okay again.' He stroked her wet hair, then, stepping from the shower, reached for a towel and dried her gently.

* * *

Dunai sat sideways on Carl's lap on top of the laundry box, cheek resting against his chest, the scent of lemon soap in her nostrils and the bath sheet warm around her shoulders.

She started awake and glanced around her. 'How long have I been asleep?'

He smiled. ''bout twenty minutes.'

'Thank you,' she said simply. His expressive eyes glittered but he said nothing, just nodded. She noticed he was still in his damp clothes.

'You can put your clothes in the dryer,' she said, getting to her feet. 'My robe's on the back of the door; you can use it till your clothes have dried.'

She went to her bedroom and pulled on a pair of blue flannel pyjama bottoms and a long-sleeved T-shirt. Carl appeared in the doorway, her white terrycloth robe reaching just below his knees and pulled tightly across his shoulders; she smiled.

They went back to the sofa, where she fell asleep again, her son in her arms, Carl against her left hip, the cats against her right and Mr Nelson on the sofa arm.

31

DUNAI sat on the passage floor outside Carl's office, the morning paper on her lap. It was Friday morning, a bank holiday, and the building was quiet around her.

Carl hadn't returned to his office yet. Dunai didn't mind waiting. She opened her bag, which was no longer one of the large totes she'd once sported. This one was small and compact, with a thick strap worn across the chest to keep both hands free. She found what she was looking for; pulled her watch from a side pocket. It had just gone nine-thirty but, as in the aftermath of Siobhan's death, time this morning had ceased to behave as it usually did.

Thoughts of that morning almost a month ago brought with it memories of Bryan. She remembered him in the passage one floor above where she sat now, coming towards her, shock and trauma on his face. 'I can't believe this is happening,' he'd said. How many hours had it been since he'd strangled the life out of Siobhan? Dunai counted eight and a half.

She remembered him bringing her tea that morning. Comforting arms around her; if she closed her eyes she'd probably be able to feel them. She stared wide-eyed at the wall opposite and raised a hand to the dressing at her throat that covered the mess of scratches and bruises that were so livid they looked as if they would burst through the skin. Swallowing, speaking above a whisper and turning her head were extremely painful but it was nothing compared to the agony of heart and mind.

The lies were almost too numerous to count, but count them she would. She would keep remembering the deceptions, trying hard to recall the exact expression on his face as he'd told them, looking for tell tale signs; more than likely finding none.

She hadn't seen Philippe since he'd taken Horse to the animal medical centre. She knew he'd gone to the hospital, where he'd remained for another half hour till they'd declared Bryan dead. Then he'd insisted on accompanying what had already become a large group of officers from various law enforcement agencies to break the news to Belle.

Dunai rubbed her eyes and spread the paper across her thighs. The headline in the *Cape Times* and, she was sure, several papers across the US was: *FBI's Most Wanted Caught in Cape Town.*

Dramatic events in Chiappini Street, Bo-Kaap last night led to the capture of a terrorist who has been sought by the FBI for 25 years. Jeffrey Alan Stappleton was wanted for his involvement in extremist activities in the US in the late 1970s and early 80s.

Stappleton was a member of the Student Liberation Army, a group responsible for killing a police officer in Baltimore, Maryland, on 9 March 1979 and a pipe bomb explosion at First Eastern Bank, Baltimore, that killed four people on 14 January 1980.

On 5 April that year, an unregistered pipe bomb was found at Stappleton's residence. He was subsequently charged with the unlawful possession of an unregistered bomb device on 7 April 1981 and with four counts of murder on 2 May 1981.

It is believed Stappleton evaded capture by fleeing to Africa, where he lived as Bryan Larsen. He settled in South Africa in 1987.

He was employed as a statistician by NGO, STOP (Strategies for Targeting Over-Population).

It is not clear whether Stappleton's capture is in any way related to the death of STOP founder and human rights activist, Siobhan Craig, who was found murdered in her office a month ago.

After a dramatic shoot-out last night, Stappleton was declared dead as a result of several bullet wounds to the chest an hour after arriving at Groote Schuur Hospital.

FBI representatives will arrive in Cape Town this morning to question his wife, Belle Larsen. He is survived by his wife and two daughters, aged eight and six.

Dunai felt enormous grief for Bryan's family. She hadn't contacted Belle yet—couldn't, didn't know what to say. She told herself she'd call later today; offer to do anything she could to make the weeks ahead bearable.

She was still unable to equate Jeffrey Stappleton with Bryan Larsen. She was sure it would be the same for his family. She'd separated him now into two men—Jeffrey Stappleton the terrorist, and Bryan Larsen, her Bryan, the man she'd known and loved. She had accepted Jeffrey Stappleton's guilt in the murder of Siobhan but not Bryan's. Dunai wondered if this delusion wasn't perhaps essential to her sanity.

She looked up as the lift doors opened and Carl got out. He came towards her, held out his hand. He had shaved and looked handsome in a tailored grey suit and open-necked shirt. He was scheduled to give a television news interview later in the day.

Dunai took his hand and he pulled her to her feet. Neither spoke as he unlocked the safety gate and door. She went to his office while he put on the coffee machine. This morning she took the seat furthest from the door.

Carl returned with two coffees and she wrapped her hands around the mug's warmth.

'You okay?' he asked. She nodded.

Carl took a sip of coffee, then placed the mug on the desk in front of him.

'They've done the post-mortem—pushed it through as a favour to the FBI.'

Dunai nodded, took another painful swig of coffee.

'There's one finding no one can figure out, though; you might be asked about it.'

Dunai met his eyes.

'They picked up a large bruise on his temple like he'd been punched or hit with something; except if he was hit with a fist it was one hell of a punch, a large man probably. There was nothing lying around at the scene, which there would have been if he'd been hit with an object, and we know he didn't connect with anything other than the carpet when he went down. Any ideas?'

Dunai looked away, shook her head. Carl waited a moment.

'How's your throat?'

'Sore,' she whispered. 'Could've been worse, though.'

'Did you know your spare room window was unlocked?'

Dunai shook her head.

'I know you don't need a lecture right now, but you do need to be more careful.'

She smiled sadly at him. 'I will, I promise.'

'There's one other mystery,' Carl added. 'No one can work out why the lights tripped.'

Dunai shrugged. 'Maybe it was one of Sister Raymunda's angels.'

'Sister what?' Carl asked, frowning.

'Sister Raymunda—one of the nuns who brought me up. She prayed from the time I was little that there'd always be an angel to look after me.'

Carl cocked his head to the side and watched her through narrowed eyes.

'There's something I'd like to ask you,' Dunai said, casting around for something to distract him. 'You lost interest in the case towards the end, didn't you? You thought the trail had gone cold and we'd never find who'd done it.'

'What makes you say that?'

'After the interview with Jerome Plaatjies—I don't think it had anything to do with my apartheid comment—you wanted to hand everything over to the police. You just didn't seem interested any more.'

Carl looked her in the eye. 'I didn't think I could trust you. And the apartheid comment *was* off-colour, by the way.'

'Trust me?'

'Yes, Dunai.'

'Why wouldn't you trust me?'

'Saturday, after you called about the threat from Brandon Cupido, I came down here to see if you were okay, and what I saw was a man who fitted the very good description you gave me of the NIA agent in the stairwell the morning after Siobhan's murder. I saw him follow you to the third floor and leave forty-five minutes later. You came out soon after, looking as if you'd seen a ghost. You should have told me what happened. Even when I probed yesterday, you chose not to tell me.'

Dunai looked down at the desk. She was silent but her brain worked furiously.

'I didn't think it was important. He said Siobhan had contacted him to say she had information for him but she'd been killed before they were due to meet. He wanted to know if I had any idea what that information was. I told him I didn't and he left. Now, of course, we know she was going to tell him about Bryan.'

'And that took forty-five minutes?' Carl asked.

'I wouldn't at first let him in or believe he was who he said he was. He had to do a bit of persuading.'

Carl's eyes narrowed, then he said, 'It's imperative you keep your partner in the loop, Dunai. That information would have given me another angle to pursue.'

'I know. I'm sorry, I should have told you. Am I forgiven?'

'If you'll come to work for me.'

There was dead silence. It took her a moment to recover.

'You want me to work for you?' she repeated, frowning.

'As a private investigator—trainee, to begin with. You've still got a lot to learn but you've got all the instincts.'

Dunai's mobile rang and for a moment she was assailed by the same primitive fear she'd felt as Stappleton's hands had closed around her neck. Other than Carl, Bryan was the only person who had ever called her on it—just to check she was carrying it on her in case of emergency. Dunai let it ring.

Carl's brow furrowed. 'You going to answer that?'

She grabbed her bag, located the mobile, then took a deep breath and answered.

'Dunai Marks?' It was a man's voice.

'Yes?'

'This is Dr Verster from Two Military Hospital. I've got your DNA results. Where would you like me to send them?'

It took her a moment to think. 'Could you fax them to me?' She gave him Carl's number, thanked him for pushing the results through so quickly, then rang off.

'What is it?' Carl asked.

'Dr Verster's going to fax through the DNA results.'

'You know where the fax is?'

Dunai nodded but made no attempt to get up.

'You okay?'

'I doubt it.'

They heard the fax start up on the reception desk next door. 'You want me to get it for you?'

She nodded.

When he returned to the office, he came to stand near her, still reading a sheet of paper. He glanced at the second page, then went back to the first. Dunai's heart hammered. Part of her wanted to tell him to get on with it. Another part wanted never to know. Perhaps she hadn't done the right thing. Sometimes ignorance really was bliss.

Carl sat on the desk beside her; there was a frown on his face.

'Just tell me,' she said, no longer able to take his silence.

'According to these results—' he waved the second page '—you've got to be an expert to read these charts.'

Frowning, Dunai tried to grab it from him. He held it out of reach.

'But,' he said, 'Dr Verster's written a summary.' He placed this page on top of the other. 'It seems you're related to the person whose DNA you supplied. That person is your mother.'

Silence followed. Justice Swanepoel-Higgs had told her the truth. She let out a long, slow breath and leaned back in her chair.

'The DNA sample you provided was Siobhan's,' Carl prompted, looking down at her.

'Yes.'

'So Siobhan was your mother. But we know Philippe is not your father.'

Dunai didn't find that funny.

'You'll have to speak to her family then.'

'She doesn't have family,' Dunai said, her stomach like a lift plummeting to basement level. She paused before saying, 'Except me.' The words sounded strange to her ears. Jesse had been the only biological link she'd had to another human being.

'Everyone has family. Chances are you have a parent who's still alive,' Carl said, placing the sheets on the desk in front of her and walking around to take his seat again.

'She never spoke of any. Not even Philippe is aware of any relatives. Only that she changed her name, so I don't even have that to go on.'

'She must have lost touch with them. Might have been her activities during apartheid. It happened. Families disowned members who they thought were traitors or terrorists.'

'So it might be possible to trace them,' she said, feeling hope, excitement and fear rush her all at the same time.

'Which you could do if you came to work for me. You could use your new skills, your contacts.'

Dunai nodded. 'I like the idea but it's too much to take in right now. D'you mind if I think about it?'

'Course not.'

'I still need to speak to Philippe; find out what's going to happen at STOP. I think we can still get through the last bit of work to get us ready for the presentation. I want to finish this for Siobhan now more than ever.'

'No rush,' Carl said. 'Oh, and by the way there is some good news. Dan Cowley announced he's stepping down as leader of the South African chapter of Men of The Covenant to concentrate on his business and family. So that's a posthumous victory for Siobhan.'

'I was so sure in the beginning he was guilty,' Dunai said.

'He might have thought about killing her,' Carl said. 'But maybe he couldn't get up the nerve. Could be why he drove around that night for almost two hours.'

'And Wayne Daniels is innocent, too.'

'Of Siobhan's murder,' Carl agreed. 'But I do believe he asked Cupido to organise a hit on Siobhan and Cupdio was in the advanced stages of doing just that, only Bryan got to her first. But law enforcement will continue to keep an eye on Cupido. One day he's bound to make a mistake. As for Daniels, he still has Thandiwe Dingake to deal with.'

'That's something,' Dunai said. 'And at least Cupido will back off now; no more story-time with Fishface.'

Carl nodded.

'And,' Dunai said, 'the NIA agent was right. He told me if I found out what information Siobhan had planned to give him the morning she was murdered, I'd find who'd killed her.'

Dunai hated lying to him about the depth of the NIA's involvement in the case but she still felt she couldn't tell him about *Cerchio di Gaia* and that Siobhan's allegiance to a listed terrorist organisation was such that she'd sacrificed Bryan to throw the authorities off her trail. Dunai knew so little about Carl and she wasn't entirely sure what he'd do with such explosive information. He was an ex-police detective, which told her he tended to lean towards the establishment, while *Cerchio di Gaia* was very definitely anti-establishment. He might try to persuade her to cooperate with the authorities. She also balked at the idea of having to reveal just how much she'd kept from him during the investigation. She remembered what he'd said just moments ago; 'I didn't think I could trust you.' He'd also said, 'It's imperative you keep your partner in the loop.' Dunai hoped by the end of the day there'd be no reason to tell him about any of it.

She hesitated before saying, 'You won't let this go any further, will you? I mean Siobhan's blackmailing activities. I know what she did was wrong but there was so much good she did and it's over now. Protecting her memory is all I have left to do for her.'

'There's no reason to tell anyone. You have my word,' Carl said. Dunai nodded.

'I think I'm ready to fetch Jesse now,' she said, getting to her feet. 'He's at St Mark's. Sister Finbar's a child trauma counsellor, so I wanted her to have a chat with him and find out what effect last night might have had so I know how to help him deal with it.'

Carl stood. 'I'll drive you.'

'No, it's okay. Thank you, but I'll be all right.'

'You sure?'

'I want to walk,' she said. 'Clear my head a little.'

'You need to have that throat scan and you need to sleep.'

'That's the plan. I want to fetch Jesse and get back to the cats and Mr Nelson. Philippe's taking me for the scan, then to fetch Horse this afternoon. I'll sleep before we go; Jesse probably will too.'

'You need anything, call, okay?'

Dunai nodded and turned to go, trying not to hear the echo of Bryan in those words. 'Dunai?' She turned back at the door. Carl was still watching her.

'Maybe you and I could have dinner some time.'

She smiled. 'I'd like that,' she said.

Carl nodded and fixed her with that penetrating gaze; only this time, instead of feeling uncomfortable, Dunai felt excited by it.

'Soon,' she said, and felt herself grin like an idiot.

32

DUNAI didn't go to fetch Jesse right away. There were things she had to do which she wanted as few people as possible to know about.

She hit some congestion at the top of Plein Street as thousands of women, some men and children, gathered outside the gates of parliament. The Women's Day marchers held banners aloft and sang and chanted slogans. They would eventually hand over petitions and memoranda to the President's representative. as they did every year.

Dunai avoided them and entered a brown high-rise, signed in at security and rode the lift to the twelfth floor.

Siobhan's lawyer, Graham Harstead, met her at the glass door to the dark and deserted legal practice.

'What do I even say, Dunai? Bryan, of all people.' He shook his head, palms held out to her briefly.

'It's going to take a long time for us to come to terms with it,' she said, but felt surprise at the hard knot of resolve in her chest. 'I don't want to take up a lot of your time,' she said, gesturing towards the passage. 'I appreciate you seeing me on a holiday.'

'Any time, Dunai,' he said. 'Let's go to my office.'

They sat opposite each other at the small conference table. He slid the document across to her and pointed with a pen. 'Here's the clause you requested in the revised will. I want you to go through it to make sure it's exactly what you want.'

Dunai nodded and dipped her head to read.

In the event of my death, the contents of safe deposit box 1113, being held at Standard Bank, Adderley Street, are to be studied by Graham Harstead, Philippe Baobi and Carl Lambrecht in consultation and a decision made regarding the appropriate steps to be taken in the light of the information contained therein. Unanimous agreement must be reached by all three of the aforementioned before action of any sort is embarked upon.

Dunai looked up and nodded. 'Yes, that's it.'

'All you need to do, then, is sign,' Graham told her.

The details and signatures of two witnesses were already filled in as she'd instructed. Dunai signed as testator and slid the document back across the table.

Outside, she pushed her way through the marchers and kept walking till she'd reached the call boxes on a relatively calm and quiet corner of Spin and Parliament Streets. She took a phone card from her purse, a business card from her pocket and dialled the number printed on it.

'Hello,' the voice said on the other end. 'This is Paula Swanepoel-Higgs.

'This is Dunai Marks,' she replied.

'Dunai. How are you feeling?'

'Alive,' Dunai said. 'Thank you. For my son too.'

'We were relieved we could help,' she said. 'Thank you for bringing Siobhan's murderer to justice.'

Dunai wanted instinctively to defend Bryan against an outsider. Her mind still refused to reduce him to the label of 'Siobhan's murderer' and, as far as Dunai was concerned, no justice had been served last night.

'I'm calling to tell you I can't join the group,' she said.

There was a second's pause. 'Why is that, Dunai?'

'I know almost nothing about the group and there're too many rumours of violence for me to join with a clear conscience.'

'Our *raison d'être* is not the creation of conflict or the per-petuation of violence,' she said, her voice resonating with au-thority. 'If violence exists, it is because there is no other way and the situation has been forced upon us. No, you do not know the workings of the circle but Siobhan did and she strove towards our aims with unquestionable loyalty to the very end. And you knew Siobhan, Dunai. Don't ever forget that.'

Dunai sighed. 'I understand what drives you, agree even with your ideology, but Siobhan always ended up sacrificing the people she loved for the cause—me as a baby, Bryan now, and I don't know how many others there've been. I loved Siobhan, always will, but I don't want to choose the same course for my life.'

'Those of us who experience a strong pull towards social jus-tice are compelled to act because we feel an intense compassion for those suffering around us, yet it is this same emotion that makes the morally ambiguous decisions so terribly hard to make. But it is only she who watches from the sidelines and does not act who avoids the risk of moral compromise and is never re-quired to make peace with her conscience.'

'Turning down your offer is not a cop out,' Dunai said, stung by the comment. 'It is a carefully considered decision. I choose to put the care of my family and friends first. I choose to be hon-est with them and live my life with a clear conscience. A deci-sion to join *Cerchio di Gaia* would put everything I care about in jeopardy and I'm not willing to do that.'

'Okay, Dunai,' she said, not bothering to disguise her disap-pointment, 'I understand you're not ready just yet. There is still so much you need to work through.'

There was a brief pause before Dunai said, 'I understand you believe you're fighting a war and I think you probably are but, for my safety and that of my son, I've made sure that until I see fit to change the stipulation, in the event of my death the entire story will come out. I don't have many facts but I know enough names the NIA would be interested in.'

There was silence for a moment. 'What would make you think you and Jesse are in any danger from the circle?'

Dunai could have mentioned the couple in the green Valiant, the assault on her that the NIA claimed had been carried out by a member of their family, and the staged rescue, but the judge could deny all this and debate was not the purpose of the call so she said nothing.

'All right, Dunai. I understand you feel the need to do this now but I think we can trust you and I predict you will eventually join the group as Siobhan believed. Did I tell you I knew your mother for twenty years?'

'Hm-m,' Dunai said.

'I think you were the only sacrifice—to the cause, as you put it—that she truly resented; something she never made peace with. But I believe losing the STOP clinics for *Cerchio di Gaia* would have broken her heart.'

It would have been hard for Dunai to explain the feelings that flitted through her just then; there were too many of them. But there was one overriding emotion and that was a strong resolve. Not so much to get her life back, because what had been before was now gone for ever, but rather a fierce desire to push forward with a life of her choosing. One in which she woke believing she had some control over what happened to her during the day, one that was based on who she knew herself to be and what she believed was right at the time.

'I plan to speak to Philippe,' Dunai said, 'about introducing a gender reconciliation component into all STOP's programmes.' There wasn't the slightest trace of uncertainty in her voice so perhaps she was her mother's daughter after all. 'I'm going to honour the good in Siobhan by choosing conciliation rather than contention and I'm going to use STOP to do it.'

'The way of the idealist,' the judge responded, and there was a hint of amusement in her voice.

Rather the idealist than this, Dunai thought, staring at the smashed nails on her right hand; there were still thin, almost invisible lines of dried blood trapped in the cuticles.

'I must tell you,' she went on, 'that every person who has joined our circle began as an idealist. And keep in mind, Dunai, that the non-violent anti-racism campaigns of civil disobedience in the fifties eventually led to an armed struggle that focused on civilian targets.'

'That's just it,' Dunai responded. 'By the time they did resort to violence they could at least comfort themselves with the fact that they'd tried every peaceful means available to them. That's why for now I must choose the pacifist route and I don't feel any need to apologise for viewing the bigger picture in a more optimistic light than you might.'

'The father of modern psychology, Viktor Frankl, believed that post-World War Two, the world needed pessimists in order to ensure activists.'

'I don't think I'm in any danger of romanticising human nature right now,' Dunai said, a hint of impatience in her voice. 'I have chosen a path of non-violence and if that makes me an optimist, then I suppose that's what I am.'

'Well,' the Justice Swanepoel-Higgs said, 'I haven't given up hope. You are by nature an activist and I believe your path will eventually lead to the circle. If you ever need us for anything you know where to get hold of me.'

'Perhaps then I'm not the only optimist, after all.'

She laughed. 'Well, Dunai Marks, the last word is yours this time,' and she rang off.

Dunai stopped at St Mark's to fetch Jesse. She found Sister Finbar alone in her office.

'He's fine,' the nun told her. 'Just be willing to talk with him about his fears and keep reassuring him he's safe. He'll be a little clingy for a while but he'll rediscover his independence when he's ready.'

She got up from behind her desk and came around to Dunai. 'And how are you holding up, little one?'

Dunai blinked, her eyes filled with tears; it was the first time Sister Finbar had used this term of endearment that had always belonged to Sister Raymunda. Dunai smiled. 'I just need to be willing to talk about my fears and keep reassuring myself that I'm safe. I'll probably be a little clingy for a while but I'll rediscover my independence when I'm ready.'

'Well put,' Sister Finbar said. 'Jesse's with Sister Raymunda. I'll let them know you're here. Why don't you take a walk in the garden in the meantime; get some sun? It's a shame to be inside on such a beautiful day.'

On their way home they stopped for milk and *bollas*, a sticky confectionary they were both particularly fond of, at the Rose Corner Café on the corner of Rose and Wale Street.

Dunai, with Jesse in his pushchair, emerged into bright sunlight and headed along Wale Street. She turned the corner at the top of Chiappini and came face to face with Jacob.

'Oh, *crap*,' she said under her breath but he obviously had good hearing.

'Pleased to see you again too,' he said. 'You did call.'

'When I said I wanted to speak to you, you didn't give a time, just said you'd catch up with me.'

'And here I am,' he said. 'I was relieved to hear you'd survived last night.'

'Thank you for your concern,' Dunai said stiffly. 'You didn't have a clue about Bryan, did you?'

Jacob's eyes narrowed. 'The unlocked window, tripped lights, hefty blow to the side of Stappleton's head,' he said. 'You get a little help from your friends?'

'Friends?' Dunai asked.

'Oh, I think we both know *Cerchio di Gaia* had a hand in last night's timely intervention.'

Dunai shook her head and sighed. 'I don't want anything to

do with any of this. That's what I called to talk to you about. I didn't ask for it and I don't want it.'

'So they have contacted you,' Jacob stated.

Dunai said nothing.

'Let's cut the crap, Dunai.'

She flinched at his tone, her nerves still raw from the events of the night before. She felt a sudden strong need to be rid of all the intrigue. This was another reason she'd decided not to tell Carl about *Cerchio di Gaia* and the reason for the NIA's interest in Siobhan's murder—because she intended to be rid of both groups. There was no need for Carl to know the details when they'd never figure in her life again.

'I am not part of the group,' she said, 'and I want you to leave me alone.'

'At least we know what happened now,' he said, ignoring her. 'Siobhan meets with a *Cerchio di Gaia* enforcer, our unmasked woman, whom she somehow finds out is under surveillance. Not so strange when you keep in mind she had military and intelligence training in the Soviet Union during apartheid and more recently had the substantial resources of *Cerchio di Gaia* at her disposal.

'Siobhan knows, of course, that because of her meeting with the enforcer she too has come under suspicion. Almost immediately the enforcer disappears and Siobhan, knowing she's being watched by international intelligence, leads an exemplary life and has no contact with *Cerchio di Gaia* that we know of for a month. Then she contacts the NIA to say that, even though it's going to cost her personally, she has important information for us.

'We know now that she was going to tell us she'd found out about Larsen's involvement in terrorist activities in the US and had used one of her old apartheid connections to confirm the Larsen/Stappelton link. It's a plausible explanation. So, by turning Larsen in, she'd have explained away her meeting with the *Cerchio di Gaia* terrorist and deflected attention away from herself and the group. Chances are it would have worked.'

Dunai had every intention of walking on, but hadn't yet moved a muscle when Jacob's hand came up to stop her. He moved a step closer.

'Siobhan was prepared to stop at nothing to conceal her involvement in the group and protect them from investigation. She was murdered as a direct result of her loyalty to them. Bringing *Cerchio di Gaia* into the open would be real justice for her murder, Dunai, and you can do that.'

He looked down at her. He was tall, solidly built, and she hated the way he interfered with her chemistry. It was as if he gave off some sort of buzz that made her unable to move away from him.

'We need you on the inside.' He spoke softly, the way you spoke to a lover the moment before touching your lips to theirs. 'You can penetrate the group. They're waging an unseen war, Dunai, but you can put a stop to the bloodshed.'

She thought then of Siobhan, Bryan, Mr Bojangles. She was only one woman and a very ordinary one at that. She seemed to have so little power to stop anything, even though she had discovered reserves of strength she'd been unaware of until her life had fallen to pieces. She stepped away from him.

'I'm sure your intentions are noble,' she said, too bone-weary to get angry now. 'But you've approached the wrong person at the wrong time. A month ago my worst fear was that I wouldn't have enough money at the end of the month to pay the vet's bills. Then, right out of the blue, someone I love and admire is murdered, as it turns out by another person I love and admire, who is now also dead. The one, it would seem, was part of a dangerous organization; the other on the *FBI's Most Wanted* list.

'I have been attacked, threatened, followed, chased. Right now, I really have no idea why I'm not a raving lunatic. I have only one aim and that is to keep holding on to my sanity and somehow get my life back. You're going to have to let this go, Jacob.'

She moved past him.

'I can't let this go because they won't.'

She began to walk away from him.

'Since you refuse to help your country and remain an un-known quantity, Dunai Marks, the government has already been advised to distance itself from STOP.'

She almost paused then, but forced herself to keep walking. He raised his voice.

'They'll always be there,' he called after her. 'And once they've got their claws into you they'll never let go. Even when you think you're alone they'll be on the periphery of your life, in the shadows, in the silences. There'll never be another coincidence in your life. Think about it, Dunai. You'll never be able to trust a stranger again; never be sure if that person really is a stranger or whether they've been sent. Even those who get closest to you, you'll just never know.'

Dunai gripped the handle of Jesse's pushcart and walked faster.

The decision to turn down both *Cerchio di Gaia* and the NIA had been the only one that had made any sense to her and she'd done it precisely because of Siobhan and Bryan. Both had crossed a line that had allowed them to believe their causes were just and worthy, not only of sacrifice, but of sacrificing a friend. And in the end they'd destroyed each other.

Dunai relaxed her grip on Jesse's pushcart, slowed her pace and tilted her face to the sun. She didn't look back to where Jacob might still be standing. She was thinking of the people she did know. All those who had proved their loyalty and love in the last few weeks, and there were so many she had to go over the list twice because she thought she might have left someone out. Then she thought of Mr Bojangles and the many faces she'd seen on the streets the morning she'd searched for him, and she felt more than a little fortunate. Her back straightened and a smile touched her lips as she turned into Chiappini Street and headed for her turquoise house.

'What we do now?' Jesse asked.

'I think it's time for a nap.'

'Oh, *crap*,' he said.

'Better not to say that, Jes.'

'It a shouting word?' He twisted in his seat to look up at her.

'Yes, it is.'

'*Dammit*,' he said, turning forward. He clapped a hand over his mouth, then threw his hands in the air. 'When I be three?' he asked.

'Don't worry about it,' Dunai said, smiling. 'When we get to that bridge we'll cross it together.'

If you enjoyed this book, then make sure you also read other titles in the Black Star Crime™ series. Order direct and we'll deliver them straight to your door. Our complete titles list is available online.

www.blackstarcrime.co.uk

Book Title/Author	ISBN & Price	Quantity
Runaway Minister Nick Curtis	978 1 848 45000 4 £3.99	
Streetwise Chris Freeman	978 1 848 45001 1 £3.99	
A Narrow Escape Faith Martin	978 1 848 45002 8 £3.99	
Murder Plot Lance Elliot	978 1 848 45003 5 £3.99	
A Perfect Evil Alex Kava	978 1 848 45004 2 £3.99	
Double Cross Tracy Gilpin	978 1 848 45005 9 £3.99	
Tuscan Termination Margaret Moore	978 1 848 45006 6 £3.99	
Homicide in the Hills Steve Garcia	978 1 848 45007 3 £3.99	
Lost and Found Vivian Roberts	978 1 848 45008 0 £3.99	
Split Second Alex Kava	978 1 848 45009 7 £3.99	

Please add 99p postage & packing per book
DELIVERY TO UK ONLY

Post to: End Page Offer, PO Box 1780, Croydon, CR9 3UH

Please ensure that you include full postal address details. Please pay by cheque or postal order (payable to Reader Service) unless ordering online. Prices and availability subject to change without notice.

Order online at: www.blackstarcrime.co.uk

Allow 28 days for delivery.

You may receive offers from Harlequin Mills & Boon and other carefully selected companies. If you would prefer not to share in this opportunity, please write to The Data Manager, PO Box 676, Richmond, TW9 1WU.